BETWEEN FAMILY

The City Between: Book Nine

W.R. GINGELL

For you:
The one who's just trying to keep their head above water.
I know you're barely holding on today, but you're going to make it and
tomorrow is going to be bright and beautiful.

CHAPTER ONE

Life has come to a pretty mess when you're starting to get paranoid about why you're still alive.

Don't get me wrong: I'm glad I'm alive. I'd just like to know *why*.

I know, I know; that sounds weird. Let me explain.

The fae butler did it.

That probably doesn't help much, but it's flamin' messy to know everything, and flamin' messy to have to think about things, so bear with me. When you've been looking for your parents' murderer for the last year with an owner who's been looking for that same murderer for the last ten or fifteen years, and it ends up being the sneaky old fae butler who you got to love somehow even though he told you not to love him...

Like I said, it's messy.

It sounds bad to say, but I think I could have forgiven the murders—not my parents, maybe, but the others—if it wasn't for the horrible magnitude of it all: the murder of my parents; the murder of countless others; Athelas wriggling his way into my life and helping on the sly until I couldn't help loving him despite his warnings; the final, dreadful betrayal of him murdering our human allies.

Oh yeah. And he tried to kill me, too.

That's where things get particularly confusing, because it was hard to know why I was still alive when Athelas had told me outright that he was going to kill me. Don't get me wrong, I'm not complaining about being alive, I just want to know *why*—and who it's gunna help to have me still alive.

I want to know why I had to spend an entire day on the phone with any of my friends who were still alive—first, to make sure they *were* still alive, and then to make sure they knew enough to stay alive.

I want life to go back to what it was.

So yeah. The fae butler did it. And if that sounds too flippant for you, you're just going to have to deal with it. Look, I never said my coping mechanisms were healthy. But if we're going to talk about coping mechanisms, well, mine are pretty healthy compared with Zero's. Zero is fae, too—technically speaking, my owner—and he'd spent the last three days in a furious welter of activity that ranged anywhere from savagely sharpening knives until three in the morning to conducting drills in the backyard that could have set the grass ablaze with the speed of them if he wasn't actually exercising somewhere between this world and the world Behind.

I didn't blame him; Athelas' betrayal had been bad enough for me, and I'd only known him for about a year. Zero had known him since he was a kid and had trusted him absolutely. It wasn't like he'd told Zero not to trust him, after all—he'd constantly warned me not to do so and I'd ignored it, like an idiot. I mean, what kind of normal person keeps warning you not to trust him? I should have realised how weird it was. I hadn't been able to stop myself trusting him, because I could have sworn that I'd seen the real Athelas emerge more, day by day, and—

Forget it. Forget him.

Only I couldn't, and that was the bit that tore shreds off my soul every time a thought of Athelas recurred. If only I could forget him, I could stop feeling the huge, gaping *pain* in my breastbone, the ache in my throat.

Zero was probably feeling something similar, so I could understand the flurry of activity. I'd thrown myself into cooking and cleaning; Zero had thrown himself into training. None of us had left the house, either, but that could have been because the house itself was being a bit protective these days. It wasn't that we couldn't get out, it was just that the house didn't like it.

Still, maybe I should be encouraging Zero to get out a bit more. He'd shown more sign of emotion in the last three days than I'd seen from him in the last year, and I didn't want to break him. It's pretty hard on a bloke when you try to encourage him to stop stifling his emotions and then something like this happens.

What about the vampire? Well, JinYeong had mostly been making himself available as a sort of self-warming pillow ever since the house became protective and inclined to shut itself off from the outside world. All right, not so much the whole world as a *part* of the world. A very specific part—a very specific person— the King of Behind, in fact. It would have been nice to be able to catch a breath before the next shock, but it's hard to do that when the flaming *King of Behind* wanders down your street, pinpoints your house, and gives you back a book you only remember losing when he gives it back to you.

A book that has your name written in it from one day when you weren't as obedient as you ought to have been. It would have been nice to think it was just a kind of *g'day, I'm the king, nice to meet you, here's something that belongs to you*. But he'd had my book; he had taken the trouble to find me and give it back to me. There was no way he didn't know I was an heirling, too.

But if he did know that, why hadn't the king tried to kill me?

I crossed my legs under me where I was sitting on the kitchen island bench in self defence against a living room that was still too...Athelasy to be comfortable sitting in. I said to the fae wall of furious polishing and bright knife points that was Zero, "It was a threat, right? Giving me the book was a threat."

"Of course it was a threat," he said briefly, testing the balance of a knife and laying it neatly next to the others. "What else would it be?"

"Dunno; but why threaten me when he could have killed me?"

Zero's voice was cut glass. "He couldn't have killed you. I'm surprised he could even see you."

"Yeah, that might have been my fault," I said, with a touch of gloom. "I saw him walking along the street, looking for something, and he stopped at our gate. I said hi first."

"He shouldn't have been able to find us in the first place," Zero said. "That wasn't your fault. He shouldn't have known about you at all."

"Yeah," I said, my gloom deepening. "That actually probably was my fault. In my defence, he was in an alley reading a book and he told me he was a librarian."

Zero's eyes closed for a brief moment. "Pet—"

"That was the day I texted you to come get me," I said, and added half-heartedly, "So you can't say I didn't tell you I was in trouble."

"Pet—"

"Who is at fault is not the question," said a voice impatiently, in Korean. Between, doing its usual, helpful best, translated the meaning directly into my mind. As it did so, a slender figure stepped up from the living room and into the kitchen and dining room, preceded by a waft of perfume.

Jin Yeong. Not my owner, like Zero, but just as much of a pain in the neck—and more, because he's a vampire. Far too beautiful for his own good, inclined to bite first and ask questions later— and apparently in love with me.

I didn't say he was clever.

"This," Jin Yeong tapped a finger on the book's cover. It had been sitting on the coffee table until this morning, when someone had brought it into the kitchen and left it on the kitchen island. Probably Zero, to make a point. "This is a *problem*."

"Tell me about it," I muttered, flipping open the cover-board as if to check that the name was still actually there, ready to give me a nasty case of the willies every time I saw it.

It was still there, all right. Still gave me a horrible chill to see it, too.

Ruth Walker.

It was a name that was never supposed to be written down—and given what I now knew about the world of humans and the world behind that, I found myself wishing it never had been written down.

A bit too late to say that now; I was the one who'd done written it down, after all.

It's no good crying over spilt milk, but when you're the one who's done the spilling, is it okay to kick yourself in the shins retrospectively?

"How bad is it, the king knowing my name?"

"That depends," said Zero, leaning his crossed forearms on the table and levelling a clear, blue gaze at me. "How much of an inconvenience is it for you to be whisked out of your bed, your house, and your world, and flung into an arena of the speaker's choice to take part in a duel to the death?"

"Heck, it's that bad?" I shivered and slipped down from the kitchen island. I might as well make pancakes and hang over the warmth of the skillet to try and get rid of the chill under my skin that kept raising goosebumps.

When I'd gotten all the ingredients together into my mixing bowl, I asked tentatively, "It's not all bad, though, right? It's not like that's my whole name, and the last name isn't even right—well, it's not what's on my birth certificate, anyway."

Jin Yeong, far warmer than a bloke who is historically supposed to be dead ought to be, stretched out his torso sinuously across the kitchen island to rest one warm hand against the arm with which I was holding the mixing bowl in place.

"It depends on who you got your magic through," Zero said. "If it was your mother, taking her maiden name has put you in a lot of danger. If it was your father, you're a single step closer to safety. What do you mean, it's not your whole name?"

"Western humans have three names, *Hyeong*," JinYeong said, looking lazily over his shoulder at Zero.

I found that I'd relaxed more to the side that was warmest and straightened myself, but JinYeong's hand moved with me, still warm and present. To Zero I said, "Hang on, how'd you know I took mum's maiden name?"

"I don't have time to play games with you, Pet," he said, instead of answering. "Even Behind, we're aware of surnames."

"Oi!" I protested. "I'm not playing games, I'm—"

"You have a name," said JinYeong. "So I will call you by it."

I gave him a bit of a look. "I didn't say you could do that."

"You are not my pet," JinYeong said. He seemed faintly offended. "I should call you by your name. You did not put me in the contract, so I am just a *person*."

There were so many replies I could have made to that, but there was only space in my suddenly shattered mind for one thought.

That thought was, *Heck*.

"Oi," I said, my throat dry. "Reckon the contract is why I'm still alive?"

I saw the almost pained expression that flitted across Zero's face, and the one of profound weariness that crossed it immediately after.

Very slowly, he said, "I had forgotten to consider the contract."

"Me too," I said. What with the king visiting and making sure everyone else in my life wasn't dead, it had been hard to spare a thought for anything else. "Reckon it's why Athelas couldn't finish off the job? He was contracted not to hurt me but he did? But if it's that, how much of it is still gunna keep me tied to him? Can he still get at me through it?"

"He broke the contract," Zero said, after a brief, almost frenzied moment of thought. With relief, he sat back again and explained, "Athelas broke the contract by attempting to kill you; it no longer has any hold over you. We can be thankful for that, at least. As you said, I shouldn't wonder if that's the thing that kept you alive by the skin of your teeth: he tried to break it and it protected you."

"The old man keeps making mistakes these days," Jin Yeong said thoughtfully. "I wonder how many of them he regrets?"

"I'm gunna make sure he regrets this one, at least," I said, my chin firming.

"We have to find him first," said Zero.

I stared at him. "You're gunna try to find him?"

Heck. That was a bad idea. Zero enraged by loss and bent on finding a nameless murderer was bad enough; Zero enraged and broken by betrayal in equal measure, bent on finding a known murderer, was downright scary.

"I'm not going to let him get away because he's Athelas," he said. "And I'm certainly not going to let him return comfortably to my father with his hand out for a prize."

Jin Yeong lifted one brow at him. "You think it will be comfortable? I do not think so."

"No, I suppose not," Zero said. "Especially once my father finds out that Pet isn't dead."

"*Ruth* is not dead," Jin Yeong said coldly. "She is alive. There is no pet."

My name coming from his lips sent a spike of something very like panic through me. Was that part of the magic mum had spoken around me when I was younger, too? Sheer terror at having someone say my name so that I would never tell it to anyone?

Shaken, I said, "That's not how you pronounce it," because I couldn't think of how else to express the deeply personal feeling of someone saying my name. Heck, maybe it was because it was Jin Yeong saying it. I didn't know. I didn't even know exactly what it was I was feeling.

Perhaps fortunately, someone knocked on the door. It wasn't a knock on the front door; it was a knock on the linen closet door. And I say *someone*, but we were all pretty well aware of who it would be. Palomena, Enforcer to the king and informant to Zero's dad by proxy.

"Don't let her in," Zero said, with the faintest edge of exasperation to his voice. Apart from Jin Yeong, I don't often get to see people other than myself wringing emotions from Zero, and it might have been fun to see if it wasn't for our current situation.

It sounds like we don't like Palomena, but that wouldn't be true: we just don't like who she represents. Whichever way you look at it, she represents either the King Behind or Zero's dad, and neither of those two options are even slightly appealing to us. She might be a nice person, all told—at least, for behindkind fae —but she was still on the wrong side of the world when it came to being an Heirling.

"I will get it," said Jin Yeong anyway, slipping from his seat and retreating to the hallway toward the back of the house, taking my warmth with him.

A moment later, I heard the linen closet door open and an unusually heavy tread cross the threshold that didn't sound remotely like the light-footed fae we usually had come to visit. Heck, what *now*?

But when the visitor appeared, it was certainly Palomena, her oiled braids sleek and tidy, stepping up into the room with a weariness I hadn't seen from her before. Her uniform was neat and orderly, and she smiled at me first like she always did, which was all nice and normal, but she wasn't walking properly. The sleeve of her uniform was getting darker as I watched, too—or maybe it was just that the dark patch was growing bigger. Zero stood up abruptly at the far end of the room just as I saw the trail of blue blood that escaped the cuff of her sleeve and dripped freely to the floor.

"Heck!" I said, my stomach lurching. I dropped the mixing bowl and grabbed a fresh tea towel, wetting it slightly at the sink. Over my shoulder, I demanded, "Who did that to you?"

"That's unfortunate," Palomena said, with a short sigh, catching sight of the mess she'd made. She stripped off her uniform jacket and set it carefully on the back of one of the chairs, then rolled up the sleeve of that arm in quick, irritated movements. "I apologise for the mess."

"Don't worry about the mess," I said, passing her the tea towel. "I'm more worried about your arm. That's flamin' deep."

"It's not so bad," she said, sweeping the trails of blood upward and then settling the tea-towel over the worst of the gash and pressing down.

Jin Yeong's eyebrow went up; he shot me a glance. I could only shrug, because I wasn't Athelas, and it wasn't like I could heal her. Zero came around the dining table toward Palomena, and Jin Yeong sank backwards until he was resting against the wall, his eyes dark and amused and watchful.

"Who did it?" asked Zero. "Did you come directly here? I know the rule that Enforcers shouldn't be seen in a weakened state in the eyes of the populace, but stopping here for succour has a few too many undertones of trust, don't you think?"

"I didn't come here for succour," Palomena said. Her voice sounded slightly dry, but maybe she was just in pain. The gash in her arm was pretty bad. "Nor did I come here directly; I do have a question, however. Perhaps the three of you can explain why unfriendly agents arrived at the humans' prior headquarters at exactly the same moment as the Enforcers? There was some disagreement between us, and between one thing and another, the entire place caught fire."

"It caught—" I stopped and said, "You mean the sorta fire that burns up shades and revenants and other stuff that isn't quite dead or alive?"

Palomena's lips curved slightly, though there was still a line of pain between her brows as she attended to her injury. "You know far too much."

"That's what I'm told," I said.

"I don't know which side threw the spell that did the damage, but it did for the rest of the scene."

"Was there much to answer for when you got back?" asked Zero, leaning over her arm and looking it up and down as if sizing up the damage.

"Not for the destruction of the place," said Palomena, blotting at another stream of blue that tried to evade the cloth and dribble down to the floor. "I'd already taken the evidence needed to verify the scene. But there was a fair bit of consternation at anyone else knowing where the scene was."

"Ah," said Zero, one huge hand supporting Palomena's arm from beneath with his fingers gently and carefully avoiding the worst of the damage. "I see."

"I'd prefer you didn't do that," Palomena said, twitching her arm away with decidedly more decision than she spoke with.

Zero's hand dropped at once. He said expressionlessly, "I wouldn't have harmed you."

I'm not sure if he meant to do it, but he turned away, too; he didn't turn away fully, and I don't think it was conscious, but he definitely pulled away with the shoulder of the arm he'd reached out to her—an almost physical sign of perceived rejection.

That was interesting. Zero had always been very good at hiding his emotions in general. The weight of Athelas' betrayal was obviously still there, taking its toll. I wondered what would happen when the weight of it all became too much for him.

"I don't think you understand," said Palomena, her dark eyes resting on his face with some consideration. "It's been decided that I should experience the full effects of my ah, incompetence."

Zero's head jerked back very slightly. "My father still does that, does he?"

"Not ostensibly," Palomena said. "But it flows through the channels, so to speak, and comes out in the ranks. If I allow anyone to heal me, I'll receive a worse punishment than this little thing."

"We really oughtta have a word with your dad," I said to Zero, my voice as snubby as my throat felt. Of Palomena, I asked, "You gunna be all right? Sit down, I'll get you something to eat. That's not a *little thing*. Flamin' heck!"

She actually sat—I think it was the first time. Zero backed away a bit more and even pulled out the chair for her, and she sat down with the faintest of nods up at him. Jin Yeong, his dark eyes still dancing, sauntered back across from the wall and slid into the stool he'd been sitting on earlier to observe the scene more thoroughly.

I fought off the grin that tried to come out, and asked Palomena, "Any rule against bandages?"

"No," she said. "But there aren't many of them Behind, given what we normally use. I wasn't going to ruin another one of my shirts—I might have decided otherwise if I knew it would do *that* to my uniform jacket, though."

"Right," I said. "Bandages first, then some food."

I let Zero do the actual bandaging—and so, to my surprise, did Palomena—and went back to making breakfast. It wasn't like Palomena's presence made the gaping hole left by Athelas' betrayal any less of a jagged tear in the atmosphere, but it did help fill the room up a bit, and it looked like it was giving Zero something to focus on, which was nice.

I started pouring pancakes onto the skillet, leaving a space on the side. I didn't know how fae bodies worked, but I knew from experience that human bodies did well with steak and eggs after a decent amount of blood loss. I took a steak from the fridge and left it on the bench to rest for a while, and sat a few eggs beside it.

As I cooked, Zero said, "We had nothing to do with whatever situation you walked into. We don't have a lot of friends that aren't already dead."

"I see," said Palomena. "Then I suppose you'd like me to tell my commanding officer that you have no knowledge of how a group called Upper Management found our scene?"

Zero thought about that for a while, bandaging slowly and carefully along her forearm. Finally, he said, "We have knowledge of them: we've faced up to them a few times in a fight. We have no friendly connections with them, and we certainly didn't tell them where to find the humans' headquarters."

"Oh well, that's more information than I expected to get." Palomena half-shrugged and winced a little. "There were quite a few of them and only three of us, which makes me think they knew what to expect. I don't like the thought that they've got so much information when we don't have anything on them."

"That seems to be their specialty," Zero said.

"Yeah, and it's a flamin' bad habit," I added. "We've managed to get the drop on them once or twice, but that was mostly by accident."

"Your father isn't going to be happy about this," said Palomena to Zero.

She said it so directly and offhandedly that it was a bit of a shock when her actual words settled into my brain and made sense. It must have taken Zero by surprise, too, because the way his eyes snapped to her face in shock and confusion was something to see. He's not a bloke who shows much emotion, even when he's still knocked sideways by the betrayal of the person closest to him, but the confusion was clear enough that even Palomena must have been able to see it.

She added, "If I had a guess, I would have said that your father was *deeply* involved in bettering your chances to get to the throne, and the fact that there are other behindkind out there who have obviously been colluding with humans is something of a shock to him. I don't know what the king knew about Upper Management, but there are now suspicions that they've been sponsoring heirlings. I'm sure you can see why your father is disturbed."

"My father's feelings are not interesting to me in the slightest," Zero said, the words swift and savage.

I hadn't heard him speak with that level of rage before, and I wasn't sure it was all directed at his dad, either.

"We only don't care about his feelings if he's not trying to kill us!" I protested. I didn't see any point in stopping Palomena from talking just because Zero needed to vent his feelings.

I approved of Zero working out his feelings in a healthy way, but I didn't want it to cost us information we might need.

As if she hadn't heard Zero say anything, Palomena continued, "Lord Sero was concerned enough about it to send us back there to rework the scene and see what the humans had come up with. We weren't able to find anything at the scene before Upper Management arrived, and then everything went to pieces, so we went straight to the human police to gather what we could there."

"What did the cops find at the scene?" I asked. I couldn't help the thread of hope that pulled at a wobbly place in my heart that was stuffed too full with blood and Athelas and shadows. I could ask Tuatu later, but I needed to know *now*. "Was there anything weird about it?"

"They matched up the body parts with each of the humans that were said to be a part of that group. The human police were surprised that there was a group living there when they all came from such different backgrounds, but they're tentatively working on the suspicion that it was a death cult. They said no one could have lived through what happened there." Palomena hesitated, and then said, "The only weirdness I'm aware of in recent events is the fact that you're alive. I don't mean to say that I'm sad about it, but I was given to believe that you would be dead at this stage and I'm happily surprised to see that you're not."

"Not to worry," I said. "There are a few people who are gunna be surprised by that, I reckon."

"I don't suppose you've got an idea about why it didn't work, do you? It's not something I'm supposed to report on, but I feel as though I'd like the information to get back to Lord Sero for a number of different reasons."

"We're inclined to think it was the pet/master contract," Zero said, surprising me. "We were discussing it before you got here."

Oh, that was weird. He didn't usually offer information that wasn't necessary for the other person to have—he didn't always offer it even if it *was*—and it was interesting to see him starting now.

Mind you, I thought suddenly, plating Palomena's steak and eggs; he wasn't the only one sharing more information than usual. I took the plate to Palomena with a knife and fork and put it down in front of her. "You're being nice and useful today," I said.

She didn't pretend to misunderstand that, either. "I'm usually limited in what I can do and say to be useful," she said, her eyes on Zero. "But for some reason, Lord Sero seems to have decided that I'm to make myself very...approachable. As a result, any information I can provide you with, outside of a few topics, is completely allowable."

Her gaze didn't drop from Zero's as she spoke. There was something being said here that I didn't have enough information to understand, but by the look on Zero's face, he understood it.

His eyes lightening with amusement, he said, "He expects you to seduce me in order to keep me close?"

"I was told that you prefer humans, but you could try not to look quite so amused," Palomena said, one brow quirking up. Now that she'd made sure Zero understood what she was saying, she seemed pretty happy to dig into the steak and eggs.

"It's not a preference, it's a coincidence," Zero said, but

although the amusement had faded from his face, he didn't seem angry.

I gave him a pile of pancakes and patted him bracingly on the shoulder as I went back for my own and Jin Yeong's pancakes. "I won't let her accost you; no need to worry."

"I am not worr—Pet, eat your breakfast and be quiet!"

Palomena grinned and got stuck into her steak again. She waited until I sat down at the table next to Jin Yeong and had a few pancakes on my plate before she asked, "You know your steward is back with Lord Sero, I suppose?"

This time I was the one who dropped the grin pretty fast, though Zero looked a bit sick, too. Suddenly my pancakes didn't seem quite so appetizing.

"Of course he is there," said Jin Yeong, reaching over me for the maple syrup. "There is no need to update us on that one. We have all the knowledge of him that we wish to have."

A silence fell at the table, but Zero surprised me by breaking it to say through a mouthful of pancake, "I find it odd that my father accepted him back with no questions. I had been under the impression that my father wanted the Pet alive for his own reasons. I can't see that Athelas would have fared well after trying to destroy one of my father's avenues of use."

Jin Yeong shot him a look across the table beneath his lashes but he must have been content with what he saw, because he went back to eating pancakes without protest.

"Lord Sero had words with him about it but was pretty quickly placated," said Palomena. "Suspiciously quickly, I would have said. I'm not sure how he's going to react to the news that she's still quite lively, given that development."

"Your dad probably told him to do whatever he needed to do if he was discovered," I said. "One dead Pet is safer than one alive, useful one."

"There was some discussion at the time about your usefulness being as assured as Lord Sero had hoped it would be. I'm very much afraid that you'll have to take precautions after I report back to him."

"Life as usual, then," I said grumpily.

"*Jaemisseo*," JinYeong said, leaning back in his chair with one arm slung over the back of my chair and his foot elegantly propped against the table leg. "Life is boring when everyone is too friendly."

"Want me to start putting banshees in your sock drawer?"

"Do not put things in my sock drawer. Do not touch my ties."

"Too late," I said, feeling a bit more cheerful.

JinYeong followed my gaze and caught sight of the tie frog hopping over into the kitchen in its usual search for sultanas. The banshees had started feeding it a few days ago, and it seemed to have developed a taste for what it was given.

"That one is allowed," he said. "No more."

"What are you gunna tell Zero's dad about the human group?" I asked Palomena. I would make no promises when it came to JinYeong's ties.

"That it's no use hoping for information from them. To the king—or at least, my commanding officer—I will report that there's no need to worry about information leakage from that direction any longer. Upper Management is another matter."

Zero nodded as if unsurprised, and I went back to my pancakes gloomily.

"At any rate," said Palomena, releasing her knife and fork with something of a contented sigh, "I've spent about enough time here to please Lord Sero. Thank you for the food and the bandages, Pet."

"I thought you were supposed to seduce me?" said Zero. It didn't seem like a complaint—more of an interested observation of someone who has had previous experience in what to expect in similar situations.

"I like to take things slowly," Palomena said, pushing away from the table. "It's no use scaring off the skittish ones."

"I *beg* your pardon?" said Zero, his face utterly astonished. "Did you say *skittish*—?"

"I'll see you all again soon," said Palomena, taking back her uniform jacket and folding it carefully over her uninjured arm. "No—no need to show me out, I know the way."

Zero, rather grimly, said, "Jin Yeong will show you out anyway."

He was probably just cranky about being called skittish. I reckon he likes to think of himself as big and impervious—which, yeah, he *is*. But he's also definitely skittish.

Jin Yeong showed Palomena out anyway. It was my job, but I had pancakes to eat and washing up to do, so I did that instead. Zero continued to eat pancakes with a dedication that was almost as terrifying as his dedication in training.

As I passed by the opening between kitchen and living room with my hands full of dishes a few minutes later, I caught Jin Yeong staring narrowly at Athelas' chair with his hands shoved in his pockets.

"Don't get rid of it," I said. "Not yet."

Jin Yeong jumped a bit, as if he hadn't realised he'd been staring at the chair—or perhaps as if he'd been startled to be read so accurately. He said, "Tomorrow, then."

"Tomorrow," I agreed, but I'm pretty sure that neither of us actually believed that was going to happen. "Definitely not today."

It couldn't be today, because today I had to go up to my parents' room—the room that Athelas had been using for nearly a year—and rid it of every piece of him that was still there. I might not be able to bring myself to let the chair downstairs go, but I was going to make sure that Mum and Dad's room was cleansed of everything that their murderer had left there.

It was something I'd been putting off for the last couple of days. No one else had volunteered to do it—no one else probably thought about doing it—but this wasn't their house. It wasn't their parents who had died, either.

So after I finished the washing up and Zero had gone outside to begin his usual exercise session, I trudged upstairs with a sick stomach. It took me a good five minutes of standing outside the door before I could bring myself to open it and go in—and when I finally made myself go in, I very nearly turned and bolted for it again.

I didn't expect Athelas to have permeated every bit of the room with his magic, or his essence, or whatever it is that fae have. I didn't expect to still be able to sense him there with my human senses, either: the scent of Athelas, the clothes of Athelas, the pocket watch I never saw him use but knew he had. His little tin of human brown shoe polish that he used despite the fact that he could have shined his shoes with magic instead.

When Jin Yeong came upstairs and found me I had sunk to the carpet in a hot, sick, overflowing bewilderment of tears, clutching my knees to my chest. He sat on the floor beside me and made a warmth against my side that was uncomfortably hot but that I didn't seem to be able to pull away from.

I heard him snap something in Korean at a couple of banshees that peeked out to see what all the fuss was about, but it mustn't have been rude because when they came back to throw things at us, what they threw was the box of tissues from downstairs.

Jin Yeong caught the box before it could clock me in the temple, then waited for me to finish sobbing before he offered it to me.

"This job is for tomorrow," he said. "Today you bandaged a friend; you should bandage this tomorrow. It will need salt to take away all of *that*."

All of that was the *eau de Athelas* fae trace, I figured.

"Reckon we're gunna need more salt than we've got if that's what it takes to cleanse this room," I said shakily, sniffing into my elbow. "I'll go out and get a proper bag of it. Yanno; for tomorrow."

"I will buy it," Jin Yeong said. "That fae woman said *Hyeong*'s father will soon know you are not dead. I think you don't want to leave the house."

He wasn't wrong. Despite the steadily-growing feeling of claustrophobia that staying in the house had brought with it over the last few days, I didn't feel safe going outside, either. It was too easy for flowers to pop up through the concrete around here and there was the king to watch out for, too. Athelas had had a pretty good try at killing me and I was going to stay alive, even if it was just to spite him.

To my surprise, JinYeong actually went out to get salt. I'd half thought that he was just distracting me, but maybe he wanted to get out of the house as well. Whatever the reason, he left me in the kitchen with a cup of coffee and a banshee that was far too interested in snotty tissues when I stopped leaking tears.

He hadn't been gone more than five minutes when the coiling burl of magic and Between that had been building in the backyard without my conscious notice grew too big to be ignored. What the heck was Zero fighting against so furiously out there?

Probably his emotions.

The thought made me smile just a little bit and sniff into my coffee. Then something big and explosive made me jump and yelp, sending coffee everywhere as I instinctively covered my head despite the fact that the explosion was more energy than anything that could be stopped with limbs or cover.

"Flamin' heck!" I whispered, jerking my knee out of the way of a scalding dribble of coffee from the kitchen island. I dropped down from the bar stool to go out and see what Zero had destroyed out in the backyard, but the back door slammed before I could do more than take a step or two toward the next room.

Pale with rage, Zero stalked into the living room and picked up Athelas' chair with one hand, then hurled it clear across living room, kitchen, and right out the window. I ducked; glass shattered; mahogany chair legs splintered.

When the whole, shocking noise of it ended, I said, "Heck!" rocking on my heels with my arms wrapped around my head. "Oi! Warn me before you do stuff like that, you flamin' chair-hurler! You nearly sent me sailing out the window!"

He didn't come up into the kitchen; he just asked, "Are you all right?"

"Yeah, just got a couple of splinters in me hair, that's all."

"Good," he said, and then sat down on the step up to the kitchen with his back to me.

He wouldn't cry—I wasn't even sure if he was capable of crying—but he sat there gulping on air in a way that would have been sobs if he had tears to cry.

"Heck," I said again, and went to wrap my arms around the back of his neck while he was within reach. I didn't like to think about how he must have lost all those tears he should have been able to cry. I couldn't do anything about them, anyway. All I could do was hug him and let my own tears drop on his shoulders if I couldn't hold them back.

We were a cheerful lot this morning.

I stayed where I was until Zero's breathing went back to normal, and then shoved him over a bit to sit next to him, massaging calf muscles that had been screaming at me for the last couple of minutes.

"This is your fault for being too big to comfortably hug," I said. "Even when you're sitting down you're flamin' inconvenient."

Zero gave a huffy sort of laugh that sounded almost resigned. "I didn't ask you to hug me."

"I know," I said. "But that's not my fault. You're flamin' bad at asking for the stuff you need."

"I didn't say that I need—"

If there had been an explosion in the backyard ten minutes earlier, this time what happened was more of an implosion. The house, the world, and the room around us were each grabbed by the equivalent of the ears and violently hauled inside out, then sealed with the most ear-popping silence that I'd ever had the misfortune to experience.

"Okay," I said into that dead silence. "It wasn't me this time."

CHAPTER TWO

Zero got up with such speed and force that he sent me tumbling to the carpet as he strode toward the front door.

I scrambled to my feet and took off after him, rattled right to the ends of my fingertips and with my heart beating far too loudly in my ears. "What's going on? What the heck was that?"

He didn't answer me. He grabbed the handle of the front door and turned it, pushing hard; then wrenched at it hard enough to have pulled it from the wood. The door rattled, but didn't open. He kicked it twice for good measure, too, but all it did was rattle more violently than before.

"I didn't do that," I said. "That wasn't me, right?"

Zero didn't answer that, either. Instead, he strode back up the hall to the back door, then went around to every window in succession, rattling them with too much strength and far too much savagery.

"Check the windows upstairs!" he snarled at me. "See if you can make them open!"

I did as I was told, taking the stairs two at a time and running a swift course around the entire upper floor, heaving at windows until my fingers went white and my shoulders popped.

Not one of them would open.

I hurried back downstairs to the sound of repeated, heavy impacts, to see that Zero was throwing his entire weight at the door.

I reckon I counted something like thirty times before he stopped and sagged against the wall, still gulping air in the same kind of dry, almost-sobs he had been doing before, the fist closest to me clenched tight as though he'd start trying to punch his way through the door next.

"The heck," I said, dazed. "You really can't get out, can you?"

Zero slid to the floor with his back against the hallway wall, his knees bent. "No one can get out," he said, staring at the wall opposite with blank eyes. "No one out, no one in. That's how it works."

"Not in my house, it's flamin' not!" I shot back, alarm radiating through my chest. He looked so lost and beaten, sitting on the ground like that, and we couldn't afford for him to look beaten. "Get off the floor! We're gunna sort this out because there's no way someone's allowed to lock up my house."

"We can't sort it out," Zero said wearily. "We've got enough food in the house for a few days, haven't we?"

"I don't *mean* that!" I said. "I mean *how the heck is JinYeong gunna get back in?*"

"He won't be able to," Zero said. "They've started."

"They've started what? And who are *they?*"

"We've reached critical mass," said Zero. "The heirling trials are about to begin, and it seems as though the king is doing things legally this time."

"Are you telling me that we're stuck inside the house until the king comes to kill us? We can't get somewhere through Between or something?"

"We can get out of the house," Zero said. "Just not into the human world. The back door will open once the house has settled into the arena, but only to let us out into the premade closed system Behind; factions will already have been forming this last half hour, and there will be fighters waiting."

"Can we get out through the broken window? Might be a sneaky way out."

"I'm certain you'll be able to get somewhere," Zero said. "I doubt it'll be anywhere you want to go, however. I told you: the heirling trials are a closed system and anyone locked into it won't be able to access the human world for the duration."

"Okay, but I don't want to experience the duration."

Zero huffed out a tired laugh. "Neither do I, but here we are."

"Hang on, what about the window, then? If there are nasties out there, they'll probably want to be nasty in here before long."

"We'll have to find a way to patch it up to stop anything getting through," he said, rubbing a hand vigorously over his face. It was a gesture of frustration; he was regretting hurling a chair through it earlier, obviously.

Still, while it was open, it wouldn't hurt to have a quick squiz.

I went to have a bit of a look, and just like the front door that rattled but didn't open, the window breathed cold air on me from an inky blackness I didn't particularly like breathing on me.

"Heck," I said at Zero, backing away. "We're really in trouble, aren't we?"

He stepped up wearily into the kitchen and upended the table with a groan. I didn't see exactly what he stuck to it, but it was magic and strong and made the table adhere to the wall so tightly that I couldn't even feel the uncomfortable fingers of cold air slipping through anymore.

"That's a bit less creepy, anyway," I said. "Are we sure nothing got through while I was upstairs and you were in the other parts of the house?"

"No," said Zero. "We'll have to check the house as well as we can and sleep in shifts for the first couple of nights."

"The first *couple* of—hang on, how long is this thing supposed to take?"

"As long as it takes," Zero told me flatly.

"I s'pose it's a good thing that the king's doing it legally, this time," I said, but it was more of a forlorn hope than anything else and I'm pretty sure I sounded more disgruntled than glad about it. What can I say? I'm a suspicious person at heart. "If he's not going to interfere with the choice—"

Zero didn't even let that hope marinate for a while before he skewered it. "He's probably hoping the herd thins out before he makes his move again; not every heirling will have been caught up in the trials."

"I'm not a wildebeest and I'm not gunna be thinned out," I said firmly. "If he tries to get into my house—"

"He won't try," said Zero, with the kind of stubbornness that suggests a person is trying to make their audience acknowledge the full extent of the situation. "He'll just wait until we heirlings find each other in the closed system Between—until alliances form, heirlings die, and there are as few left as possible—and then he'll likely kill the survivors out there in the layers of the world until the victor emerges. This is exactly what my father was trying to prevent."

"Yeah, by taking it on himself to make sure all the heirlings were killed," I said; but I said it quietly. We both knew who had done the actual killing, and we didn't really have any more chairs that could be thrown through windows, even if the windows would allow themselves to be smashed now that we were...not in the human world.

"Right," I said. "I'm having coffee."

Zero gazed at me with the same kind of blankness he'd stared at the hallway wall earlier, but he took the coffee cup I gave him when it was ready.

He also answered me when I asked, "Reckon they'll let him get away with it? The king, I mean."

"Who do you think will stop him?"

"Isn't it against your laws, what he's been doing?"

He huffed out an impatient sigh. "Yes."

"Yeah, so—"

"He's the *king*."

"Yeah, and he's been breaking the law!"

"He's the king: he is the law."

"That's garbage," I said. "A king is supposed to protect his people from lawbreakers, not become a lawbreaker to keep power."

"Once we start judging the king, we've opened the door to anarchy."

"Yeah, because the worlds Between and Behind are so flamin' orderly and well-balanced!" I muttered, and left him in the kitchen so I could do one last circuit of the house.

If I hadn't seen the empty blackness out the broken window and witnessed Zero trying and failing to open the door and windows, it would have been hard to believe that anything was wrong. I could see everything I could usually see from most of the windows; only the windows facing the backyard were cloudy and uncertain. From the upper storey I could see the street, the neighbouring yards, the backyard; from the lower story I could see the front and side yards all around, a glimpse of the neighbouring roofs above the fence, and the clearness of space across the road that had once been filled with the house across the road.

That house had disappeared about a year ago, while the four of us were trying not to disappear along with it and after someone had reported the whole place as an outpost of Upper Management—though we hadn't known it was Upper Management then.

Athelas had said that it wasn't him—actually, he hadn't. Not outright. Who was I trying to fool? He must have been the one who told Zero's dad; there was no one else who had known what we knew and had had access to Lord Sero.

He'd even said a tranquil little, "What a shame!" about it happening. Well, not about it happening—about Zero mentioning that they would have to dismantle the waystation themselves.

Twisty old tea drinker had probably already been figuring out how he was going to get away and report to Lord Sero without us knowing about it.

I shivered away the memory and trudged upstairs again with my coffee to have another look at the silent, untouchable human world from a better vantage. It wasn't creepy until you realised that there was no sound from that sight and that every window was absolutely frigid to the touch. The branches that should have tapped and scraped against the glass just mimed their actions without any sound of their movement reaching me; I felt the shudder of the wind rattling the windows but couldn't hear the sound of it.

I perched on the windowsill that gave me a view of the road out front and the house of our new neighbour, my foot propped against the side table there for balance, and sipped my coffee as I tried to call Jin Yeong.

I didn't even get a dial tone for my efforts—just the complete silence of a dead phone. I pulled it away from my ear and checked the battery despite the fact that I'd literally just seen the screen light up as I tried to call. It was fine; everything was fine. I just didn't have a dial tone.

Heck. It really was a closed system.

I finished my cuppa, watching the road for Jin Yeong, then reluctantly went back downstairs to try and discover why a nippy little breeze was sweeping upstairs from the general direction of the laundry. When the whole house is closed up, a breeze slipping through is a bit of a curiosity; when the whole house is closed up via magic for a combative contest to the death, it gets downright worrisome.

So I made sure there were no dregs left in my mug and, clutching it a bit tighter by way of having a weapon if I did chance to see something, I went cautiously down the stairs into the hallway, and stopped just outside the laundry room.

That was when I discovered the old mad bloke paddling

happily in the laundry sink with his bare, browned feet, gnawing happily on the fat stick of salami I'd bought to put on pizza later in the week.

"You loopy old galah!" I said exasperatedly. The arm with the coffee mug relaxed. "Who told you you could sneak into the house and get into my fridge!"

Not to mention *how* he'd done it, with Zero in the house!

"I won't soil the carpet, lady," he said, smiling anxiously at me. "See? I'm washing my feet."

"Yeah, I saw. How come you went for the salami? It's full of salt—not much good for you."

He wagged the salami at me remonstratingly. "Lady, salt is good for humans."

"Yeah, but not too *much* of—hang on. Salt is what Jin Yeong said would get rid of fae presence. You sneaky old duffer!"

"Don't talk with your mouth full," he mumbled, but I was pretty sure he was talking to himself more than to me.

I sighed and asked, "How'd you get in, anyway?"

"There's an open window," he said, admonishing me with the salami. "You shouldn't have done that."

"I didn't do it; Zero chucked a chair through it. You came through there? Heck, you must have got in pretty quick, then! There were only a couple of minutes between Zero breaking it and the whole house doing...whatever it is that's happening."

"I am quick, but I must have a bath."

"Okay, but you better not go making trouble around the house —and *don't* annoy Zero. I'll go let him know you're here. Don't move."

He blinked at me a couple of times and then splashed one foot in a questioning sort of way, as if making sure it was all right to move *just* that foot.

"I meant *stay in the room*," I explained. "I'll be back."

Goodness knew where he had been hiding the entire time Zero had been charging around the house to rattle the windows, and then later when he'd been making sure nothing would get through any of the windows or doors.

I found Zero back in the kitchen, inspecting the edges of whatever he'd done to the kitchen window—carefully checking them for signs of tampering, probably. No doubt he'd felt the bit of a breeze that was still seeping through the place from the laundry.

"Oi," I said to his broad back. "We got a problem."

Jin Yeong got back a few minutes after I finished persuading the old mad bloke to get down off the top of the fridge by getting Zero out of the kitchen and into the living room. When I managed to get the old fella to sit on the table instead of the fridge and went back into the living room to make nasty remarks at Zero, who had scared the old duffer up onto the fridge in the first place, there was movement behind my and Jin Yeong's couch.

Zero, concentrating on the heirling sword—which was softly glowing blue—didn't seem to see it, and it was so swift and silent that I almost missed it, too. Across the room there was someone at the window—a blue-suited figure I recognised at once. Jin Yeong, his hand dropping, was just turning away from the window. It looked as though he'd been there for a while trying to get someone's attention and was just about to give up.

"Jin Yeong!" I yelped, and dashed across the room before he could turn away fully.

He almost didn't see me, either; the lack of sound was the most inhibitive thing about the entire situation, and it looked as though it worked both ways. My mad rush did some good, though; Jin Yeong's head snapped around as I made contact with the windowsill and he caught my eyes.

I beckoned him to come back and to my surprise he hesitated, his body still angled away as if he meant to go anyway.

I scowled at him and vigorously beckoned him again. "Come back here, you wally!" I snapped.

Jin Yeong's face changed—in fact, it very nearly crumpled in an expression that I didn't remember seeing on him before. Whatever it was, it sent the blood rushing to his ears and lips, and liquified his eyes.

"Jin Yeong?" I said again, uncertainly.

And then I realised what that expression was: it was relief. Deep, stark-fear-to-bright-hope *relief.* The actual *heck?* Had he thought—? He had. He'd thought that we knew he was there and were ignoring him until he went away. What had Zero done last time when he went off on his own that had left Jin Yeong so sure that we would abandon him at a moment's notice?

I didn't know, but I was going to have words with Zero about that later. There was no way Jin Yeong should be feeling so insecure about the partnership all three of us had that he thought we'd abandoned him at the first sign of distance.

In the meantime, it was more important to see if we could communicate with Jin Yeong at all. Maybe he could do something from the outside that we couldn't from the inside.

I jerked a thumb at the room behind me and raised my brows. *You know what's going on?*

Jin Yeong shrugged; spoke. His mouth moved but I couldn't tell what he was saying, and it took far too long for me to realise that I couldn't understand it because he was speaking in Korean, as usual. Only with me here in the arena and him there on the outside, Between didn't seem to be doing the translating like it normally did.

I motioned for him to stop and pointed at my ears, then shook my head. *Can't hear you.* No good trying to write notes to him, either; Jin Yeong didn't read English, and I couldn't read Korean.

Moodily, he nodded. He'd already guessed that. He jerked his chin at me, and I thought I saw him mouth the words *No hae bwa.*

Heck. He thought *I* could do something about this? He wanted me to try?

I took in a quick, uncertain breath, then gave a half-shrug and a nod. Might as well try. Zero hadn't been able to do anything, but I wasn't even supposed to be able to see Between, let alone use it, so I was already an anomaly.

Jin Yeong nodded, bracing himself there with his palms resting on the outside windowsill and his forehead on the glass, eyes on me.

Heck. He really did think I could do something, and he was waiting for me to do it.

I stepped closer again and rested my own hands on the windowsill, reaching out to the sight and feel of Between that I'd gotten so used to sensing all around me. It was still there; I could still feel it and touch it. I could even still influence it. But instead of being a mellow, touchable stream of gently moving pieces that I could turn into what I wanted it to be, now it was vibrating; moving so fast and so furiously that it felt as though it would tear itself to pieces—or maybe just turn itself inside out—and then tear back into being again to do it all over again.

I was no longer in synch with it in the same way that the inside of my house was no longer in synch with the human world I could see through the windows. Here in the house everything was still mellow and gentle; between me and the outside world was a tumbling skirl of Between that couldn't be contained or stopped.

And behind that furious movement I sensed emptiness—an awful and vast emptiness that might have been time as well as space, and that separated me and the living room in my house from Jin Yeong and the outside world in Australia as thoroughly as if I'd taken the entire house into the underworld with me. Heck, it was basically the same thing.

"No one gets to shift my house into the underworld without my permission," I said, through my teeth. I rested my forehead against the glass too, meeting JinYeong's gaze for another brief moment. I saw his lips curl in anticipation and the expectant brightness of his eyes, and felt myself shaken, not quite able to catch a breath.

He couldn't be sure I was going to be able to do anything, but he somehow was.

"Pet, what are you doing?" demanded Zero, alert and alarmed.

"*Now* you see something!" I snapped. And, grasping all that fast, furious swirl of Between that would have torn through my physical hands if I'd tried to use them, I shoved it back at itself and the wall and Between with everything I had.

Ever heard monsoon rain on a tin roof? That battering, shattering, louder-than-screaming assault of sound that comes with the first thunderstorms of the season? It was like that—if the monsoon rain was on both sides of the tin roof instead of just the outside; howling, battering, and trying to shatter against itself.

Somewhere in the eye of that storm, something shifted, and for just a moment I could have sworn I smelt the faintest whiff of JinYeong's cologne and felt the smoothness of his forehead against mine instead of glass.

Then it vanished and the downpour disappeared. Every bit of Between that I had pushed into the wall to try and pry open the shifting mass of Between turned inward and ate itself, then sealed in a fizz of too-quick-to-see motion that sped around the entire house before I could draw in a shocked breath.

JinYeong seemed to catch his breath, too. He gave me an encouraging sort of smile, and the bitter frustration of having to accept that I hadn't been able to do what he had trusted me to do seared right through me.

I didn't mean to kick the wall as hard as I did.

Definitely didn't mean to put a hole in the wall. But now my foot hurt and there was a hole in the wall, so it was definitely me that had done it. Somewhere further along the wall, a banshee yelled, and I pulled my foot out of the powdery mess of gyprock pretty quickly. I didn't want to get whatever I could catch from one of them biting me. Jin Yeong's head tilted as I did so, and for just a moment there was amusement in every line of his pouty little mouth.

A huge hand grabbed me by the hoodie and jerked me away from the wall. I saw Jin Yeong bare his teeth, and said nastily over my shoulder at Zero, "What, you can throw chairs through windows but I can't kick a hole in the wall?"

"You don't kick holes in walls."

"Maybe I've picked up the habit from being around blokes who throw stuff when they're annoyed!" I shot back, pulling myself away and hunching my shoulders as I went back to the window.

Zero narrowed his eyes at Jin Yeong's glare and stepped closer to the window as well. "Whatever you did, don't do it again," he said to me. "You've tightened the whole thing."

Echoing the disapproval, the old mad bloke's voice floated into the living room from the kitchen. "Lady, this house is *squeezing* me."

"Sorry!" I called. "I was just trying something! Just eat your salami; it's gunna be fine."

Jin Yeong levelled his gaze on Zero, then jerked his chin forward. The message was clear: *Go away, Hyeong.* Zero huffed out a small, sardonic breath, but went back to the couch and the heirling sword.

Jin Yeong pulled his phone out of his breast pocket and wiggled it at me.

"I *tried*," I said, but he didn't seem to understand that, so I took my own phone out and showed him as I tried to call his number. Jin Yeong's sharp eyes flicked from my phone to his and back again, and his mouth grew sulky—or perhaps just discontented.

"I'm not real happy about it either," I said, tucking my phone away again when it was evident that it wasn't working.

"The Between thing doesn't seem to work between here and there."

"If you can't communicate with him, let him go away and do something useful," Zero said, from the couch. "We're wasting time."

"What time?" I demanded. "We're not doing anything, anyway! And what do you think he can do to help us out there?"

"He can't do anything to help us," said Zero, laying a hand flat on the blade of the sword, which glowed faintly bluer in response. "No one can. He can find somewhere else to stay for a little while; it's no use hanging around the windows."

"He's my emotional support vampire," I shot back at him. "And not everything has to have a tangible use, you know!"

Zero only said crushingly, "Jin Yeong is no use to us in this situation, tangible or otherwise. He'd be well advised to go to ground for the duration of the trials."

"He thinks you might get hurt," I said to Jin Yeong, jerking my thumb at Zero. "Don't listen to him; you're very useful."

Jin Yeong's eyebrow quirked, and I saw the faintest hint of laughter to his lips once again.

"I didn't say that!"

"All right, all right, no need to get your knickers in a twist!"

Jin Yeong tapped the pad of one finger against the glass and tipped his head back and sideways a bit, lips moving.

I was fairly sure he'd said the Korean equivalent of *I'll be back*, but I was no expert in lipreading, especially lipreading Korean. I must have been right, though, because he backed away, eyes on me, and gave me a final smile before he turned and vaulted over the fence.

I turned away from the window when I couldn't see his blue-suited back any longer, and asked Zero moodily, "What are you doing, anyway?"

"We are working the sword," said the old mad bloke, popping up from behind the couch. It was very nearly the most complete sentence he'd ever said, and it still made no sense. "While it's blue, there's danger."

Zero shot a look at him over his shoulder, making the old bloke dance back a few feet and wave a shaking finger in Zero's direction.

"Sit down properly or go back to the kitchen," Zero said. To me, he said, "The sword acknowledges those it considers worthy to be in the trials."

"It goes blue when it approves of someone? Heck, that's handy."

"Blue is good if you want to be king," said the old mad bloke. It must have suited him to be ignored, because he sidled around Zero's couch and sidled into the spare chair, too. Before long, he had crossed his freshly washed feet beneath him and was waggling fingers in the general direction of the sword as if he was influencing it by his aura or something.

"What if it doesn't go blue but you're an heirling?"

"Then you might live through the trials if you give up your right to compete by joining with someone it does go blue for, and make yourself useful," said Zero.

"Or maybe you'll get a knife in your back one night," said the old mad bloke, momentarily less woo-woo and more shell-shocked. "Fae are always stabby-stabby."

I went and got the biscuits to give him something to gnaw on, and asked Zero when I came back, "What about when it's yellow?"

"I don't know. I told you: I'm not the one who made it yellow."

"Oh." That was a bit disturbing, but at least it meant the sword hadn't picked me, right? "Cool! Guess you're the one I'll stick myself to—if you stab me in the back I'm gunna flamin' complain, though."

"No stabbing," said the old bloke. "I already have too many holes in my shirt."

"Oi," I said to him. "What are we supposed to call you?"

I'd never known his name, and although I assumed Detective Tuatu must have, there was no real way for me to contact the detective—not that it would stop me from trying later, of course.

"Don't give him a name!" Zero said sharply. "It's no use getting fond of the Harbinger unless you want to be king."

The old mad bloke stared at him with wide eyes. He whispered, "Who said so? I didn't say so!"

He was pretty earnest about it, too; his hands shook for a good few seconds before he clutched them together on his legs, and he looked as though he might start crying any minute.

"I didn't say it, either!" I said hastily. "You don't have to be the Harbinger if you don't want to be!"

"Do *not* make friends with him!" Zero said exasperatedly. "The sword is already blue, and if you're going to bind the Harbinger to it as well—!"

"I just asked what we could call him!" I protested. "I can't keep calling him the old mad bloke!"

The old mad bloke wagged his finger at me again, shaky but slightly more normal than before. "Names are dangerous, lady."

"Yeah, I know. I didn't ask you for your name—I asked you what we could call you."

"Clever lady!" he said in delight. "I am the Avenger Without a Sword."

"That's a bit long, isn't it? What about we call you Avva, then —nope, that won't work. Everyone'll want to say 'avva cuppa tea?' at you."

"Nobody in the heirling trials will do any such thing," said Zero. He seemed to have given up, because despite the comment his eyes were back on the sword instead of us. That was all right. He'd come around later.

"Without a sword, swordless—oi, what about we call you Les?"

"A boon!" cried the old mad bloke. "A name has been granted to me!"

"All right, Les, avenger without a sword—reckon you can stop spilling coffee on the carpet? You can either dance or drink coffee; doing both isn't allowed in my house."

"Yes, lady!" he said happily. "And now, I will do the dishes. Les, doer of dishes, avenger without a—"

He burbled happily to himself as he disappeared into the kitchen, and I heard him burbling to the little cracked tile above the sink later, too. We'd probably end up with a few broken dishes, but he seemed to like doing the washing up so I let him do it. I didn't see much point in it: if you might die in the afternoon, why worry about doing the dishes? Still, if you're going to die in the afternoon and you want to do the dishes, you might as well.

I NEARLY DIDN'T BOTHER to try calling Morgana's phone—after all, why would it work when I couldn't get hold of Jin Yeong? But I tried after lunch anyway because why not? It wasn't like I could do much more, and Zero was too busy fortifying the house to answer questions with anything other than monosyllables. Not that it was much different to how he'd always been, but now that he'd just started answering questions, I found that I didn't have much patience for not being answered properly. I'm not sure he would have answered questions even if he wasn't busy, mind you; the situation had drawn out a few bad habits again. He seemed to find it a relief to do something with his hands, though, so I left him to it and threw myself on the couch to call Morgana even though I knew it was a ridiculous thing to do.

Only when I tapped her profile and put the phone to my ear, it was actually ringing.

"Heck!" I said, and nearly dropped the phone.

"Pet!" squealed Morgana in my ear a moment later, nearly deafening me. "You're safe! I was *so worried!*"

"*You* were worried! I'm fine—what about you? Is the house— are you guys—"

"The house went weird and the kids are pretty upset, and now there are people camped outside but it's actually inside something, apparently. Daniel says that a trial has started."

My heart sank. "They got you too?"

"I suppose so," she said. "People have been trying to get in through the windows at the front of the house, but when I look out the windows, there's nothing there."

"Yeah, they're not outside in the human world," I said, cold right through. "How about your back windows?"

"Those ones are a bit cloudy still," she said. "But we can see... things out in the backyard. The kids think we'll be able to see clearly soon, but I'm not sure any of us want to know what's really out there."

"Daniel's still there, yeah? What about the others?"

"Half are here; the other half were off doing something secret. They tried to get in this morning and couldn't. Daniel says he thinks it's a closed system, but I already knew there was something wrong. The house isn't...sitting right in the world."

"Yeah," I said. "That's the problem. We can't get out, either— me or Zero. Jin Yeong's outside in the human world."

She tried to say something, but all I heard was a barrage of thumping, yelling, and almost tangible impacts. When it died down, Morgana said, "That's the people outside. Outside the house, I mean—they're still inside whatever this is, and they really want to get into the house."

"How many?"

"We don't know yet: it's too hard to see. Enough to make that kind of a racket, and *big*. They don't know about the kids, but they seem to know there aren't many of us here in the house."

"You got supplies?" I asked. I didn't say *brains* because I didn't need to; Morgana might be a zombie, but she'd never eaten brains yet, and she was still pretty sensitive about the subject.

"Yeah," she said. "I don't want—I really don't want to use them, Pet! But I will if I have to."

"Don't worry," I told her. "Me and Zero will be there in a bit. Just make sure you've got everything to hand in case they get in first, all right? And keep Daniel close."

"You're going to go *out there?*"

"I've got Zero," I said. "I'd like to see anyone mess with him. Don't worry, we'll be fine. See you later."

I jogged up the stairs to where I was pretty sure Zero was poking around and found him in my parents' room. He must have found it as unpleasantly reminiscent of Athelas as I had, because he had a frozen, almost pained look to his face, and I reckon he must have been standing in the same place for a while.

To take his mind off things, I wiggled my phone at him and said accusingly, "You said we can't contact anyone."

"We can't."

"All right, then how come I could call Morgana? She and Daniel are trapped in her house just like us."

Zero's eyebrows twitched together for a moment before the momentary puzzlement cleared. "I told you that the heirling trials is a closed system. It could work like that closed system the merman made for us when we dealt with the sirens."

"Okay, that's something," I said. It was still hard to breathe properly, but at least I could breathe. We weren't dead yet, and we weren't likely to be dead if Zero had anything to say about it. I just had to stay behind him. "That's something, right? We've got contact with Morgana."

"Contact with the zombie offers us nothing," Zero said shortly. "We'll all be best if we stay in our own areas and don't venture out."

"You reckon everyone else is gunna think like that?"

"Of course not. I told you that we need to reinforce the house against attack."

"What about Morgana?"

"She has a house and she has the wolf."

"Yeah, but she's not used to this world, and she doesn't eat...

the right stuff. And there are already people trying to get into her house, unlike ours."

"Pet," said Zero, after a long, pregnant pause. "Are you trying to tell me that you want to go and find the zombie?"

"Got it in one."

"I wish," he said, with a flash of heat that was as sudden as it was surprising, "that you would put forth one tenth of the same effort you put toward the safety of your loved ones, toward yourself!"

"That's flamin' rich, from a bloke who helped out a human girl who was on the turn to lycanthrope even though he knew he could die if she bit him."

"I knew you wouldn't bite me."

"Garbage. We gunna do this?"

"What's your plan? What are you hoping to achieve?"

"Get to Morgana, first of all. We can probably stay there with her once we get through: hole ourselves in and wait it out like you wanted to do in the first place."

He shook his head. "The zombie has no idea how to control or appoint her house. We'll have to get them back here safely if we can. This house knows what it's doing, and it's well trained to obey you."

Like my house was a dog, or something. In spite of everything that horrible day, I couldn't help grinning. "Look at you, saying nice things about me," I said. "All right, so we're gunna have two dangerous trips, but it should be a bit safer on the way back when we have Daniel and the others. What about Les? Should we try to find him and bring him along?"

"He can stay or go as he pleases," Zero said briefly. "If he hadn't been sneaking into the house, he wouldn't be in this mess —and if anyone is equipped to deal with Between and Behind, he's the human for it. If even—if even Athelas couldn't kill him after three or four attempts—"

"Good point," I said.

Heck. Zero was just standing there, staring at nothing, a line between his brows and his eyes distant.

Hastily, I added, "All right, but if he follows us, you don't know what he'll do. He's as likely to cause trouble as he is to help, so if he does anything bad, you're responsible."

That seemed to twitch Zero out of his silent contemplation with a slight smile. "Really, Pet?" he said. "After all the drinks you've left for him and pies you've allowed him to eat?"

"First of all, he pinched that pie. Second of all, you're the one who chucked a chair through the window and left it open for anyone to get through."

Zero's eyes grew lighter, comforting me. I'd wanted him to learn to deal with his feelings, but I hadn't expected for him to have to deal with quite so many—or quite so soon.

He said, "Very well. I'll accept the blame."

"Accept it?" I said, happy to relieve my own feelings at the same time as helping him with his. "You're to blame!"

"Didn't I say I'd accept it?" he said, but there was the faintest curve to his lips.

I grabbed his hand and pulled him toward the doorway. "C'mon; let's get ready to go. You need to strap on all of your little knives and get the big sword that sticks out past your ear."

To my surprise, Zero allowed himself to be pulled: right out of the room and into the upstairs living room, then down the stairs and to his alcove to get out all the hardware we'd probably need to make it to Morgana's and back in one piece.

By the time he emerged from the alcove with two knife belts, an assortment of other knives, and the pommel of a giant sword sticking up past his ear, there was a flurry of blue at the window again. It was JinYeong, and he had Five by the scruff of the neck. Five wasn't too happy about that, but if I was as short as the leprechaun and was being scruffed by someone of JinYeong's comparative height, I'd be pretty unhappy, too.

"Heck," I said, startled out of my composure. "What are you doing back here already?"

Five shot me a glare through the window and tried unsuccessfully to free himself from JinYeong's claw-like grasp. That failing, he windmilled with his arms to turn his face in JinYeong's general direction and silently bellowed something at the vampire that I couldn't follow. JinYeong leaned further over and snarled into his face.

I heard a knife belt drop on the floor, and Zero's voice said, "What in the everloving—!"

"Looks like JinYeong went to grab Five," I said. "Literally. Reckon he's trying to get him to do something about getting us out of here—don't reckon Five knows how, though. Look—now he's probably telling JinYeong that he hasn't *got* his *station*, and everyone knows a leprechaun can't do anything without his station."

Outside, JinYeong lifted Five by the scruff and bared his teeth in the most flagrantly threatening gesture I'd seen from him in a while.

"Good grief, what does he expect Five to do?" I asked.

"JinYeong isn't thinking; he's grasping at straws," said Zero. "The leprechaun can follow a money trail to the loftiest echelons of Behind, but he's useless when it comes to trying to get out of a closed system."

Five must have managed to convince JinYeong of his uselessness—or maybe just of his need for his beloved station—because after another few minutes of silent, vigorous conversation, JinYeong grimly hauled Five away again. Before he went, he mouthed the same thing at me that he'd said earlier—the thing I'd suspected was *I'll be back.*

"Heck," I muttered beneath my breath. "Wonder who he's gunna bring back with him next time, though?"

"The merman, I suppose," said Zero. His eyes were a touch bluer again, which was a good sign.

"At least he's trying," I said. It was comforting, in a way. We'd already lost one member of our household, and I didn't want to lose another one, even for a day. "Maybe he'll figure out a way in."

"There is traditionally no way in without being an heirling or a hanger-on of an heirling," Zero said, the amusement fading. "A few more heirlings might make their way in as the system finds them, but lone outsiders are shut off. We should be moving as soon as possible; the longer we wait, the more dangerous it will become out there."

"How do we tell Jin Yeong what we're doing?"

"We don't," said Zero. "You can try, and he might understand a little, but—"

"But not much. And I won't be able to understand anything he says," I agreed gloomily. "All right; we'll just get on with it, then. Hopefully he won't come back while we're gone, or he'll think we've vanished on him."

"Jin Yeong will be fine," Zero said shortly.

"You didn't see his face before," I retorted. "We are *not* going to make Jin Yeong think we've abandoned him."

Zero checked his larger knives with swift, professional fingers. "Oh, are you commanding this excursion, Pet?"

"Yes, I flamin' *am*," I said. "We're gunna nip out and find Morgana, bring her and anyone else in the house with us, and nip back in before Jin Yeong gets back. You got it?"

He still looked a bit too amused for my liking, but he kept checking weapons, and eventually nodded. "Very well. The dangerous part will be immediately after we leave the house— we'll also have to do a thorough check on this house when we get back. Once we leave it, it's fair game to outsiders."

"No, it's flamin' *not*," I said firmly. "It's my house. We taking the heirling sword?"

"I'm not going to leave it here," said Zero shortly. "Not for anyone to find."

"Is it gunna make things more difficult?"

Zero gave a small sniff that was nearly a laugh. "It will make things more dangerous. Anyone who sees it and knows what it is will attack us to try and take the sword for themselves."

"'Cos everyone else is probably gunna want to be king."

"No," said Zero, unclipping his cuffs and testing the freedom of his shoulders to move within his leather jacket. "Some of them just want to survive; being king is a risk that comes with that desire. The heirlings don't always die, and once one of them is king, the others only have a certain amount of time to contest it. I told you that. The current king is the only one who made sure no one else could do so."

"I remember," I said. "It's how you ended up being in utero for twenty years."

"Exactly. The heirling sword is an attribute to anyone who wants to survive, and an even bigger one to anyone who wants to become king. It's also our biggest weapon."

"Nah, you're our biggest weapon," I said, patting his shoulder in passing. "C'mon, let's go."

CHAPTER THREE

I called Morgana again just before we left. "We're coming to get you now."

I was pretty sure it was relief in her voice as she asked, "You sure?"

"We're coming to get you," I repeated, more firmly.

"Daniel says it's dangerous out there," she said, after a pause. "You probably shouldn't come."

"I've got Zero," I said breezily. "Don't worry about it. Reckon we're a lot safer if we all stick together, anyway."

"Are you going to stay with us when you get here?"

"Doesn't sound like it; our place is a bit easier to defend, I reckon—unless the kids are making themselves useful."

"They already have been," she said. Was it a grin I heard in her voice? I thought so. "I don't think the...people outside know what they are. The kids have been pinching stuff from them and setting booby traps on the lower floor in case they get in."

"I'll make sure to let Zero know to watch out for the bottom floor," I said. "See you soon, all right?"

I had barely hung up before Zero asked shortly, "Ready?" as if he was the one who had been trying to convince me, and I had been dragging my feet. Flamin' rude, that.

"Yep," I said, and found Les at my elbow in his full old mad bloke form.

"Tea, lady," he said solemnly. "Don't forget tea!"

He had a travel mug with him, too; he swished it at me, sorta voodoo-style.

"What are you bringing, bubble tea?" I asked him. "Or are you trying to put a spell on me?"

"Bubble tea is for flower men," he said disapprovingly.

"Actually, any liquid seems to work for 'em," I pointed out. "So there was no reason for it to be bubble tea except—hang on, this has nothing to do with anything. What are you bringing?"

"Tea!" he said happily, and scuttled away to the back door.

"What is *that*?" demanded Zero, pointing after Les with one of his knives.

"You said he could come or stay if he wanted," I remarked. "Looks like he wants to come. Seems like we'll have a bit of company."

"Only for as long as he stays alive," Zero said grimly, and strode away to the back door, too.

I said, "Well, aren't we all flamin' cheerful today," and followed.

THE BACK DOOR actually opened for us by the time we were ready to go. Zero had said it would—as soon as we were settled properly into the arena.

So I guess we were properly in the arena now. Oh yay.

The Behind version of the backyard was dark but not unwelcoming, with tiny familiar touches that would have let me know where I was even if I hadn't stepped out of my own back door. I don't know what I expected—a bloody red hell-scape, maybe; or something so untouchably beautiful that it hurt to breathe the air

—but the twilight softness of the world outside wasn't it. Huge hedges that grew roughly where the next-door fences ought to have been flanked us and led forward toward a huge wall of greenery: another hedge. I had the suspicion that if I could see over the hedges, there would be a heck of a lot more of them out there—a vast labyrinth making up the closed system of the heirling trials.

Still, it was more twilight than fiery-dying-of-the-sun, and when Zero shut the back door behind us, everything felt more like an adventure than a dangerous mission. Even the air wasn't too cold, and the scent of lemon myrtle hung in the air, comforting and then worrying me.

Checking on that sudden suspicion, I asked Zero, "What's it smell like to you out here?"

"Lavender," he said.

"Let me guess," I said. "It's a comforting smell to you."

He nodded, though there was a deep cleft between his brows. "Someone is trying to put contestants at their ease. We'll have to be more careful in areas that feel more comfortable to us."

"They're trying to lull us into a false sense of security?"

"Exactly," he said. "Follow closely, Pet; swords drawn."

I did as I was told, and it seemed as though the scent of lemon myrtle faded a little in the suddenly clear air.

"Oi," I said to Les, who had popped up beside me and was standing far too close for comfort. "What's it smell like to you?"

"Apple pie," he said, beaming down at me.

"You gotta have other good memories!" I said, shocked. There was no way that pinching apple pie from me was the best of his memories.

"Pay *attention*, Pet," said Zero, through his teeth. "Forward."

So I paid attention and moved forward with a slim, unsheathed sword in either hand, slightly damp at the palm. There would be time later to feel sad about an old, mad, human bloke who had been so much beset by faery and behindkind that his best memories were of stealing or being given food by a small human. For now, I needed to make sure I stayed alive long enough for there to *be* time later.

We didn't even get out of where my backyard would have been if it were overlaid on the trials. As we approached the faintly misty T-section of hedge, figures coalesced from either side and into our space, dark and menacing, weapons already drawn.

Longswords, short-swords—heck, even an axe or two. There were at least eight of them, and I couldn't help feeling that today was going to be the day that I lost an arm or a leg. If it came to losing either, I'd probably prefer to—

"Finally!" said one of them, putting a stop to that particular train of thought. "We've been waiting for someone to come out for ages."

"Were you waiting for anyone in particular?" asked Zero. "Or were you going to take anyone who came?"

One of the women stepped forward: a tall, tightly-braided woman who might have reminded me of Palomena if Palomena had ever worn such a contemptuous expression.

She said, "We were given some information that we might like to find the person who lives here. If I'd known we were going to meet up with the younger Lord Sero, I'd have told the boys to wear their best hankies."

They all laughed at that, and a couple of them even nudged each other. This woman obviously knew her audience.

"I didn't think I was of much interest now that I'm no longer allied with my father," Zero said coolly. "On the other hand, you have a better chance trying to endear yourself to my father by killing me than you do trying to endear yourself to me."

"Oh, is that how you're going to play the game?" the leader said, one eyebrow winging upward. "Pretending that you're not interested in the throne and that your dad wants you dead, too? The great Lord Sero the younger, striking out on his own!"

"Yeah, I don't think she cares whether you are or aren't with your dad," I said to Zero. "She's gunna try to kill you, anyway."

The leader shrugged. "Well, that's what we're all here for, isn't it? Slaughter or be slaughtered? Be king or be dead?"

"I'm here because someone pinched me house," I said. "I'm not going to go around killing people because of that, regardless of what fiction says about house pinching and dropping houses on people going together."

"I have no idea what you're talking about."

"That's all right," I said, jerking a thumb at Zero. "Neither does he. You would if you were human."

"If I were human, I would be dead by now."

"Doubt it," I said. "Humans like you usually end up popping up on top, too."

She narrowed her eyes at me. "I don't like the way the things you say sound like they should be compliments but feel like insults."

"Neither does he," I said again, jerking my thumb at Zero once more.

"Be quiet, Pet," Zero said in exasperation. "Nobody likes that."

"Pretty sure it's just control freaks who don't like it, but okay," I said. "Look, if you reckon you're gunna get accolades from Lord Sero Senior for killing his son—"

"I'm not going to try and get anything from him," said the leader, with a heartfelt frankness that would have amused me from anyone else. "He's got a finger in every pie and far too long of a reach when it comes to the world Behind."

"For someone in as much awe of my family as you, it seems ridiculous to make a move against me."

The leader laughed. "What's your dad going to do with you in here? Fight for you?"

"I don't need my father to fight for me," Zero said.

"'F'you ask me, he'd fight his father before he fought you lot," I told them. "And I don't want the crown, either, for what that's worth."

"I hate heirlings like you most of all," said the leader. "You pretend you'd never shed blood and don't want the throne, and then you wait until everyone kills each other to come out of hiding and stab the winner in the back."

"That sounds like a beef with someone else," I told her. "Not us. If someone in your family got slaughtered back in the day—"

"Stop talking, Pet," said Zero. "They don't care."

"It's not about whether they care or not," I argued. "I'm just giving them a chance to save their own lives. I'm not going to go around killing people just for snarling at me."

"Shut up, Pet," said one of the behindkind, and sliced at me from high over his shoulder.

I parried by pure instinct, restricted by Les on one side and stepping forward into the attack instead of toward the side. My upper, right sword blocked and scraped; my left was already darting forward in a short, sharp thrust. He had one sword, and it was already engaged; I had two. I ran him through and stepped back, disengaging both blades as he fell, and immediately fell back another step to block a high, heavy slash that would have cut my head open.

After that I didn't know where the old mad bloke was, but I had a good idea of Zero, too huge and light-blocking to miss. I ducked, parried, slashed, slipped in blood, fell into the hedge, thrust—did everything in my power to stay close to Zero so that no one could come at me from behind.

Maybe all the training had finally done some good, because this time I was aware of each of the attackers around me instead of being constantly on the defensive, barely blocking anything that came close enough to make me aware of it.

The fight didn't feel long, but I was gasping before it was half over, and my arms were shaking when there were no more attacks to fend off and no standing enemies to pursue. I looked wearily around the bloody section of grass and hedge, staggering a bit, and said, "Heck, I'm tired."

"You should be," Zero said shortly, cleaning his sword. "We were fighting for half an hour or so—your stamina will increase if you stay alive long enough, but you'll have to get used to being tired in the meantime."

Half an hour. We'd been fighting *half* an *hour?*

"They were a bit tougher than the usual behindkind, weren't they?" I asked. I hoped so. Heck, JinYeong wouldn't half be annoyed if I didn't show back up at the window later on because I'd been so tired from dealing with one bunch of heirlings that the next lot did me in.

"They weren't tougher than the usual behindkind, they were just better used to combat. All the training in the world won't get you ready for the duration of a fight where the other side aren't just rank and file. They can afford to get the best training and the best in-field practise; they know how to stay alive instead of just throwing themselves on swords."

"Okay, well maybe I'm just getting old," I said, still breathing too deeply but not quite able to catch my breath as I cleaned my swords. "Because that pretty nearly killed me."

"You fought extremely well," Zero said. "You weren't in any danger of dying, and you won't be in the next match, either. You might feel as though you are, but once you push through the burn of your arms—"

"Are you seriously trying to hype me up for the next fight?" I demanded, following him down the left hand lane of the labyrinth. "*Push* through the *burn?* What are you, a fitness instructor?"

Zero cleared his throat a bit—to hide a laugh, if I was any judge—and said, "Do you ever stop making remarks long enough to catch your breath, or should I assume that even a half hour fight isn't enough to exhaust you despite your claims?"

"First of all, *rude*. Second of all, if I don't keep making remarks you'll be able to hear my teeth chattering, and that's flamin' embarrassing."

"Your teeth aren't chattering," said Zero, as we left the last, lingering scent of lemon myrtle behind us and turned down a new green-lined lane.

We squabbled a bit all down the lane while we gathered our breath, then took the left-hand turn at the end of it. By that time, my arms weren't shaking anymore; I was still walking pretty slowly, though. Maybe that was just because it was impossible to see what was coming at us in here, or maybe it was because things were so unbelievably peaceful. You know things are bad when everything looks peaceful—well, you do when it's got anything to do with Behind, anyway.

Les just followed along behind us like a particularly muddy border collie, looking around the world with interest. I hadn't seen him do the same kind of damage that Zero had done during the fight, but he'd been in the fray all right: flask of tea clutched to his chest with one hand, and what looked like a knobkerry in the other. I don't know why he went with a blunt weapon instead of a sharp one, but he seemed comfortable with it.

He didn't seem to have spilled much tea, either, so I said, "Good job staying alive," and flashed the thumbs-up at him.

"Alive is my state; fresh, wriggling bait," he sang softly to himself.

"That's a bit dire," I muttered, and moved forward to walk with Zero again.

The old mad bloke lingered behind, still singing to himself, until we came to another T-section of the lanes and he caught up again.

Much to my surprise, we stopped there while Zero looked up and down the lanes. To our right, the lane seemed marginally more floral and perhaps a bit lighter in tone; to the left, the hedge grew darker and had a shiny black patch between the leaves every so often.

Maybe it was a hard choice for him. I waited for Zero to make his decision, and found that the old mad bloke was gazing at me as if he was waiting for me to make that same decision.

Then Zero asked, "Which way?"

The question sent a thread of pure, shocking terror through me. "You asking *me*? I thought you knew where you were going!"

"I have no idea where we're going," he said. "I got us away from the place that felt safe, that's all. You know your friend, and this is a closed system; there are a finite amount of choices that lead to her. Which direction should we go?"

"Oh," I said. "Right. Well, in that case, we might as well go this way."

I took us down the left-hand path for no other reason than that there was a bit of shiny black to the leaves on the hedges there. It would be just like the road to Morgana's place to be dark and shiny and gothic here Behind.

As we walked, the darkness increased and the leaves on the hedges became draped in moonlit spiderwebs, though there wasn't any moon to reflect off them. I don't like spiders, but the sight of the webs cheered me up, anyway; the tickle of hope that I had somehow found the way to Morgana's house kept me cheerful enough to not mind the thought of spiders crawling around some-where in the leaves, just waiting to come out.

And as we walked, it really did feel as though I could sense us getting closer to where we were supposed to be getting; a kind of sixth sense that would be useless anywhere except in the environ-ment we were currently in.

"Is the closed system supposed to help heirlings?" I asked.

"No; it just accepts that there are things some heirlings can do and allows those things to happen."

I threw a quick look up at him. "So there could be heirlings in here who can't even use Between?"

There was a very brief pause before he said, "They won't be here for long."

"Yeah, that's what I was worried about," I said. And because he looked faintly guilty, I added, "It's not like you did it; you don't have to look so upset about it."

"I wasn't—I didn't look upset."

"It wasn't an insult," I said, and took the road straight ahead at the next cross-section, still following that vague feeling that this way led to black crepe and Morgana.

We were nearly at that intangible goal when I realised that Les had disappeared.

"Flamin' heck!" I said, more indignant than worried. "The old mad bloke's gone again."

"He can look after himself," was all Zero said. "Keep going. We shouldn't stop out here."

"I know," I said; but I didn't like it. The old mad bloke had survived too much to die here Behind instead of comfortably in the human world. At least in the human world he could get bubble tea and apple pie to make up for the lack of a steady life. "We'll see if we can pick him up on the way back."

A moment later, we turned a blind corner and the back of Morgana's house was framed between the two hedges before us: stark, almost two-dimensional in appearance, and glowing faintly pearl between the black lines. It looked as though someone had drawn the house on cardboard, cut it out, and made a thin, barely three-dimensional version of it for a pop-up card.

The array of behindkind that were clustered around the windows and the back door were pretty flamin' solid, though. If they hadn't been moving, I would have thought they were just rock formations, and I didn't like to think about rock formations that could move and fight.

"Good grief!" I said below my breath. "What the heck are *those?*"

"Rock dusters," said Zero, re-sheathing the smaller heirling sword and bringing out his double-handed broadsword instead. "See if you can find anything heavier to fight with; double-handed if you can manage, single if not. You'll need something sturdy, and you'll need to make sure that the smaller ones don't knock you to the ground for the bigger ones to squash."

So that's why there were smaller ones as well.

"Perfect," I said, through dry lips. "Oi, they don't have weapons."

"Their bodies are weapons."

"Like JinYeong," I said, with a small laugh that caught in my throat. Heck. It would have been nice to have JinYeong here too, even if he was only complaining that his favourite suit was going to be ruined.

Zero ignored my aside and instructed, "Don't pull back or give way through a mistaken sense of fair play; rock dusters grind living things to death for the fun of it."

"Which one do you reckon is the heirling?" I asked, spotting a promising sort of pruned branch within the hedge. I reached for it and felt a grippy handle within my fingers instead of a branch. "'F'we get that one first, the others might scatter, right?"

"It's possible," said Zero, but his tone was dampening. "Have you got something?"

"Yep," I said, hauling on the grippy handle I'd found.

I could have sworn I tried to pull out a sturdy, mid-sized sword that wasn't too heavy for me to lift, but not light enough to be smashed. What came out instead was a cricket bat.

I stared at it, and so did Zero.

"You really have a type," he said. "That'll do. Go for their heads; the rest of them is nearly as hard as rock, but the dome of their heads is as close to shale as you can get in a living being."

"Head shot only," I said. "Got it."

They sent a wave of the smaller rock dusters at us as soon as they saw us: a knee-high, bruising avalanche that fairly shook the ground and unsettled me enough to send my back foot stuttering backward.

"Mind your toes," instructed Zero.

I hastily brought my feet back together, and maybe it was

instinct, but I turned side-on and found myself in batting position. It was all instinct after that; one of the rock dusters charged right at me and I played a straight shot, sending a rapid jolt of Between down the haft of the cricket bat to hit the rock duster with the suggestion that it was very light instead of very heavy—and lofted the little beggar for six right over the top of the house.

That seemed to worry the whole group of them, because there was a moment of absolute stillness that Zero broke by saying, "Good job, Pet. Do that to all of them, if you can," before the smaller rock dusters rumbled forward again, this time more cautiously.

I wasn't cautious. I coated my entire bat in the essence-of-be-light Between to make anything I hit light, and played shot after shot: drive, square drive, sweep—anything I could start low and send high. I don't know where the little beggars went after they sailed over the house or hedges, but none of them came back, and that was good enough.

Zero left the last of them for me and strode on toward the bigger rock dusters, which was okay by me. There were only about six of the mongrels, but they were *huge* and I didn't like my chances against them even if I did have a bat that could make them think they were light.

I took care of my smaller rock dusters and then hurried into the fight closer to the house with aching arms once again. I might as well have left Zero to do it himself, for all the good it felt that I did. Every hit I managed to get in shook me to my bones but didn't seem to make much of an impact on the rock dusters, and Zero had already taken care of three of them. He was slowing down a bit now, but he was at a good height to get at their heads, unlike me. The rocky bozos could hit *hard*, and Zero's torso was mottled blue and purple where I could see it through the tear in his shirt.

Obviously, I couldn't leave the fight, even if it didn't look like I was achieving much. I ducked under another swing that would have made tomato paste of my brains and darted toward the steps. I needed a height advantage. As I dodged a swing from a rock duster closer to the stairs and skipped right, something heavy and terracotta smashed on the ground a few feet away, sending pottery shards flying.

I risked a glance up, narrowly avoiding a punch that would have had me on my back permanently looking up, and saw shutters open with a froth of children at each window: windmilling limbs, shoving projectiles at each other, and hanging precariously out into Behind to line up the next unsuspecting victim.

The kids! Those homicidal, flower pot-wielding little menaces were up at the windows, taking literal pot shots at the rock dusters below, with little thought and probably not too much care whether it was an enemy or a friend that they actually hit.

Another pot grazed my shoulder and hit the ground with shin-stinging force. I yelped and jumped sideways, instinctively ducking and covering—which probably saved my life, because a ringing *clang* just above my head took out one of the metal portico supports that framed the back stairs.

"Heck!" I said, taking the steps two at a time and ducking for cover beneath the now-drunkenly-leaning portico. "Oi! You cock-eyed little cabinet dwellers! You nearly hit me!"

They only giggled, but the next pot shot missed me completely and hit the behindkind at the base of the stairs right on the top of his head, caving in his skull with a sickening sort of wet sound. I wiped his blood from my face and batted away the smaller rock duster that tried to cannonball my legs and tumble me down the stairs again.

A few feet away, Zero set his sword at shoulder height and shoved it through the eye socket of the last standing rock duster as if it was paper mâché, shifting back briefly at the hips to avoid the last, powerless swing of the duster.

"That's flamin' gross," I said, then dropped my bat with a yelp as the back door was wrenched open behind me.

"Pay *attention* to your surroundings, Pet!" said Zero through his teeth.

Luckily for me, it was only Morgana and Daniel in the open doorway, not more rock dusters. Morgana, her face absolutely white, cried, "Pet!" and grabbed me as I turned around.

I allowed it, but warned, "Careful! You'll get blood all over you."

"I don't care about blood!" she said, but she'd already closed her eyes. "If I can't see it, it's not there."

"It'll still get all over your clothes, even if you can't see it," I protested, but she kept hugging me anyway.

"Just let her hug you," Daniel said. He seemed resigned. "She won't feel better until she does, and it's not like it hurts you. You can go wash off the blood afterward when she knows you're still going to come back alive."

"I am *right here*," said Morgana, with some dignity. The dignity was slightly ruined by the fact that although she turned her head to glare at him, she still hadn't opened her eyes. "You should come in before any more of those things start trying to get through the door."

"Not to worry; you shouldn't get any more of those ones coming through," I said.

"They'll be different ones next time," Zero said, ruining the moment. He took the stairs three at a time in two easy strides, and brushed past all of us to enter the house. "They'll probably be more dangerous ones, too. Where are your things? We should leave while we can."

"We've already packed," Daniel said, following him into the hallway.

That left me with Morgana, who let go of me while carefully looking away so she wouldn't see the blood, and wafted down the hall after the other two.

"Hang on!" I said, far too late. "You're standing up!"

"I don't want to talk about it," she said, still carefully not looking at me. I had a feeling it wasn't because of the blood this time.

"All right," I said, nice and easy, like she might run for it if I wasn't careful enough. I knew what it had taken to get her on her feet, but I couldn't regret it when I saw her standing up for the first time since I'd known her. It wasn't right to expect her not to regret it, though. It was fair enough to not want to eat brains. "What's the go with the kids? Are they coming with us?"

"We've said our goodbyes," Morgana said sadly. "We had a bit of a talk while you haven't been around, me and the kids. I think they're locked onto the house—Daniel told me that they were all murdered here, and I don't think they can leave. It's why they were so annoyed at those things outside."

"Yeah, I noticed," I said, grinning. I pinched someone's tshirt from the pile of clean laundry on the couch in passing and cleaned my face off so that Morgana could look at me without fainting from the sight of the blood. "They were pretty helpful; got rid of a few rock dusters for me that were pretty flamin' inconvenient."

The next question I had to ask was even more touchy, so I waited until I'd finished cleaning my face before I asked, "What about your parents?"

"I couldn't get into their room," she said quietly, after a moment. "I had to try and explain from outside the door."

"If it helps, I don't reckon there's anything here in the arena that can hurt 'em," I told her. If it wasn't for Morgana's feelings, I wouldn't have cared if there was something that *could* hurt her parents. They'd bargained with Morgana's life to escape death, and they deserved everything they got.

The house didn't echo quite right, a bit like a house that's empty and ready to be moved out of, and before Morgana had a chance to reply, I heard Zero's voice saying quite clearly from the kitchen, "We need to leave as quickly as possible. The sooner we get back, the less likely it is that anyone will have found the bodies we left behind us."

Morgana shot me an accusing look that banished the uncertainty that had lingered in her eyes, and I said, "We just killed a few fae who found the house and wanted to kill us. We haven't been going around and killing people for the fun of it."

I nearly added, "Well, not all of us, anyway," but that made me feel weird and squishy on the inside, so I sniffed away the words.

"We're ready to go," Daniel's voice said, also from the kitchen.

Zero's voice asked, "Just you and the zombie?"

"I have a name," said Morgana indignantly, starting forward into the kitchen ahead of me in her indignation.

"We're coming, too," said a voice.

"Yeah, we're not staying here," said another.

I craned my head around the corner and saw five bulging cooler bags stacked together in the kitchen, along with three fat travel bags and six other lycanthropes.

I opened my mouth to say, "Flamin' heck, what's all that!" at the cooler bags, but shut it as soon as Daniel glared at me. They were cooler bags and Morgana was walking—there were brains in those coolers, dead cert.

Instead, I said, "Three bags for the eight of you?"

"We already have another change," said one of the lycanthropes, winking at me.

Zero shot him a cold look, and he gulped and looked away.

Daniel said, "We've got what we need, and we already know it's dangerous out there. The lighter we travel, the better; one bag per person. How long did you say we'd be shut up in your house?"

"I didn't," said Zero, to whom the question was addressed. His voice was grim, but that was pretty normal.

"Only until we figure a way out of the trials," I said. No one had asked me, but there was no way I was going to be imprisoned in my own house where the only permanent way out was to foray into fairyland and fight to the death. There was no way I was going to let people shut Jin Yeong out of the house, either. "Once we figure a way out, they can stay in here and fight to the death while we send a message that we don't want to be heirlings."

"We can do that?" asked Morgana, her eyes lighting up. "I don't want to fight, either."

"Coulda fooled me," said one of the lycanthropes, and was ruthlessly smacked across the ears from about four different directions.

Morgana's chin crinkled very slightly and then grew firm. "I told them not to come into the house," she said.

"We had a few visitors before the rock dusters," explained Daniel. "They took us by surprise, especially since they got into the house, so—"

"You said we shouldn't stay here for too long," Morgana said, grabbing one of the bags. "So let's get going and leave the stories for later."

Morgana took another few minutes to say a second goodbye to the ghost kiddies before we left. I don't think Daniel was too happy about it, but the kids had a tendency to try and drop things on his head from the upper floors when he was on the stairs, so I didn't really blame him. And even if there were no rock dusters outside, the same sense of menace still hung over the whole house, tickling around my ears like a cold breeze that shouldn't be where it was.

I hunched my shoulders, wondering at the familiarity of the feeling, but didn't have time to figure it out. Zero, who had followed Morgana up to the second level but no further, stuck his head around the balustrade and caught sight of me.

"Pet," he said, in a low voice. "You should see this."

"Dunno if I want to," I muttered, but I went up the stairs anyway. Morgana's house was nearly as familiar as mine: I'd spent a while here not long ago, and if I was judging right, Zero had just come from the bathroom. Given there were now multiple lycanthropes in the house instead of one zombie girl and about a dozen ghosts—none of whom had any basic bodily functions any longer, despite the fact that they seemed to be able to eat—it probably wasn't going to be very pretty.

It turned out Zero had come from Morgana's room, not the bathroom. That gave me a few moments of relief until I followed him through the room and into her little attached kitchen and saw what was there.

I'm not sure what I expected to see; what I *didn't* expect was to feel the renewed knife of cold breeze as soon as I entered. The window there in the kitchenette was inky blackness, just like the window in our kitchen had been before Zero blocked it up, a cold not-breeze billowing the tiny curtains. Apart from that, the kitchen was all black and white and red tiles; nice and gothic, except that the black and white was tile and the red was blood— lots of it. I mean, I suppose that's gothic, too. It wasn't supposed to be on the walls, though.

The real mess was on the floor; four more-or-less human-looking bodies tumbled on top of each other in a pool of blood that seemed to end at about...neck level. In other words, all of the bodies were headless—or nearly headless—the remains of their jawbones and skull cavities loose and dangling like the remains of popped balloons. Some of that popped balloon had made it all the way back into the carpeted part of Morgana's room.

I would have said, "Wonder where the brains went," but I was pretty sure I already knew. Instead, I asked Zero, "You reckon she ate 'em straight outta the skull? Or did Daniel and the others clean 'em out afterward and pack 'em for supplies?"

"These two are clean," said Zero, pointing to two of the bodies in turn. "Cleaner, at any rate; no teeth marks."

I struggled with my breakfast for a few moments before I said thickly, "So she ate two?"

"Warm from the body," he agreed.

"Thanks for that," I said, swallowing. I prodded the closest body with the toe of my boot. "Looks like she was hungry."

Zero shrugged. "Hungry, or angry. There's human blood in here, and—"

"Oh," I said, because I saw the coffee cups at the same time. One lay partway beneath a body, spilt coffee long over-run and thickened by blood; the other listed drunkenly on the countertop with a broken handle, a slowly-drying stream of coffee leading tackily toward the edge of the counter and the entire lot sprinkled with blood. "Doesn't look like she had trouble with fainting in here."

Morgana had seen something come through her kitchen window while someone prepared coffee for her—something that attacked whoever was there. And true to her word, she hadn't needed to get to the fridge to make sure she was fed.

"Well," I said, when I was pretty sure my breakfast wasn't going to come back up, "I s'pose at least we know we don't have to worry about Morgana being dead weight, right?"

CHAPTER FOUR

YOU COULD SAY IT WAS LUCKY THAT WE MADE IT HOME without having to fight again, but by that stage I wasn't exactly sure who it was lucky for. Judging from the bodies I'd seen in the kitchen back in Morgana's house, we weren't short on muscle power ourselves.

It was a relief, anyway. The old mad bloke was waiting for us on the back step when we got back, too, which sent another spark of relief fizzing through me.

Daniel said suspiciously, "What's *he* doing here?"

"Waiting for us to open the door, I reckon," I said flippantly. "Dunno why he can't get in this time; he seems to be able to get in whenever he wants to any other time."

"I mean why is he here at all!" snapped Daniel. "It's only supposed to be heirlings in here, and—"

"You're here," I pointed out. "And a whole lot of rock dusters who weren't all heirlings, not to mention the lycanthropes you two brought along with you. It looks like whoever's with you when this thing starts up is who comes along for the ride."

"I thought the trials had to be made up of all the heirlings and *only* the heirlings," complained Daniel. "They don't tell us lycan-thropes anything."

"You and vampires both," I said, grinning at Les as I stepped up to open the back door. "That's what happens when you're a second-class citizen."

"Tell me about it," he muttered, following close behind me with Morgana sandwiched between us. That was pretty funny, because Morgana probably could have outfought the both of us, judging by the carnage in the kitchen earlier.

"Maybe someone knows too many names," I suggested.

I caught a glimpse of Zero following behind Daniel. He said, "The arena does its best with a series of presets that pull away anyone likely to be an heirling with their surroundings, and plants them in the arena. If the heirling names were known, another heirling, the king, or the harbinger could call them to combat—it would be a mess. Occasionally the harbinger has been known to call two finalists to combat when they were dragging their feet, but heirlings are usually careful not to let their names be known."

"Hear that?" I said to the old mad bloke. "You're supposed to go calling the king and whoever wants to fight by their names so they can fight and leave the rest of the heirlings out of it."

Les threw me a suspicious look. "You want to fight, lady?"

"Heck no!" I said hastily. "I just want to—Jin Yeong!"

I heard Daniel groan and there was an accompanying, short sigh from Zero, but I didn't care because I could see Jin Yeong slouched beside the window as I came out of the back hallway and into the living room.

He straightened as soon as he saw me and I grinned and waved at him, crossing the living room at a trot. I might not be able to talk to him in a way that he could hear, but it was nice to see his face anyway. I didn't want him to think that we'd nicked off and left him alone out there. It might be safer out there than it was in here, but that didn't make it any less lonely and I was pretty sure that JinYeong was more of a people person than he liked to pretend.

"Lady," said Les, tugging at my sleeve confidentially just as I made it to the window. "You really shouldn't want to fight."

"I don't want to fight," I said, beaming at JinYeong. There was a flutter of movement to his left, just out of sight, so he must have brought someone with him. "I just want to get my people out of here safely."

"Am I your people?"

"'Course," I said, surprised. "Gave you apple pie, didn't I?"

"Stole it," he muttered, but he looked pleased anyway. JinYeong scowled at him and he scurried away again, though I wasn't sure where he went. I never was, anyway; the old mad bloke was basically a larger version of the banshees, who hid in the rafters, skirting boards, and bookcases, not to mention the washing machine.

Once we were alone again, JinYeong held up his index finger, looking very pleased with himself—as if to say, *Just a moment, please.* Then, with the air of someone giving a present for which he knows he will receive suitable thanks, he tugged the unseen person into sight—or at least, dragged him.

Heck. This time, he'd brought Marazul along. Marazul didn't look very happy about it, but at least it didn't look like JinYeong had dragged him along by the scruff like he had with Five; he had certainly wheeled Marazul into eyesight, but the fact that the merman seemed startled and discomforted by the action gave me hope it was a new indignity rather than a continuance of it.

"Don't do that," I said, pointing at Marazul's wheelchair and frowning at JinYeong. "It's flamin' rude to drag people around by their chairs."

JinYeong cocked his head, one eyebrow rising, and touched the handle of the wheelchair once again as if to ask, *This? You're annoyed about this?*

"Yes," I said emphatically, nodding so that he wouldn't be in any doubt. "You can't just wheel people around without their permission!"

His eyes narrowed thoughtfully while Marazul looked up at him in exasperation and some trepidation; then Jin Yeong released the handle with a little flick of his fingers and made the slightest bow toward Marazul, who looked about as flabbergasted as I felt.

I blinked a bit and gave Marazul the thumbs-up, which he returned tentatively, then I smiled happily at Jin Yeong. "See! You can stop yourself from being a prat when you want to!"

Jin Yeong's eyes narrowed again, as if trying to decide whether or not to be offended, but I thought I caught a gleam of laughter in the darkness of them anyway. He tilted his head toward Marazul and I saw his lips move in a way that seemed to be, *"Jal dwill ko kata."*

I think it will be fine.

I couldn't help the small smile that crossed my lips, or the warmth in my heart.

"We'll see," I said to him, leaning against my side of the window and making an almost mirror image of him. I didn't dare to hope too much, even if Marazul and I together had defended a café from goblins and rescued a good handful of humans from a slow, siphoning death by emailing them out of the café and into the closest library. If anyone could figure out what to do in this situation, it was probably Marazul; he was very good at wriggling out of dangerous situations.

I wondered for a brief moment if that was just sour grapes on my part, since Marazul had wriggled out of a dangerous situation by selling me out to Zero not so long ago; but the thought wasn't as bitter as it had been. Jin Yeong seemed to have gotten over his dislike of the merman for long enough to ask for his help, too—or had he?

I took a quick look at Jin Yeong's profile, wishing I could see his face properly; he was still there, still close, but his attention was on Marazul. For a brief second, I found myself very nearly as cranky about that as Jin Yeong had been about being interrupted by Les earlier, and hastily looked away.

Good grief, what was wrong with me?

I suppose that once you've shared a house with someone for a year they start to work their way into the regular rhythms of your life—enough to make a bit of a hole when they're suddenly not there any longer. Athelas had left a hole, too, even if it was a different kind of hole.

It wasn't as though we had been separated from Jin Yeong for very long: barely a day in the human world. It wasn't as though I couldn't see him, either. He was right there, even if I couldn't touch him or smell him.

Good grief, when had I got so used to having him beside me—warmth and all, cologne and all—that I'd become addicted? Because that's what it must be. I was so used to having my emotional support vampire there that I was going into withdrawal when I couldn't have him.

"I'm fine without you," I muttered at his profile, and tried very hard to concentrate on what I could lipread of his and Marazul's conversation.

Far too late, I realised that I couldn't understand a thing they were saying. Why couldn't I understand at least Marazul? I'd been able to do a bit of lipreading with Five, so why was it even harder to understand Marazul than it was to understand Jin Yeong?

It wasn't until I saw Marazul mouth something I was certain was *"Si, si, bene!"* that I dredged up the last remnants of the Italian I had learned with mum and realised what was happening. The sneaky merman must have been speaking in Italian the whole time I knew him: he had been using Between to translate everything he said, just like Jin Yeong did when he wanted to be understood. Only I had known that Jin Yeong was doing it, and I had taken it for granted that Marazul was speaking to me in English.

Well. This was just great—the two of them having a conversation; JinYeong in Korean, Marazul in Italian. They understood each other out there, but from inside the house I couldn't understand either.

"This is flamin' garbage," I said grumpily.

Zero said questioningly, "Pet?"

"Nothing," I said. "Just something else making life harder. Not sure Marazul will be much help."

"I didn't think he would," was all Zero said, before turning back to Morgana.

I managed not to roll my eyes and turned back to the window just in time to see Marazul pull out his laptop, set it up on his knees, and start threading a clever electronic sort of working around the window frame that fizzed as it joined at the top. It made a buzz in the room, too—a buzz that had one of the wolf-form lycanthropes shaking his head and whining, and even Zero looked up in my peripheral, startled and worried.

"What are you doing, Pet?"

"It's not me!" I said, grinning, my eyes on Marazul, who seemed to be struggling with the working.

At any rate, he was holding onto his laptop pretty tight, and if I had to guess, I would have said he was vibrating slightly, too. He didn't look worried, but he did look increasingly rueful.

"'Zul's having a go at something," I added. "I don't think it's working, but it seems to be doing something, anyway."

The buzz took a while to die down, even after Marazul had evidently stopped his working; a slight fuzz of it still hung in the air after Marazul and JinYeong stopped arguing back and forth and turned their attention on me.

The merman met my eyes as he opened his mouth, then stopped, thought, and started to speak very slowly and carefully—in English. It looked as though he understood what he was seeing and why it didn't work; that, moreover, he needed to make it easy for me to lip-read.

I couldn't understand everything he said, but I got the gist of it. Marazul had thought that he might be able to open up communication by tracking the vibrations of the window as we spoke, but for some reason—"neither side is synched with the other" was what I thought he said—he couldn't get it to work.

JinYeong, his lips compressed and his eyes dark and dangerous, just glared at him.

"Don't blame Marazul for not being able to do something," I said. "It's not like he hasn't tried."

"What has he tried?" asked Zero. I hadn't heard him sneak up behind me, but I often didn't; he's far too light-footed for someone of his size. "That buzzing might have drawn unwanted attention from outside if anyone was near enough to sense it—I'd rather he didn't do it again."

"Reckon he was trying to read the vibrations from the glass as we speak and feed it into one of his little magic computers," I said. "He says things aren't synched up and that's why he can't."

"Molecules vibrate," called Morgana, perched upright on the couch with her legs crossed and her back straight and proud. "That's how living stuff *is* and behaves and interacts. I suppose with magic it'd be possible to make the outside and inside molecules vibrate just enough out of synch with each other so that we can't interact. It's surprising we can still see each other."

The look that Zero shot her was equal parts respect and confusion. "Does this apply only to the human world?"

Morgana shrugged, but said, "Doubt it. The way some of you can...do stuff that you call magic seems to follow a lot of the same principles, even if you don't know the right words to call 'em."

"Who have you been watching do magic?" I asked, huffing a surprised laugh.

"We're not just animals you know," said either Darren or Dylan. "We can do stuff other behindkind can do."

"Beaut," I muttered. "Just what we need, lycanthropes doing magic."

Zero left me alone at the window, much to Jin Yeong's surprised amusement, and sat down in his own couch, casually displacing a lycanthrope to do so. "What is your position upon magic, then, zombie?"

"First of all, my name is Morgana. I don't call you fae boy, do I? Secondly, my position is that magic is just really hands-on science. Basically, I think you behindkind have a really good grip on your physical body and on the vibrations of the world around you. That's my guess, anyway. Every time you do something with magic, I bet it's just the vibrations working for you—not to mention the fact that you seem to vibrate on the right level to actually interact with non-physical things."

Zero, looking about as alert and normal as he'd looked in far too long, leaned forward with his arms on his knees, fully engaged. "Fae scholars have debated about the connection between the physical world and the application of science and magic for—"

"Good grief," I grumbled. I caught Daniel's eyes briefly as I turned my attention back to the now slightly-pouting Jin Yeong, and understood the expression of mingled fondness and rue the lycanthrope wore. Morgana must have been talking about this for longer than a few minutes.

Even though I knew he couldn't hear me, I said to Jin Yeong, "Sorry about that. Morgana and Zero are having a heart-to-heart about how magic is actually just science when people know how to touch the science with the right vibes."

Jin Yeong's mouth quirked. He might not understand, but he knew when I was being sarcastic. He tipped his head at Marazul and gave an apologetic sort of half-shrug. He might as well have said, *This one was useless, too. I shall try again.*

"You don't have to keep trying," I said. "And you don't have to keep kidnapping our friends to get them to try and do something about all of this. We'll figure out another way."

Jin Yeong grinned at me, his eyes bright and mischievous, and blew me a kiss. Then he sauntered away, leaving Marazul to follow behind him at a much slower rate on the grass.

"*Oi!*" I yelled. "I said you *don't* have to—flamin' heck, there he goes! Wonder who he's gunna bring back next."

"So long as it's not my father, I don't care," said Zero. "There's nothing that can be done to get us out of here."

Even Daniel, as naturally gloomy as he was, seemed to find that annoying. "What are we gunna do, then? You know, if we're not going to try and escape and everything's hopeless?"

"Stay in the house," Zero said briefly. "Barricade ourselves as best we can and try not to die for as long as it takes for the trials to end."

"I thought it was fight to the death kinda stuff?" Daniel said.

"It is—until the sword declares a victor, or until only one heir-ling is left and the others are dead or have sworn fealty."

I said flatly, "No matter what happens, heaps of us are gunna die."

"Yes," said Zero. I wasn't sure the thought worried him too much, but the look he shot at me seemed to show that he was worried about it bothering me, and that was nice. "We can't do anything about it; all we can do is survive and try to keep everyone we love alive."

"Yeah, but what if—"

"There are no *what ifs!*" he said. "The trials are a closed system that require a victor, in some capacity, to unlock."

"And I assume we're not going to be helping anyone to be the victor," said Daniel. "So it will probably take a while."

"You assume correctly," said Zero.

I was secretly relieved by how immediately he said it—more by how absolutely he said it.

"We might as well get comfortable and eat something, then," said one of the lycanthropes. Kevin, probably. Maybe Kyle.

"Hope you lot like rice," I said. "'Cos we're gunna be eating a lot of it."

. . .

I MADE a big batch of rice with a nice, creamy curry to go along with it in hopes of spinning out the food we had. We had a fair bit of rice and coconut cream in the cupboards, along with a lot of milk in the fridge, so I might as well work to our strengths until we could get out into the real world for more food.

I ate dinner with the half of everyone sitting on the floor in the dining room, keeping an ear out for the half in the living room to make sure no one was stuffing curry down the back of the couch. Mind you, it wasn't like the ones in the dining room weren't going to be stuffing curry—they were just more likely to be stuffing it in their mouths.

I started making tea and coffee while the lycanthropes were still fighting over the last dribble of curry in the pot, hoping to fill up their stomachs for a bit longer. If Zero was determined to keep to his plan, we would have trouble keeping up with the demand for food. Morgana hadn't eaten dinner, which had made Daniel watch her with a frown between his brows, but her food wasn't in short supply. I had seen enough brain unloaded into my refrigerator to last any self-respecting zombie for a good fortnight. I didn't like to ask how much of it was behindkind and how much was animal, either. I wondered, grinning a bit, how long it would be before Morgana realised that she'd already seen blood—a *lot* of blood—without fainting, and that her zombie form seemed to be lacking the weakness that her human body had had.

So instead of asking awkward questions, I took tea and coffee out to everyone. We could talk about brains tomorrow. For now, Morgana was walking and the lycanthropes were fed; it was time for coffee.

I hadn't realised how few coffee mugs we had, and the cupboard was nearly empty by the time I found myself gazing dumbly at Athelas' teacup. The hand I had raised to take out another mug shook a little bit, fingers curling back into my palm, but then Zero looked over and I found myself hurriedly pushing the teacup to the back of the cupboard with a shock of worry.

It was a useless, protective gesture; I didn't want Zero to break the teacup, too. Which was absolutely ridiculous, because the teacup belonged to the murderer of my parents. I shouldn't *want* to have it in the house.

But I couldn't bring myself to either take it out of the cupboard and use it *or* let Zero at it.

Heck. I wasn't going to cry right here in the kitchen, was I?

Nope. I wasn't going to let it get to me. I was going to get my own coffee, then I was going to check and see that JinYeong hadn't come back again and take a look at all the windows in the house to see if I could get something, *anything* through to the outside. If I could get something through to the outside, maybe there was a chance that I could get some*one* through to the outside.

And there it was again: that tickly little thought that there had to be something I could do to get us out of here. Some way of seeing the world in just the right way or making it interact with *us* in just the right way to get out while we could.

Still caught with the idea, I took my coffee mug upstairs with me and started on the windows in my own room first. I didn't get too far in there, so I came back out into the upstairs living room, hoping I would be able to get a bit more of a grip on the windows I had used to sneak in and out of the house so often before the psychos came into my life. It wasn't so much that I thought that those windows would treat me better, as such—more that Between seems to have a thing about recurring patterns, and where there are repeated patterns, it's easier for...*stuff* to get through.

Whether or not you want that stuff to get through is entirely dependent on whether or not you're the stuff, or whether you know what that stuff is.

The living room windows weren't much good, either. I tried

out there for a good half hour, always thinking I had a handle on *something*—that *something* was about to connect in just the right way—before everything slipped through my fingers and dispersed into a whirlpool again.

It wasn't that I couldn't feel what was happening now that I knew what it was; even before Morgana had mentioned anything about vibrations and things being on the right wavelengths, I'd noticed the way that Between was acting. Now that I suspected it was folding back over itself because it couldn't come to grips with the differently vibrating section of the human world it should have connected with, it was easier to really see what was happening.

I only wished that it made it easier to do something about it.

When I couldn't do more to the windows in the living room than cause them to become a bit less stable than I was comfortable with, I headed on into Mum and Dad's room. Nothing could be done there, either, but that might have been because I was unsettled by more than the situation I found myself in.

Still, it was oddly peaceful in there with the faint hum of the household below my feet, despite the fact that the back-facing windows were beginning to show more of what was actually outside in the backyard than what was in the human world. I found myself lingering, caught as much by the quiet, mismatching array of items around the room that had been left to loiter in the dust by Athelas as I was by the peace. Somehow, I could still smell the faint scent he always carried with him. I should really start getting rid of some of the things he'd left behind—without crying, preferably. I caught sight of the little collection of items on the dresser top, lit warmly with evening sunlight: a key, a plain banded ring made of what looked like citrine, and a little round badge-type thing that could have been a button pin if I hadn't known it was actually a small component of a private network—the magical tech by which we'd secured our phones between us and prevented anyone from the outside from being able to hack into our phones.

I turned it over in my fingers, wondering if Athelas had meant to keep it or if it had merely been forgotten.

A lycanthrope voice said from the doorway, "This where we're sleeping?"

"Nope!" I said firmly, shoving the badge and key into my pocket and striding out of the room so I could close it in front of that far-too-inquisitive nose. I would have grabbed the ring as well, but I knocked it to the ground and under the bed instead, and I didn't want to stoop for it while a lycanthrope was looking. "No one sleeps in here."

"Bed looks comfy," he said, eyes narrowing.

"Your face looks punchable," I retorted. "No need to judge based on looks, mate. No one sleeps in that room."

The grin he sent in my direction was lazy and unphased. "What, you reckon you're going to sort me out?"

"Don't have to," I said. "I'll get Morgana to sort you out."

That wiped the grin off his face pretty quick. "Hang on, there's no need to go telling the missus on me!" he protested.

"The *missus*?"

"Alpha's missus," he said, surprised. "Zombie girl."

"All right, I know who you're talking about, I was just wondering why the heck you were calling her *the missus*. The bunch of you are flamin' old as the hills! You should find some new slang."

"I'm not old, I'm only fifteen!" he said. "And my dad used to call my mum *the missus* all the time, so—"

My phone went *ping*!

"Heck!" I said, interrupting him. "Belt up for a tick, yeah?"

My phone shouldn't be making any noises, let alone the ping for a text, because anyone who should be able to text me was already in the house and could yell for me instead. I grabbed it and stared at the lit screen. Not a text—it was a missed call. Tuatu had tried to call me three times in the last hour, and the notifications had all come through right now. Every single one of them—the texts that I had missed from him as well.

How the heck had they got through?

Hang on. *Hang* on. If call notifications from Detective Tuatu had somehow got through, did that mean I could call the detective back?

I started grinning and fished the badge out of my pocket again. What was the bet that the private network Marazul had made for us was still up and running? What was the bet that Detective Tuatu's phone had just connected with mine and I'd received backed-up notifications that had been sent over the course of the day?

"What?" asked Kyle or Kevin, looking worried. "I didn't do anything, and I'll tell the missus if you bash me."

"Never you mind," I said. "Just had a thought, that's all. You go back downstairs; I've got a call to make."

He stared at me, perplexed. "I thought we couldn't use our phones to call the human world while we're in here. Mine doesn't work."

"We can't," I said. "That's why I've got an idea."

"Still dunno what you're talking about."

"You don't have to," I told him. "Off you go. I have a private call to make."

"No one can make calls!" he called out over his shoulder, stubborn to the end.

He did leave and go back downstairs, though, leaving me free to unlock my phone and pause for a second before I could bring myself to press the button to call the detective. Every instinct told me to hurry while there might still be a chance that I could get through, while the lead feeling in my stomach told me that I'd missed the window and it was no use hoping it would work.

When I found my thumb twitching, I hastily tapped Detective Tuatu's profile. I was so busy trying to make the thumb stop twitching that I almost didn't notice that I could hear the phone ringing—actually ringing.

"Heck!" I said, slapping the phone against my ear just in time to hear the detective's disgruntled voice.

"Hello? Pet? I've been trying to call you all day!"

"Oi, Tuatu," I said, bright with relief. So he *had* kept the token on him! Rapidly, I added, "Don't throw away that little network chip you got from us, whatever you do!"

Tuatu said something beneath his breath that was pretty rude. "So *that's* why my phone's been cutting out every time I walk into this part of the room!"

"You on the move right now?"

"No, I'm sitting at my table; I chucked the chip into the fruit bowl and forgot about it."

"All right; just don't move away from it while we're talking, all right? I'll be cut off if you do that."

"Pet, what's going on? Weird stuff has been happening since this morning and I've tried to call you four times in the last few hours."

"It's a long story."

"North just got *very sane* and I don't know what to do with her. I'm terrified."

"Yeah, she probably knows that everything's about to go to pot."

"What do you mean, it's about to go to pot? I've never seen her like this! I think her little friend disappeared again, and if she's got to go through what she went through last time—!"

"Heck, they got Sarah, too? We'll look for her in here. Tell North not to worry."

"Where is *in here?*"

"You won't understand: just tell North that the trials have started, we're trapped in the arena with the other heirlings, and that we'll look out for Sarah. I bet she's in here, too. I need you to do something."

He audibly took a breath. "Are you all right, Pet?"

"I'm alive, and I've got Zero—we've also got some lycan-thropes and a zombie, so we're looking good for now. Apparently this is a gladiator, last-man-standing kind of deal, so—wait, that's not important. What's important is that I need you to do some stuff."

"Yes, sorry. What do you need?"

"I need you to get one of those chips to Jin Yeong so we can talk to him. And I need you to find someone for me."

"Who? And where am I going to get another chip? The other humans are—"

"Dead. Yeah, I know. You won't be able to get back to the house, either, I reckon. Do you think they'll have some of 'em in evidence in your lockup? Your blokes took evidence, didn't they? Before everything went to pieces?"

"I'll look. What's the name of the person you need to find?"

"Don't know that. I know he owns a particular bit of land in the city; I'll text you the address. It might take a bit to find the bloke, though; I reckon he'll be hidden behind a few false names and fake companies, as well as a lot of paperwork."

"Is he someone you're after for one of your cases?"

"Nope," I said, busily texting the address while I was talking. I didn't want to lose the connection midway through our talk and leave him with nothing. "Oh, and you'll have to be careful when you start looking; it could be dangerous. Make sure North knows that you're doing it, okay?"

"I don't need North's help to stay safe."

"No, but you can't deny it's nice to have," I reminded him.

He didn't deny it, but he did ask, "What's this one done to you?"

"Gave me a book and sent off a fae lord who was trying to drag me out into the street."

"I can see why you're so worried about it: he sounds like a

dangerous man. Shouldn't you be getting me to do more to help you out of your current predicament?"

"Nah, that's something you can't help with. And sarcasm aside, it might not sound like much, but the bloke knows my name—he threatened me with it—and I wanna return the favour if I can."

Tuatu might have sounded very slightly miffed. "He knows your name, and I don't?"

"It's not 'cos I told him!" I protested. "And you won't even tell North your first name, so it's not like you have a leg to stand on!"

"That's fair," he said, after a brief pause. It sounded as though he was smiling. "I'll look into it for you."

"There's a leprechaun who'll be able to help you," I said. "Especially if there's a money trail to follow. You give him access to your computer systems and the internal and external internet, and he can follow a money trail across the internet. Just give him a lot of choc chip bikkies and a few crisp fifties and he'll be all yours."

There was another pause, but this time it didn't sound like Detective Tuatu was smiling when he said, "You expect me to take a...a *leprechaun* who can be bribed into the police department?"

"You've had Zero and Athelas in there," I said, and my voice caught. "At least Five won't be pinching bodies and doing weird voodoo in your morgue. He'll just plug himself into your computers and follow any money trail through the internet until he finds his little pot of gold at the end of the 'net."

"Isn't there anything else I can do? Those three are always getting you into trouble, but this is the first time it's been trouble I've seen North worried about."

"She's right to be worried," I said soberly. "But there's nothing you can do from out there. We have to play by the rules to get out, apparently. We'll see about that, but I don't reckon anything can be done from the outside. Once Jin Yeong is all mic'd up we'll be able to get everyone together if we think we can attempt a breakout."

"Make sure you call me if you need me," he said. "I'll have the chip on me all the time."

"You won't be able to take other calls," I warned him.

"I was due for holidays anyway," he said, and hung up.

It was a cheerful feeling, knowing that we had people on the outside. The reflection that soon we'd have contact with Jin Yeong properly again was also a nice, cheerful one; it would help to balance out the stark necessity of leaving the house again in search of poor little human Sarah, who had already escaped Behind once.

There was no use waiting to tell everyone; it was growing dark outside in the human world now, and there were sure to be things wanting to come into the house if they could. It wasn't like we were going to sleep. Not all of us, anyway.

So I went downstairs to find the lycanthropes having an arm-wrestling competition that was apparently supposed to work right up until the winner faced off with Zero. They were about halfway through the ranks when I got back downstairs, and more than one set of eyes fastened on me as I stepped down onto the carpet.

I dunno; maybe I have a portentous walk. At any rate, there was no use wasting the entrance I'd managed to effect. "Got bad news and good news," I said to the lot of them. "Which one do you want first?"

Morgana shot me a look and said, "Bad news. We've got zombies, lycanthropes, fae, and a smelly old man. What's badder than us? We'll be fine."

"Don't play games," said Zero, unimpressed. Maybe he'd heard me on the phone with Tuatu.

"Right; so the bad news is that we need to go outside the house again. Sarah's out there—probably her parents, too—and North wants us to go get her and keep her with us."

Zero didn't even blink. Maybe he'd given up—maybe he'd just

decided that if everyone around him was going to die or betray him he might as well join hands with humans again. "So we need to find the girl and bring her safely home. What's the good news?"

"Good news is that I was able to call Detective Tuatu, which is how I know—and he's on the outside."

Lycanthrope ears pricked up; Zero's face went stiff with shock. Okay, so he hadn't heard me on the phone. Only Morgana was unreservedly joyful.

"That's fantastic! We've got a line to the outside world! We've hacked the trials!"

Zero asked, "How—?"

I grinned at him. "Remember those little chips that we got from 'Zul so that Abigail and her lot could help us with the sirens? He was nearby his chip when I called, so I managed to get through; I got lucky and he was home for the day."

"I'm not getting what the good news is," Daniel said.

"We can get into contact with Jin Yeong," I said happily. "We'll be able to talk to him as soon as Tuatu can get another badge to him!"

"I'm still not getting what the good news is," said Daniel, then grunted a bit when Morgana elbowed him in the gut.

Bouncing just a little, she said, "It's a cheat code, right? It's a cheat code to give us extras that no one else has. Jin Yeong is our outside man."

"Exactly!" I said triumphantly. "And with everyone we've got on the outside—Jin Yeong, North, Marazul, Five, Tuatu—we'll have a flamin' good edge. I reckon we've got a good chance of getting out."

"But first we have to rescue your friend Sarah," Zero said.

I had the feeling he was humouring me with my idea of getting out, but so long as he was on board to help rescue Sarah, I didn't mind.

"We already went and got Morgana," I pointed out. "It can't be much harder than that, can it?"

"We faced rock dusters and a group of barely adult fae," he said bluntly. "Nothing compared with what will be further in—and nothing compared with who will remain after a day or two has passed. Only the strong survive, and the longer the survival, the stronger will be the remaining heirlings. We've only faced brute strength so far, and not much of that—later, we'll find heirlings who know how to manipulate Between as well as the king himself does."

"Maybe we better try and find Ralph, too, then," I said. "He's probably in here."

"Ralph will look after himself," Zero said, exasperated. "That wasn't what I was suggesting! He's already dead, and I very much doubt he'd be able to convince the sword that he was a good choice. Nobody will care about him."

"Yeah, but he's flamin' good at using Between," I pointed out. "All right, all right; don't get your knickers in a knot! We'll just go out after Sarah—see if we can find her."

I was also pretty sure that Ralph could defend himself against anything that could possibly get into his house here Behind—if anything managed to get in there at all. He would be a useful ally. Not that we were planning on fighting to the death, but if and when we needed to defend the house, it was sure to be safer with more friends rather than less, especially when those friends knew how to use Between like Ralph did.

"Who'll go?" asked Daniel.

Zero's gaze flicked across to him and they seemed to share a look. "We'll discuss that later," he said.

"So long as you don't mean just you two when you say "we"," I said suspiciously, turning over the badge between my fingers.

"Let me see that," Zero said, pinching it away from me.

I said, "Oi!" more from conviction than the idea that it was useful. It wasn't like anyone on the private network would be trying to call Zero—there weren't enough of them left alive who weren't already in the room—and even if there had been, he would have been able to answer the call without taking the badge from me. That meant he had taken it from me deliberately for another reason.

Whatever that reason was, I didn't get a chance to ask about it; as Zero took the badge from me, bringing it into closer proximity to the lycanthropes hanging over the back of his couch, something chirped from behind his couch.

"Heck!" I said, jumping. "What's that?"

"Sorry," one of the lycanthropes said guiltily. "Brought me speaker along."

Daniel glared at her. "When we were pressed for space, you brought a *speaker* with us?"

"We weren't using the space for brai—supplies! And it's small."

"It might be small, but it's flamin' loud," I said. "What is it, Bluetooth?"

"Yeah," said the lycanthrope, disappearing behind the couch to grab the speaker out of the nearest bag and flourishing it triumphantly. "Dunno what it's connecting to, though."

"Our private network, probably," I said, grinning. "Chuck it on the coffee table, see what it's hearing."

It probably hadn't connected with anything other than Tuatu's phone, but that could be fun, too.

Only instead of Tuatu, it was Abigail's voice that I heard saying sharply, "Who's that?"

"It's the old man," said Ezri's ghostly voice, her voice surprised but welcoming. "How's the stomach?"

"Nothing that a few days of healing won't fix," Abigail's voice said impatiently. "You know what they're like! Worry about your own injury."

"Not much use worrying about it," Ezri said bluntly. "It's not like it's gunna grow back if I do."

I met Zero's eyes over the coffee table: he looked sick, and I'm pretty sure I looked much the same. Voices from the dead—or in this case, ghosts in the system. I looked away pretty quickly and fixed my eyes on the speaker instead.

As if in the distance, voices called urgently; shouting, warning, brawling.

"What's that?" demanded Abigail's voice. "What's the fuss? Speak one at a time!"

"Trouble, I am very much afraid," said a cool grey voice that I knew far too well.

CHAPTER FIVE

I looked up numbly and into Zero's eyes once again, and found them shocked, dazed, and dark with pain.

Through the speaker, Abigail's voice yelled, "No! Get it away! Ezri!"

The female lycanthrope stuffed the speaker into her pocket, eyes wide, but I could still hear the yelling and scuffling. Soon, I knew, there would be fighting and screaming, because I'd already seen the aftermath of that particular moment in time.

Zero almost whispered, "What is that?"

"Ghosts, I reckon," I said thickly. I snatched the badge away from him—away from the speaker—and the voices died away. "Echoes in the private network. I should have known that there might be other stuff caught in there. Sorry 'bout that. Oi, Chantelle—"

"Chelsea."

"Sorry, Chelsea; reckon you can keep that thing upstairs where we won't accidentally hear people in their death throes?"

"Yeah, sorry," she said, slipping off the couch. "I'll be right back."

"It's gone," I said to Zero, even though he must have seen that it was. He was still a bit too stunned-looking for my liking.

One of the lycanthropes said, "What do you mean, echoes in the private network?"

"The voices you're hearing are dead people," I told her. "They must have got trapped in there somehow."

"Shades in the sound vibrations?" asked Morgana, brightening.

"Yeah," I said.

To Zero, she said excitedly, "Okay, but this just means that what we said before about vibrations in a contained space—"

"We'll talk about it another time," Zero said. He didn't wait for her to reply; he rose abruptly and disappeared down the hall.

I heard the back door open and close, and wondered if he'd remembered exactly where that door led to right now. It wasn't like he could practise out in the backyard for a while—he was likely to have company before too long if he did that.

Morgana stared at me. "What did I say? He's—did you break him or something? He's been fragile all day and now he looks like he's going to snap if anyone says a word!"

Daniel asked, "Was it the shade-sound in the speaker that threw him off?"

"Yeah," I said. "Some friends of ours died in a bad way while they still had those badges on 'em."

"Oh!" Morgana said. "It was *those* friends? Oh no! I was just excited—he's the only one I've been able to discuss this with, and it's been *killing* me, not being able to discuss it with someone who understands! I'll go check on him."

I nearly stopped her and went myself, but it wouldn't do Zero any harm to have to interact with other people on an emotional level, and while Morgana was still fairly powered up by her brain consumption, she wasn't likely to be in any danger that the two of them couldn't sort out.

I said to Daniel, "I didn't expect the sound to still be in there, though. I didn't know that could happen."

"I didn't know you could fuse magic and technology before I met you," he said, shrugging. "And I'd bet that there's a lot those thre—Zero has been learning since he met you, too."

I couldn't help grinning, even if it was a bit of a sick grin. "Yeah, that's what they—he keeps telling me."

"I've never seen one of them upset by human deaths before," he said. "One of the fae, I mean. Every now and then they'll get fond of one human, but it's only ever one. Even other behindkind can get friendly with humans, but the fae..."

"Yeah," I said. "Noticed that."

It shouldn't have comforted me. It shouldn't have warmed me to have confirmation that Zero was as cut up by the deaths of our friends as I was—Abigail and the others were still dead, and Zero still had to go through the aftermath of that. But it *was* comforting. It was good to know that the changes I'd seen in Zero weren't just my imagination. It was good to know that his human side wasn't being squashed into oblivion anymore.

WHATEVER MORGANA SAID TO ZERO, it must have worked—either that, or they'd run into a bit of trouble in the backyard, which was more likely—because Zero was definitely looking brighter and less stricken about the eyes when he came back in. I was pretty sure that the blood splatter on his arm had once been confined to his shoulder, too.

"We're going Sarah-hunting!" Morgana said happily as they entered the room.

I exchanged a glance with Daniel then looked across at Zero, who didn't sit down in his usual spot—which usually meant he was getting ready to go out again straight away.

"What, we're going now?" I asked, jumping to my feet. "All right, but—"

"Only three of us need to go," Zero said, without looking at me. "The less of us wandering around together, the better. We want to be able to move quickly."

"I can move quickly."

"I'll go," said Daniel. "You'll probably need a better nose, and I know what she smells like. Chels is a pretty good tracker, too."

"Both of you with me, then," Zero said.

"Having good noses is important, but so is having fighters," I protested. I didn't like being left out of the action now that I'd just started getting used to being treated almost as an equal.

"We need fighters at home, too; I want you here," said Zero, more pointedly. He seemed to stifle a sigh, and added, "I'm not ordering you to stay here."

"It flamin' *sounded* like it," I remarked. "All right. We need fighters at home as well as out there. Fine. But can you find Sarah without me?"

"Pet, I've been wandering through Behind and Between since I was ten! I'm more likely to be able to find her than you are!"

"First of all, it's rude to be so flamin' honest," I told him. "Second, fine; I'll do as I'm told."

Zero, who had opened his mouth to retort, looked bewildered for a few moments before he said, "I thought you'd argue more."

"There you go being rude again," I said, grinning. "Try not to die, all right? And if you see the old mad bloke out there, tell him to stop wandering off."

Mind you, for all I knew he was off with the banshees; I hadn't seen him since he ate with the others, and I had a feeling—that was more of a knowledge—that he was no longer in the house. If he kept on going like this, I was going to have to stop worrying about him. It was either that or get a stomach ulcer.

Zero said briefly, "Get a drink if you need it, and make sure you have all the weapons you'll—"

"Yeah, yeah, we'll make sure we go to the loo before we leave," Daniel interrupted.

"You're going right now?" I asked, but I wasn't really surprised.

"Best to get in and out while we can," said Zero.

"We do better in the dark, anyway," said Daniel, grinning. It was a grin for Morgana, but I appreciated it despite that.

To show my appreciation, I said, "It's all twilight out there, you galah. It won't change even if you wait for the morning."

Only the human world-facing windows would.

"Shut up, Pet," he said cheerfully. "You ready, Chels?"

"Good to go, boss," Chelsea said.

Morgana and I went with them to the back door like two ladies seeing off their knights—if you didn't count the fact that one of us had on black lipstick and a bloodstain or two around the neck, and the other was in dusty jeans and black boots that had a bit too much of what counted for blood with rock dusters on them.

"I'll make pancakes for you when you get back," I said to Zero, standing on tiptoes to peer around the three of them and make sure the coast was clear. Once they left the back patio they'd be in for whatever was waiting out there in the labyrinth—and maybe even before, if the chunk that was newly missing from the over-hang was any indicator.

I would have said something else, too, but before I could even finish scanning the yard-turning-to-Behind-labyrinth behind them, I was whisked forward and up and squashed into close proximity with the crossed knife-belts that circled Zero's chest.

Good grief. Zero was actually hugging me without me having to hug him first.

"Heck," I said into that broad chest, because I didn't think I could deal with too many more surprises today.

"Please don't die," he said quietly. "Keep the others safe, and don't do anything hasty."

"When did I ever do anything hasty?" I asked him, as he put me back down on the patio.

"I don't have long enough to stop and enumerate the times, Pet. Not to mention that—"

"All right, all right!" I said hastily, pulling away from him. "Make sure you don't die, yourself. And you better bring back the other two as well."

"Yeah, we want pancakes, too," said Daniel, lingering behind as Zero turned to step down from the patio. He surprised me—but not, by the looks, Morgana—by stepping forward to kiss her on the cheek. "Don't let Pet boss you around," he added.

"Oi!" I said indignantly, but he only grinned at me and followed Zero and Chelsea across the lawn.

I shut the back door just as they disappeared into the hedges, and found Morgana watching me with her black lips pursed and her eyes narrowed.

"First time he's done that?" she asked, arching her brows at me.

"Don't do that at me," I said. "And yeah. Reckon he's worried he won't be able to worry about me much longer."

She looked sceptical. "You think that's the reason?

I shrugged one shoulder. "So long as I'm still here to worry about, it gives him a reason to keep processing stuff instead of blocking it out. Last time, I don't think he had anyone to keep trying for; reckon he's just trying to keep connected."

"Last time— What last time?"

"Last time someone...went away," I said. "Well, last time someone died, too. I don't reckon Jin Yeong counts—or he didn't, back then. Not enough. That might have changed now."

"I think you're going to be taken by surprise one of these days," Morgana said, unconvinced. "Love is pretty hard to hide, and I'm telling you—"

"Yes, yes, I remember," I said quickly, and started back down the hall so that I didn't have to listen. I'd only just got back to a normal sort of equilibrium with Zero after Morgana had put ideas in my head in the first place, and I refused to let go of that tentative equilibrium.

"*And* you've got the vampire hanging around at the window," she said, trotting after me. "What are you going to do about that?"

"Try and let him in, for starters," I said. "Can't leave him out there, getting into trouble—and the others say he keeps glaring at them, so—"

"I mean, what are you going to do about the two of them? Zero's probably just heroic enough to keep his mouth shut and say nothing if it looks like Jin Yeong already has you."

"First of all, Zero's definitely not keeping his mouth shut," I said plaintively. "He's been throwing Jin Yeong through walls and warning him off. *Secondly*, do we have to talk about this?"

"You're the one who asked for advice a little while ago," she pointed out. "I'm just asking if you actually know what you want? If they were both there outside the window with their hearts in their hands and you could only let one of 'em in, which one would it be?"

"Dunno," I said. But I did know—sort of. With Zero, I would always be the weak one, the frail one—the one who wasn't quite as good, or fast, or as *much* of a person. I couldn't do anything about it because it was how he thought. No matter what I did, so long as it was his thought process, that's how he'd see me. And he'd give his life for me—but to him I would always be slightly less of a person than he was. I could love him, but I didn't think I could ever be *in love* with him.

With Jin Yeong, I was even. He was physically stronger than me, faster and definitely more likely to win in a fight, but somehow he could acknowledge where I was capable of the things he wasn't. And I knew that in his eyes I was no less of a person for being a human. He knew where he came from too well for that. In a world of half-humans, corrupted humans, and fae, we corrupted humans were most likely to recognise each other. If it came to a choice of being loved without respect or respected and not loved, I wanted to be respected.

And Jin Yeong promised both.

"Liar," said Morgana, far too sharp. She seemed content enough not to ask anything else, though; maybe she knew I was as confused as she was about her choice to either eat or not eat brains.

All I knew with any certainty was that if there was a choice between Jin Yeong and Zero, I would pick Jin Yeong every time. But *was* it a choice between them? Did I have to choose anyone? Did I *want* to choose someone? That was the biggest thing I wasn't sure about, and until I was sure about it, it didn't seem fair to try things out with anyone. Especially not when the vampire was already emotionally unsteady and the fae had recently become emotionally unsteady.

Especially not when the world as we knew it was winding up like a jack-in-the-box, getting ready to leap out in all its dangerous behindkind conflict at human passersby.

WE TRIED to have a quiet cuppa to while away the time, but lycanthropes don't really do quiet cuppas when there's nothing on the telly; they ferret through cupboards and start snarling and fighting at a moment's notice, then tumble through the whole house, snapping and growling.

Morgana and I left the kitchen when it looked as though we were likely to be knocked over in the fight, guarding our mugs from flying wolf fur, and went upstairs instead. Luckily for me, Morgana left the discussion of hearts downstairs too; she was happy to sit in the beanbag in my room, displacing a few of the collected papers there, and sip at her coffee while I did the same on the floor opposite her with my back against the wall. I hadn't slept in or sat on my bed for...well, a few nights now. Hadn't been able to bring myself to do it, which meant that once the beanbag was taken, the floor was all that was left.

Morgana seemed happy not to talk at all, in fact. She made a happy little indent in the beanbag with her coffee cup on her stomach and lifted first one foot and then the other to rotate as she observed it. At first, I thought she was just admiring her shoes —I didn't remember her wearing shoes before—because they were about as goth as she was while still being absolutely beautiful. Then it occurred to me that she was quietly marvelling over the fact that her feet moved—that her legs were at her own command—and I realised that even the most minute movements were beautiful to her.

I let Morgana delight in the movement of her feet until the coffee was gone and she discovered the stack of papers still behind the beanbag by the simple expedient of putting her coffee cup down on it.

"Good grief, what's this?" she asked, slipping them out from beneath the coffee cup. "Hey! This has my address on it!"

"It's stuff that Athelas made someone collect for him," I said. "I found out about it and was able to get my hands on a copy."

Morgana's left foot froze where it was. "I still see him in my nightmares," she said.

"Yeah," I said. I didn't need to say *me too*, because Morgana already knew; we'd talked about it a few days ago. She'd had a right to know that we found the bloke who was responsible for making her what she was.

Hoping to turn the subject to something a little bit less fraught, I added, "One of the bits of info is missing, though: a copy of my great-grandma's driving license. I haven't been able to find it for a while, and I even moved the couches out there to make sure it wasn't under anything."

Morgana's mouth compressed in a thoughtful black rosebud. "Could either of *them* have taken it?"

"Don't know what Zero would want with it, and I can't ask

JinYeong about it," I said. "I thought it might have been Athelas but he would already have known about it without having to see copies again."

"Yes," said Morgana, relaxing a little again. She pivoted her toe and pointed it, then did the whole routine backwards. "That's something that really makes me curious. This one with my address—the record of your great-grandma—what did he want them for?"

"We think he was trying to find out who else had access to all of this information," I said. "Someone's been paying the power and water bills here for years before the psychos arrived—and yours. A lot of kids like us who were housebound for one reason or another had their electric and water kept on because someone was paying for it."

"You think someone has been looking after heirlings?"

"Something like that," I said. "And Athelas was looking for that person—to kill them, I suppose. Or maybe just to find out how many heirlings slipped past him."

"Why get your detective to do it, though?" she asked. "That's just asking for trouble, and I don't think Athelas is stupid."

"The detective was a bit too hasty with telling Athelas he owed him," I said gloomily. "This was the result, I suppose. He couldn't help but do as he was told and keep quiet about it."

"Yes, but anyone can tell that Detective Tuatu is mulish and will do his best to scupper sneaky people," she argued. "And you have the papers, so obviously—"

Someone downstairs yelped—a short, sharp, high thing that had Morgana sitting up straight in front of the beanbag, red about the eyes—and I scrambled to my feet, staggering in the sudden distortion of the room around me.

Something was pulling at the house. Pulling hard and pulling with more than purely physical means.

"I bet it's that flamin' window again," I said, starting for the stairs at a run.

There was an almighty crash before I got all the way down, followed by snarling so vicious and wild that I almost stopped running toward it. I tumbled around the corner of the stairs and into the living room, and saw blades—no, claws!—so long and curved that they didn't seem practical, protruding into the living room and then drawn back.

A lycanthrope in wolf form went flying through the divide between kitchen and living room, tumbling into the couch, and I heard Morgana switch directions behind me. Without a word, I darted for the kitchen and she went for the living room.

I lunged up the slight rise into the kitchen and straight into an instinctive roll, barely avoiding a slashing attempt from the same huge claws I'd seen extend into the living room. It was an undirected attack, but my roll was pretty undirected, too, and I nearly collided with the kitchen island while the claws stabbed into the wall and seemed to be caught for the time being.

I used that moment to look around and assess what was happening. Nearby, blood pooled in the kitchen from something hairy that was mostly out of sight behind the kitchen island. A quick step around settled my stomach, because although the lycanthrope there was in a bad way, she was still alive. Chantelle, her name was; she was torn and panting hard, and I didn't think she'd be moving any time soon, but she was still breathing.

The window was the problem. The broken table listed drunkenly below the window with two broken legs, and in the window…

Heck. What *was* it in the window?

At first glance it could have been a huge protrusion of the kind of reeds that you find beside a dam or a waterhole—fatter and rounder than grass, but smaller than bullrushes—if someone had gotten about half-a-house's-worth of the stuff and shoved it through someone else's window. And if that half-a-house's-worth of grass had grown sly, stupid, muddy eyes, pointed ears with tufts of grass at the tops, and stupidly long arms with elbows that couldn't help digging into the floor while the huge hands at the end of the other half of them either waved wildly or kept close to the body with huge claws that had already torn chunks out of the room.

Those claws were ridiculous in their size—almost too big to be useable. Heck, the *arms* were ridiculous. But it had done a lot of damage with those claws, and it was still only halfway through the window, its almost marsupial body stuck at the back haunches while its free arm jerked in a paroxysm of furious desire for freedom and the other clutched what looked like a lifeless lycanthrope to its reedy chest.

That body made me think there should be a tail out there somewhere, but if it was anything like the horror that was its arms, I didn't really want to have the chance to check.

"Flamin' heck," I breathed, unable to stop staring. "It's a bunyip, isn't it? It's a flamin' bunyip."

It was a bunyip that was struggling pretty hard to get its claws out of the wall, too—which meant that I needed to find weapons *now*. I sent another look around the room, looking for options, and lunged at the knife block.

A second later I had the chef's knife in one hand and the santoku in the other; I shook out my shoulders and flicked my wrists outward, and those blades extended until they were the same length and shape, much to my relief. I was used to fighting with twin swords when I fought with two swords, and an unbalanced pair of weapons would have thrown me off completely.

Hopefully they'd turn back into knives after all of this was done: they were a good set of knives, and I didn't want to have to buy another set now that I'd got used to them.

"Pet!" called Morgana, interrupting my thoughts. "Where are you?"

"Dining room!" I yelled. "Better stay there. There's a wolf in the kitchen that needs some help, but she'll be fine until I get this thing out of the window."

Plaster and paint exploded as the bunyip finally tore its claws from the wall. I covered my eyes with the crook of my arm to keep off the worst of the chips and dust, but took it away pretty quickly at the first shifting of rubble that meant movement from the arm.

The bunyip was already drawing back its arm at the elbow, broken ceiling and wall trailing from it. I don't know what kind of joint it had in there, but it used its elbow as a pivot to sweep and flick those claws at me. I leaped over that sweep, but one of the claws caught the slight heel of my boot and my leap forward turned into another tumble, this one only slightly more deliberate than the first, right past the hairy elbow that was planted where the dining table ought to be.

I scrambled to my feet, shedding plaster and paint as I rose, and met a fresh onslaught with my blades braced and crossed. I let it knock me to the floor without taking the edge of the blade-like claws and slithered out of my defence to spin in place on my butt and stab through the muscly part of the arm.

The bunyip yowled high and wild, like a feral cat, and dropped the lycanthrope to swipe at me with the other hand. Luckily for me, it hit with the back of its hand and not the claws, sending me sliding across the floor on my rear.

Heck. That was gunna be good for the seat of my pants.

I rolled with the last of my momentum, and heard Morgana's voice from the living room, too deep and guttural to be quite human.

"Pet," it said. "*Are you alive?*"

"I'm fine!" I yelled, coughing up dust. "But I hope ripped jeans are gunna come back into fashion because I'm gunna be fashionable for the first time in my life and I don't wanna waste the opportunity!"

"I need to get to Chantelle in the kitchen! Can you cover me?"

"Gimme a sec! Get ready!"

I vaulted over the bunyip's elbow again, avoiding the bristly spikes, spun in place to send another stab right through the flesh and muscle there, and wrenched the sword free just in time to duck beneath the fresh attack that action brought on. Low and dusty, I scrambled toward the living room opening and turned back to face the bunyip. For the first time since entering the room, I got a chance to see its face instead of just concentrating on its gangling arms, and the sheer, stupid malevolence of its expression chilled me like the scything blades of its claws hadn't.

Stupid was good. Malevolent wasn't. Malevolent usually meant that something would keep stabbing something that looked dead, even though it was dead. I didn't like what that meant for the injured lycanthropes in the vicinity. Chantelle wasn't in too bad of a position, but Kyle—or was it Kevin?—was still in a very bad place. We only had enough manpower to get one lycanthrope out of the battle ground right now, and Chantelle was very definitely alive. I didn't like to give up on anyone, but the sooner we could get Chantelle out of the line of fire, the better; I would just have to hope that Kyle wasn't dead, and that the bunyip didn't become enraged enough to have another go at him.

The bunyip had another swipe at me; I met the onslaught and redirected it, sending the claws into what was left of the wall between dining room and living room.

"Go, go, go!" I yelled.

Morgana shot through behind me and straight into the kitchen, far too quick to be human, and I scrambled onto the kitchen island just in time to bat away another loose, not-quite-properly-aimed swing that passed overhead and took out the upper kitchen cupboards on the same wall as the window.

I stretched and planted one booted foot on the opposite bench, hacking at the wrist as if it were a vine in the rainforest, and was very nearly knocked flying when the bunyip wrenched its arm away, sending cupboard doors flying off their hinges and into the other rooms. I gave it a good shave along the lower side of the arm as that arm passed over my head and shoved back with my extended leg to retreat along the kitchen island again.

I couldn't take the time to look, but I heard scrabbling behind and below me as Morgana tried to move Chantelle—heard the small whimper that movement caused. The lycanthrope beneath the window growled at that, deep and savage, and stirred. He staggered to his feet like a newborn lamb, the pelt on his left shoulder sagging a bit too much to be normal and freely running red.

"Play dead!" I yelled at him, bright with relief that he was alive but agonisingly aware that any signs of life would draw the attention of the bunyip once again. It seemed to like lively prey.

He didn't have the chance to play dead: before I could even jump down from the benchtop, the bunyip curled in with one of those ridiculously long arms and snatched up Kevin, or Kyle.

I yelled to try and capture its attention, and maybe it decided that things were getting too hot to handle. It looked at me with its stupid brown eyes and then, lycanthrope in grasp, heaved itself back through the window, reed-like hair slapping against the lopsided window frame as it went. The claws scythed after it like quicksilver, disappearing into the dark in a moment, and I leaped from the kitchen island, slicing too late to get anything but a resounding *clang* from the last claw.

I caught myself in the window frame, my boots dusty with rubble from the damage and my right hand catching the remaining wall above the space. From here, I could just see the bunyip as it tried to swim and sink into the darkness as if it were dam water, the suspicion of a tail coiling behind it, sinuous and deadly.

"Pet!" yelled Morgana.

I threw a glance over my shoulder and met blood-red eyes that should have been frightening but were too sorrowful to really frighten me. A lycanthrope, halfway between wolf and human girl, was cradled in Morgana's arms, shivering with her side cut open and bleeding far too much. But back in the darkness of the window was a rapidly vanishing lycanthrope in the clutches of a bunyip, and he didn't have anyone to help him.

Heck. Looked like I could only obey one of Zero's commands: Keep the Others Safe *or* Not do Anything Hasty.

"Look after the others," I said to Morgana; then, seizing on that last flicker of the essence of Kevin or Kyle that nearly snuffed out in the blink of an eye between thinking and jumping, I leapt out into the cold, deadly darkness.

CHAPTER SIX

I said it was dark looking out from the window, but it was worse outside the window. Darker. Less real. More like being inside a spherical, bouncy black trampoline where you didn't know which way was up because there was no *up*. No sign of the window, either.

I wasn't standing on anything, either. I was literally standing on darkness, nothingness; and it definitely didn't feel solid. Worst of all, I couldn't sense Kevin any longer, and there was no sign of the bunyip.

Well. I was out here in solid darkness and there was nothing to do but walk forward. If it *was* forward I was walking, anyway. Foot up, foot down; moving onward (presumably) moving forward (hopefully); desperately trusting that the trampoline of darkness beneath me wasn't becoming less solid as I walked.

I had a few nasty moments where it seemed like the ground might actually be getting less solid beneath me before it occurred to me that rather than getting thinner, it was actually getting *lighter*. By the time I'd realised that, the lighter, straw-like patches of ground that made the earth look see-through were beginning to take on the appearance of light-edged grass and sticks instead as the earth itself turned to soil that was *almost* not see-through.

I kept walking as light gathered, glancing around for signs of Kevin or the bunyip—or even an idea of where I was. I saw no sign of any other living thing, but the confusing criss-cross of dark strands and shadows that made up the tunnel-like world around me was distractingly familiar. It would have taken two of Zero to reach out a hand to either side and just touch fingers in the middle; it was higher than my house, with a few speckled motes of dirt or mould fluttering gently downward toward me.

Nope, not mould: leaves.

"Flamin' heck," I said, my voice too thin and scratchy. "I'm inside the hedges!"

That was exactly where I was: I was inside the hedges that made up the labyrinth out in the heirling trials arena. Through the criss-crossed branches and leaves I could vaguely see the world outside, but with the same kind of muddiness that seemed to overlay the sounds I should have heard from inside. I could clearly see birds darting along the path in the labyrinth; but in here, I couldn't hear more than the very faint suggestion of birdcall.

My kitchen window led to the inside of the labyrinth walls? That was sure to come in handy—or turn dangerous, more likely. There had to be a benefit to it, though; something we could use, something that gave us an edge. Maybe something that gave us an out.

I didn't have time to think about that right now, though; I had a lycanthrope to rescue. I was still in a labyrinth, but it was a labyrinth of a different kind. I didn't know which way the bunyip had gone, except that if it had gone the same way I was facing, I was pretty sure it would have left a few more marks on the inside of the hedge.

And *thinking* of marks on the inside of the hedge—there was no way the bunyip wouldn't have left a good trail through here.

Even if it was able to control the claws on the end of its gangling arms, which I had reason to doubt, there were other claws spurring out from its knobbly elbows, and those would take nice big chunks out of any hedge it passed through.

Sure enough, there were gouges here and there along the hedge to my left: a deep cut in the branches to the left, then a slash in the branches to the right, as if the bunyip bumbled from side to side as it walked. It probably did. Despite the claws, it hadn't struck me as being a particularly graceful creature.

Even when it had been slashing at me with its elbow planted and its claws slicing, it had been too slow and clumsy to really worry me, which made me wonder exactly how the lycanthropes had been so quickly and badly injured. There was also the fact that Kevin hadn't seemed to be slashed so much as punctured, and I wondered again at the tail I thought I had seen as the bunyip vanished. Huge claws and uncanny-valley-esque arms were more frightening than dangerous, so what was so dangerous about the bunyip?

I bet it was that flamin' tail. It probably sat in the front of its lair to frighten people off with the big claws, ugly face, and stupid arms; the real danger was probably that tail. I remembered reading about bunyips a long time ago, but apart from the fact that they lived in waterholes and dams and poked their heads out to scare passersby, I didn't know too much. If it was a possibility that there were other dangers about it, I'd have to be more careful when I was on the bunyip's turf.

In the meantime, I thought, stepping carefully along the path too quickly to avoid every noisy twig but too slowly for my peace of mind, at least I wasn't as likely to be attacked in here. It *had* to be safer in here, right? I was surrounded by sticks and leaves that looked a bit too alive for comfort, and I was on the trail of a bunyip, but at least all of the contestants were outside.

I hoped so, anyway.

I was soon to know that at least a few of them were, at any

rate: the birds in the lane that ran beside the hedge scattered with the faintest of warning cries and something else moved through the lane, footsteps heavy and percussive rather than audible. It was big and it looked dangerous, but somehow it didn't look very self-assured in its dangerousness; with shoulders like a gorilla and arms nearly as long, a sword bigger than Zero's strapped to its back, it should have been strutting along the lane. Instead, as I watched, it sorta sidled along the pathway, one arm hanging awkwardly. I thought it was injured at first, but after a little while of watching it, I was pretty sure it was just dead scared and tentative about moving around.

Flamin' heck. If something the size of your average station-wagon and the reach of a gorilla was scared to be walking along in the labyrinth lanes, I had probably been a bit too casual about my jaunt out to Morgana's place with Zero. We'd had to fight our way through, yeah, but I didn't see either the rock dusters or the group we'd faced worrying something this big and well-armed. Not everything big was a good fighter, but I could see the muscles on the creature, as well as the number of scars; this fella had been through a lot.

Whoever he was, he drew even with me in heavy silence then passed by just as a blink of light and darkness fluttered near the end of the lane. It drew my attention immediately, since the twilight world around me was already shades of dark and light rather than colour, and I distinctly saw two figures striding swiftly and confidently around the corner and into the lane that ran alongside my hedge.

I was pretty sure that these ones were fae; well-armed and well-practised, they carried themselves like Zero. They knew how to fight, and even if they were half his size, I was pretty sure they would do more than a bit of damage together. Were they both heirlings, or had they both come into the trial arena because they were together when it started? They were identical in appearance except for their hair, and so beautiful that even with one of them wearing what looked like a more masculine style of hair, both could have been either male or female.

Twin heirlings, I decided, my eyes flicking up ahead to the mastodon who had just passed. He hadn't looked around, but I was pretty sure he knew the twins were there; he had begun to move more quickly, though not at a run, and now instead of seeming cautious and worried, his walk was purposeful and intent. He definitely knew they were there, and he definitely didn't want to turn around and face them.

I had a lycanthrope to rescue or I might have tried to help the lone fighter. As it was, I didn't dare leave Kevin on his own for as long as it would take to find out how to get through the hedge and into the labyrinth again, not to mention the time it would take to help the lone creature in the fight—or defend myself from him if he decided that it was better for only one champion to be around at the end of things.

I couldn't help feeling guilty as I kept going, despite that. I heard the faint clash of metal meeting metal and a yell as I passed on, and something wet hit the hedge in a spray that fluttered across the leaves. I hurried on, gritting my teeth and turning my attention back to the gouges in the hedge branches that marked the path to Kevin. If I didn't get to him soon, I didn't think he was likely to make it.

I walked for longer than I'd hoped to walk, turning corners and following the gouges in the hedge, until they stopped. Heck. What now? Maybe I should have brought one of the other lycanthropes with me to help smell out my quarry. My training in life hadn't taught me how to track bunyips through the inner parts of a labyrinth hedge, and Zero hadn't done much to help in that way, either.

It was probable that the bunyip had somehow left the inside of the hedge to get into the labyrinth section, but I was more inclined to think that it was likely to still be inside. Just maybe in a more expanded part of the hedge.

I threw a look around and found a couple of hedge branches that had been unceremoniously cut from higher up, tumbling down into the lower branches just a few steps on from where I was. On the other hand, if I looked behind me there was a distinct glimmer of Between to the hedge that suggested there was a path there to be taken if I could trust it.

Unbidden, I heard Athelas' voice in my head. *What about that path? That one looks promising.*

"Shut up, Athelas," I said. Then I took the path that hadn't prompted that wormy little voice to speak, distrusting the voice on principle even though my own subconscious had been the author of it.

I pushed through the hedge between the shorn branches, but somehow I didn't exactly leave the inside of the hedge. Instead of finding myself pushing through the branches to the outside of the hedge, the hedge itself stretched out until it was heat shimmer or sky, or mountain far away, and suddenly there was a swelling plain spreading out in front of me. A few steps forward brought me properly into that world, though I could fancy I still felt the twiggy, leafy ground beneath my boots instead of the grass that my eyes told me was there. Ahead of me was a waterhole partially bounded by trees. Half the size of a football field, that waterhole was nearly perfectly round in shape, with an overhang of rocks that opened out in what was very nearly a path in my direction.

I didn't know how, but the hedge was still somehow there above my head, too; above me wasn't quite sky and wasn't quite hedge, and that made me uneasy. I could have been in Queensland, if the sun was shining down brightly on my head. It even smelt like Queensland, and the waterhole that rippled gently every now and then—rippled suspiciously *toward* the cluster of trees and overhang of rock instead of away from it—could have been any waterhole out west: brown, muddy, and ringed with mud from the gradually dropping water level.

So, what? When the trials started up, they hadn't just

brought heirlings in with them, they'd patched in random monsters to do a bit of killing or be killed? That was all well and good, but why bring traditional Aussie nightmares in to round out the lot?

Something rustled in the reedy part of the billabong just beyond the overhang of rock and further into the cluster of trees, and my head snapped around. It was Kevin, and he was still in his wolf form. This time he had his left flank toward me, and that was how I could finally tell for sure that it was Kevin; Kyle had more of a golden touch to his coat, while Kevin was distinctly red over his left flank.

Even better, he was on all four paws instead of in a pile on the ground, which must mean he was feeling a bit stronger.

"Nice work, Kevin!" I called, in a congratulatory sort of voice, and his head whipped around as if to say, Now *you remember my name!* "Must have been a bit hard not to pass out with those claws in you!"

He made a half-dodge, as if trying to bring himself to dart toward me and safety, but stopped low on his haunches, ears pricked and eyes cautious.

Heck. It really was playing with him.

"Oi, Kevin," I said, stepping forward lightly and quickly. "It's the tail, right? That's the bit you gotta watch out for?"

He whined once, and shook his muzzle, blood went flying from a red-stained patch near his chest. Right. So I'd been right. That would be why he was limping now too, no doubt. It must have had a go at him since it'd got him back to its lair: looked like I'd been right about bunyips liking to play with their food. I couldn't see the bunyip itself, but judging from where Kevin was, midway between the thicker trees and the outcropping of rock that was still suspicious, he had been put down in exactly the right place for proximity and fun.

Head low, Kevin turned his muzzle this way and that, watchful for the next attack. I moved closer with more speed than caution, and saw the briefest movement below the rock outcrop where rock met water.

Heck. Here came the claws and those flamin' weird arms again.

I broke into a trot as claws and arms parted the reeds by the water's edge, with barely a flicker through the trees to show that something else sinister was moving in the greenery. I didn't slow down, hoping to convince the bunyip that I had been completely fooled by the claws, heading full pelt up and over the rock ridge to leap down on the other side. Kevin startled and snarled as I landed beside him, crouching low, but I didn't have time to reassure him; a thin, whippy tail came snaking out from the trees, lightening fast and bright-tipped. I was nearly too slow even though I was waiting for it, and my hurried defence slapped the flat of my swords against it rather than slashing through it as I'd hoped to do.

But that moment was enough for Kevin to lunge forward, snarling; another moment and he had it in his teeth, snarling and shaking it as though he was trying to break its nonexistent neck. I took off across the clearing, leaping claws and muddy-green bunyip arm, felt the hot breath and saw the teeth of the bunyip as I leaped for the reeds that were its whiskers.

The bunyip tried to curve in on itself and protect its tail, but it had been too sneaky, curling its tail through the other end of its cave to attack us, and there was too much solid rock between it and its tail. I met that forward lunge and rotting-sheep breath with two swords thrusting up and forward, right through the roof of its roaring mouth, and took a glancing cut from its rancid teeth that worried me by being instantly hot.

The bunyip died in a last rictus of assault, nearly sweeping my legs out from beneath me with its jerking arms, and I had to climb over them to get back to Kevin, who was still shaking the tail with all the savagery of a puppy with a leaf and about the same stability on his feet.

"It's dead," I told him. "And I know you're tired, but it doesn't have a neck in its tail; it's not like you're gunna do much good by doing that."

He just growled at me and gnawed on the tail for a few moments longer before he let it drop, looking faintly ashamed. I didn't know if that was because he had let his wolf nature get the better of him or because he realised he'd been fighting a dead beast for the last thirty seconds.

"Just figured you'd want to save your energy to get home," I said. "It's a little way back, and if anyone figures out we're in the hedges, things are gunna get nasty pretty quick. I saw a bloke get —well, I reckon he got the worst of it from a pair of fae, and fae are pretty good at seeing through stuff, so the sooner we get home, the better. You want to try and change back to heal a bit?"

Kevin didn't answer, but he didn't stop, either; he took off down the way we'd come and I saw his nose flaring as he passed me.

"Fine," I grumbled, leaving my swords to grow up near the billabong as bullrushes and jogging after him. "But if you outrun me you're gunna have trouble finding your way back to the—"

He might as well have snorted at me, for all the notice he took of me. That wasn't surprising, since it was obvious he already had the right scent in his nose, following it without a pause right back to the point where I'd stepped into this particular patch of stretchy hedge.

He didn't know how to get right back into the proper hedge, though. After a few abortive starts he stopped and sat, whining as if he were a dog, until I caught up.

"Nope," I said, grinning. "Having the scent isn't gunna help you here: reckon we've gotta close this up behind us as we go back inside the hedge. And there's no way I'm going back through all that black stuff later on, so we're gunna have to find a way to get back out into the labyrinth before we get home, too."

He growled a bit, but since he couldn't get back to the scent that was annoying him without my help, I was pretty sure he'd listen to me when the time came for us to leave the hedge.

Still, if he needed me, it turned out it was much quicker going back the way I'd come with a lycanthrope nose to tell me when to stop, too. On the other hand, this time things were a lot more nerve-wracking. I don't know if most of the heirlings, like us, had been hiding out in their respective houses until now and had just come out to fight in the last half a day, but we saw at least five different groups of heirlings, and a few single travellers, too—each of them passing by us almost silently but still far too close for comfort.

"Heck," I said anxiously to Kevin after the fourth group. "Wonder how many heirlings Zero has had to get through to get to Sarah? If there are this many close to our place, I wonder how many are further in?"

Kevin didn't reply or show any signs of turning human, but I was pretty sure his trot sped up a bit. He obviously wasn't feeling too comfortable about being out here, either. Fortunately, we hadn't so far seen anything like what I'd witnessed on my way to find Kevin, though I'd caught sight of a huge, prone body as we passed down the inside of the hedge on our way back.

The twin heirlings were still patrolling the area, too; I knew they couldn't actually see or hear us, but they were sharp and watchful anyway, and when they sank quickly back out of sight into a stony, decorative alcove in the hedge opposite, I already knew what was about to happen.

Kevin stopped, growling, his hackles up. Into the lane beside us trotted a slender little wolf, his nose to the ground and his ears pricked. I saw the male fae grin; saw the glitter of Between-laced magic that was hiding their scent.

"That's not on," I muttered. "He's just a kid!"

The two fae exchanged a look, and the female rolled her eyes. She might as well have echoed *Just a kid!* but her emotion was more contempt than pity, and the closer the little wolf grew, the more contemptuous that expression became.

The two fae pounced on the wolf as one before I was ready for it, and Kevin snarled and leapt for the closest twin. This time I didn't try to stop my instinct; I shoved myself into the hedge, trusting that it would work just like it had worked to get out to the bunyip's lair.

That was when I discovered I couldn't get through hedges when there was no glittering of Between to indicate a way through. Branches tore and stabbed at me, forcing me backward, and Kevin, who had been right beside me, fell back onto the ground in a tumble of limbs and tail, scattering blood.

"All right, settle down," I said, pressing a hand against his flank to keep him where he was. "It's too late, anyway. The kid's dead."

I'd seen the first and final blow even while I was trying to force myself through the hedges; the poor kid hadn't stood a chance. One of the twins had taken off his head with a single blow —they hadn't even stopped to check he was dead, just kept striding along the lane. The second twin kicked the body aside and they did another quick patrol of the lane while Kevin snarled and staggered to his feet, and the female fae stopped abruptly, her head snapping around. She stared at the hedge—stared almost directly at us—her brow sharpened in concentration, for far too long. I found myself holding my breath. Could she really see us?

To my relief, she looked away a moment later and strode away to catch up with her brother. They passed up and down the lane again, this time more slowly, and I realised what I hadn't before.

"They're waiting for someone," I said, dread seeping into my bones. "Patrolling the same place where they know that someone has to pass by. Reckon it's Zero?"

There was no reply, of course; I didn't expect one. Kevin seemed more defeated now than he'd been earlier despite his injuries and the danger in which he stood, but I didn't like to try and make him feel better by reminding him that the dead kid would probably have tried to kill us both if he was trying to become king. There wasn't any point, and I wasn't sure it was true.

It wouldn't have made any more sense of him being slaughtered like an animal, either.

Kevin was staggering, his sides heaving, by the time we got back to where I'd found myself walking through the inside of the hedge. I might not have known it was where I'd begun if he hadn't stopped, sat, and whined a bit.

I stopped, too, and that's when I saw the slightly darker edges to the leaves and the faint limning of Between to them.

"We *can* go that way," I said to Kevin, my voice doubtful. "But no promises on me being able to actually get us back to the house."

The bunyip had managed it well enough, but I was pretty sure it had been working on instinct and hunger, and even if I did work on instinct more often than not, walking boldly back into that darkness again wasn't something I really wanted to do.

Kevin must have agreed, because he gave another small whine that was nearly a yelp and got up to trot back down the path again. We walked for another few metres until I found one of those patches that looked like you could get out of the hedge if you really tried; a place where everything was a bit Betweeny but not shadowy.

I called back Kevin, who seemed determined to run ahead, and experimentally pushed a hand through the branches. It went easily—and to my relief, came back whole, which meant there were no fae twins just waiting outside to cut off limbs—and when I pulled it back in, a faint trace of Between lingered for just a moment, silvery in the darkness of the hedge.

"This is us," I said, jerking my head at the branches.

Kevin didn't much like it when I grabbed him by the scruff, but he probably would have liked it less if I'd left him behind, so I didn't let his offended growling worry me too much.

This time, instead of being prodded and cut when we forced ourselves through the hedge, there was the softest of sensations across our faces—leaves that weren't quite solid any longer but weren't quite bodiless either. Being on the outside of the hedge brought with it a perilous sense of openness and danger, however, and Kevin must have felt the same, because his muzzle lowered, hackles up as he shot a suspicious look up and down the lane we found ourselves in.

"Not to worry," I said, in what was meant to be a cheerful voice but just came out a bit too loud. "I know the way from here."

It wasn't so much that I *knew* the way as that I could *sense* the way. Kevin and the other lycanthropes had their sense of smell; I had my sense of Between, and home. There's something very comforting in having a home that tries to pull you back toward it when you're trying to find it, too.

Kevin made a snuffling sort of sound that could have been either dismissive or a sneeze, but he followed me regardless, and maybe he caught the scent of us from yesterday, because his ears and tail both lifted slightly as we walked.

I think we both felt as though we were on the homeward run, and with the sense of acute danger behind us we didn't slow down, though the flowers growing up the edge of the next turning ought to have warned us that there was something nasty coming our way. It should have just been a turn or two away from our backyard, so we walked around the edge of a break in the hedge that led to a new section of the labyrinth without first checking to see what was there.

What was there, I discovered, as I froze just a step into the open with Kevin behind me, was a tall, handsome, terrifyingly cold fae with bare feet and flowers in his hair, surrounded by the usual retinue of assorted fae, behindkind, and footsoldiers.

I tried to remember to breathe without breathing too heavily and attracting notice, far too much in the open for comfort. How the *heck* had Lord Sero managed to wriggle in here? More importantly, why had he come personally instead of sending minions? Obviously he'd brought minions with him, but that was pretty flamin' different to sending them on their own.

As if being an heirling in the heirling trials wasn't bad enough, now we had to contend with Lord Sero as well?

I felt, rather than heard, a low, rumbling growl, and that reminded me that even if I wasn't susceptible to all of Lord Sero's nasty little tricks, Kevin definitely would be. More importantly, I'd told Zero that I would keep the lycanthropes safe, and there was no way I could keep Kevin safe from Lord Sero if he stayed with me. I had the feeling that home wasn't far away—if we could just get there.

I gathered all of the filaments of Between that I could feel in the air around me and used those glittering strands to shove Kevin, who grunted in surprise and went sailing back through the hedge next to me—and every other one in the vicinity, if I was any judge.

Heck. I'd meant to use Between, but I hadn't thought I'd be able to gather *that* much power! Hopefully I'd sent him in the right direction—or at least back to the inside of the hedge from which he'd be able to make a break for the kitchen window—because the motion of it had drawn all of those cold, fae eyes, and there was no chance of me going after him to make sure he was fine.

Not when it would just draw Lord Sero after us and right to the house.

"How the flaming *heck* did you get in?" I asked him, with some bitterness. "This isn't Hobart, and you shouldn't be wandering around as if you own the place."

Lord Sero's face hadn't exactly lit up, but a smile of deep satisfaction spread across his face, and for the first time I saw his eyes match up with the emotion on his lips.

"So you really aren't dead," he said. "I've been hoping to meet you again since it was told to me that you yet lived."

I saw the slight look he threw behind him and slightly to the left. I followed that look and caught sight of Athelas: a grey shadow just behind and beside his master. My stomach clenched, and at the familiar sight of his eyebrows rising just a little, grew sick.

"How expedient," said Lord Sero, pulling my attention away from the sickening whirl of thoughts that had begun in my mind. "I hadn't expected to see you in this situation, but you will be quite useful to us, I believe. I will also enjoy calling you to account for your lack of usefulness thus far."

"What do you want *now*?" I demanded. It was too late to mind my tongue, and I didn't think there was much use in doing it now, anyway. Whatever was going to happen was inevitable, unthinkable, and extremely unpleasant. Might as well go out showing this garbage can pretending to be a person exactly what I thought of him. "I'm flamin' tired of you turning up like a bad smell every time I leave the house."

"You and I had an agreement," said Sero, his smile frosty and completely unamused.

"No, we didn't. We had a you-telling-me-what-to-do and me-trying-not-to-die thing going on. You're fae; you know nothing's set in stone without a contract."

"I certainly do," Sero said, and I didn't miss the absolutely venomous look he flicked at Athelas beneath his lashes. "Some of my underlings would have been well advised to remember that."

"To be fair, he was pretty busy trying to kill me at the time," I said. I saw Athelas' eyes lower briefly to the ground, and the very slight curve of his lips that was at odds with the greyness of his face. I said directly to him, "You don't get to be amused at the Pet anymore. Wipe that expression off your face."

I didn't watch to see how he reacted; I turned my attention back on Lord Sero, who said coldly, "Don't play with my steward; he has nothing further to do with you and I don't choose to observe byplays in which I have no part."

"Yeah, figured you were the sort to think you were the main act," I said. "You're not, you know. You're just an overdressed galah who can't stop spreading flowers everywhere he goes. One day you're gunna run into a bloke with a mower and you won't know what hit you."

Sero's brows rose very slightly. "Very little of what you say makes sense. We'll have to fix that during our discussion before you're put down."

If I'd been the centre of attention before, I was pinned by nearly thirty sets of eyes now: fae eyes, behindkind eyes, lizard eyes. I even saw a few hackles go up with some of the less humanoid behindkind. All of them waiting for the word—the gesture—that would sic them on me and start the bloodbath. They might be trying to grab me, but I'd be fighting back as hard as I could, and I was pretty sure that was the kind of situation in which I ended up dead—especially now that I didn't have to pretend that Lord Sero's voice held any power over me.

Into that bristling instant of menace, a voice said mildly, "Might I suggest, my lord...?"

It made me feel sick to hear that gentle voice say *my lord* to Lord Sero after saying it for so long to Zero. I would have said Lord Sero didn't deserve it, except that Athelas was a traitor and a murderer, and Lord Sero deserved the respect and loyalty of exactly that kind of person.

Sero's nostrils flared very slightly, but he turned his attention on Athelas. "Well?"

"We have no way of knowing if the king himself has entered

the construct, nor do we know how many of his minions are available to assist the Pet. Given his interest in her...”

“Are you suggesting we retreat?”

“Certainly not, my lord. Merely that we take the Pet prisoner and question it in the comfort of our own surroundings rather than question it here where anyone could happen along to... disturb us.”

Lord Sero gave it a moment or two of thought, then said imperiously to me, “Come along with us.”

“Yeah, nah.”

He hadn’t waited. He’d actually just turned and started sweeping off, and at the flatness of my words, he turned back to stare incredulously at me.

“*What* did you say?”

Heck, maybe I should have used the time to run. I wouldn’t have got far, but I would have got a little way away.

“Did you *refuse* my *summons*?”

I probably would have laughed at the pitch of his voice if I hadn’t been feeling too sick to give in to the urge. Was he personally offended because I wasn’t susceptible to fae manipulation?

“Hey, it’s not just you; I can refuse anyone’s commands if I want to,” I told him. “Nothing personal, mate.”

“Our agreement—”

“Told ya,” I said, shoving my hands into my pockets. “We didn’t have an agreement. You don’t have my name and you can’t speak stuff about me into existence without it, so why don’t you just shut your yap and get on with things?”

“It’s unfortunate that I was mistaken about your part in all of this,” said Sero, his lips curling a little in fastidious distaste. “Such a waste of time and effort! I did think that you would prove very useful, but after...debriefing one or two final sources, it would seem that I was misled. My comfort is that at least one other had the same suspicion and seems to be acting upon it. That should be amusing. In the meantime, once you’ve answered a few questions, I have no further need for you. Our agreement is dissolved."

"You just said a heck of a lot of words to say what I did when I said we don't have an agreement," I said. I would have liked to have thought about what it meant that he had had to say it aloud to me before he allowed himself to openly attack me, but I didn't have that time. Open attack was coming, and I had to be ready to die as strenuously as possible.

"You may regret that, Pet. I would have taken you away gently, but now I'm more inclined to see you injured first. If you give up and beg for leniency, I may spare you some pain now."

"Nope," I said, grinning a grin that hurt my cheeks. "I'm gunna fight."

Actually, I was going to die—whether here and now or after a lot of painful questioning—but there wasn't much point in telling him that: he already knew.

He said a single, contemptuous word. "Ridiculous."

Flamin' rude, that. I drew a sword from one side of the path and another from the opposite side—swords that should have been fenceposts in the human world and saplings in the world Behind, but made themselves into what I needed them to be instead.

"Bring the Pet," said Lord Sero.

Welp. This was it. I was gunna die somewhere Behind without being able to do anything about the fae who had killed my parents or the fae who had ordered him to do it. It wasn't going to be an easy death, either, and Zero was going to have to come across the body of *another* human he hadn't been able to do anything about saving. Who was going to be there to make sure he didn't turn into a block of ice again, that's what I wanted to know?

"Sorry," I muttered beneath my breath. "Looks like you're on your own."

Then I dropped a bit lower into my guard stance, swords at the ready, and waited for the rush, for the swell forward that would envelop me, crush me, and kill me. I waited for the first person to step forward and attack.

But nobody did.

And Lord Sero was just...walking away. Some people never learn. He'd spoken, then turned around and walked away, as if the world always had and always would work exactly as he wanted it to. Maybe he was right in general, but for some reason *right now* he was wrong.

They tried to move. I saw their muscles straining; I saw the bigger ones at the back pushing the ones in front, but none of them seemed to be able to move past a very small pebble that had bounced down from between hedge roots a moment ago.

I locked eyes with Athelas without meaning to and saw that his brows had gone up. He was startled but he was also amused, and that cut my heart so painfully that I actually pressed a hand that was fisted around a sword to my chest as I looked away, wishing it didn't hurt to breathe.

"My lord," he said. "There would seem to be a problem."

Something much bigger tumbled down suddenly through the roots of the hedge, and now that I was in fighting stance it was really hard not to take it as an attack. And I couldn't really attack, because it wasn't a rock this time, but the Old Mad Bloke.

He uncurled in a dusty tangle of limbs and beard and said to me in a confidential sort of way, "Standing is nice. Very nice. But right now, running is better."

"Got it," I said hastily. "Let's get outta here. Hang on, I need to make sure Kevin is—"

"Your dog went home," he said, grabbing around my right hand, sword hilt and all. "Lady, nest is best so follow the dog!"

"Lycanthrope," I said, but he didn't seem to care.

Giggling, Les towed me right back across to the other side of the T-piece I'd arrived at just before I saw Lord Sero, and we fairly sprinted down the lane with the shouts of Lord Sero's minions behind us. I don't know if we actually followed Kevin's path, but Les seemed to know where he was going, and he wasn't dead yet. I decided to trust him.

That turned out to be a good decision, because by the time we had skidded around far too many left turns for us to be going in the right direction, we tumbled out into our backyard, which was as much of a relief as it was a worry.

Neither of us slowed down; we jogged toward the back patio, where Kevin was sitting with all the stubbornness of a dog who refuses to be taken to the vet while Morgana pulled at his scruff and vainly tried to convince him to get inside. He rose as soon as he saw us, and we all made a mad dash into the house in a tumble of laboured breathing, bloody shoving, and muttered recriminations.

"Flamin' heck!" I said, when the door was shut behind us and the cold chills on the back of my neck had a chance to go down. "What were you doing sitting out on the back patio, you dipstick?"

Indignation did what nothing earlier in the day had done, and prompted Kevin to ripple out of his fur and into a slightly less injured, naked young man who could snap at me, "You *threw* me through the hedges!"

"Yeah, sorry about that."

"No you're not!"

"Yeah, well, you'll have to get over it. I told Morgana I'd bring you back safely."

"I could have helped you fight!"

"I know," I said. "But I didn't want to fight. I ran away. I just made sure you were out of the way so that he didn't know which way to chase."

He stared at me. "You ran away, too?"

"I'm not stupid enough to fight Lord Sero alone," I said bluntly. "We're trying *not* to die."

"Nobody died, and that's the important thing," said Morgana.

"Kevin, *please* go and put on some clothes! I know you don't care, but some of us want to be able to eat later!"

"That's flamin' rude," he said, but he went upstairs anyway.

Morgana hugged me with far greater strength than I remembered her having and made a small snuffling sound somewhere near my ear that eventually became, "Thank you for bringing Kevin back."

"How are the others?" I asked, pulling away. We could probably all do with a cuppa, but I didn't know if I had it in me to make tea and coffee.

"Chantelle's doing fine; once I got her to change back she started healing up all right. They'll probably need to rest for a day or so and they'll be fighting each other the same as usual. Is that thing dead—the bunyip?"

"As a doornail," I said, yawning. "Any more fun here?"

"No, but we haven't been able to get the table back up against the window," Morgana said, leading the way up the hall toward the living room. "I mean, we can get it there, but we can't keep it there."

I'd forgotten the amount of damage to the house in the rush to get Kevin back; we had to pick our way through debris and powder just to get to the living room. Once there, I was able to see that I wasn't the only one surveying the mess with raised brows—Jin Yeong was at the window, his mouth pursed and his brows up.

"Oh yes," said Morgana. "And someone's been waiting to see you."

CHAPTER SEVEN

I grinned and waved at him, picking my way across the worst of the mess in the living room and completely forgetting that I must look about as messy as the room did until I was standing in front of the window and found that Jin Yeong was surveying me with his brows pinched together and his right forefinger tapping against the windowsill as if he wanted to be doing something else with his hands but couldn't.

Mwoh haesseo? was what I thought he mouthed at me. *What happened?*

I shrugged a bit and pointed to the mess behind me, and the darkness of the still-broken window behind that. "Had a bit of trouble with a bunyip," I said. "It's all fine now, but I can't talk for long; I have to fix up that mess."

Jin Yeong nodded, and it seemed to me that his jaw became firmer, if that was possible. I don't think he understood me, but he didn't stay long, and despite the fact that I was the one who had said I couldn't talk for long, I was left standing by the window with the dissatisfied feeling that time had somehow become very short lately and the conclusion that it would be nice if it would slow down every now and then. Jin Yeong must be on his way to go and see someone else—though goodness knew who else he could drag over here. Hopefully he'd go after North next—at least then Tuatu might be able to get a network badge to Jin Yeong so I could speak with him on the phone. I didn't like how disconnected my family was feeling lately.

I wandered over to the kitchen again, stumbling over plaster and splinters of wood as I did so and Morgana sent me a sympathetic sort of smile that I didn't exactly understand. I was disgruntled, not in need of sympathy.

There wasn't much left of the kitchen table when I stepped up into the kitchen dining area, which was a pain in the neck. I'd been hoping to try something like Zero had done with it earlier to block off the window. Failing that, I was going to have to try and get tricky with Between, and I had no idea how I was going to do that.

Morgana came into the kitchen while I was still gazing on the mess with a kind of bemused futility and said, "You have no idea what to do, do you?"

"Not a clue!" I agreed. "That's all right. That seems to be my default mode."

"You never look like it," she said. "You always seem like you know what you're doing. Did you know that your house looks like its knitting itself back together over there?"

"Heck!" I said, impressed. "Where?"

Morgana pointed to the section of wall that formed the dining room wall on one side and the back hall on the other; a huge chunk of it had been punched right out, forming a curved, almost bite mark section of wall instead of the straight edge it should have been. That bite mark was looking just a little bit flatter on the curve than it had been just an hour or so earlier when I leaped out of the window to go after the bunyip. Around the section that seemed to be knitting itself together, I saw the wriggling of a million little filaments of Between; in the rubble that was the back hallway, something else wriggled and seemed to move closer.

"It's been healing itself quicker since you got back, too," said Morgana, moving over to get a closer look. "I think your house is alive, like mine—probably more, though. Is that an heirling thing, too?"

"Being able to control Between is an heirling thing, or so I hear," I said, with the tickling of an idea in the back of my mind. "Houses are mostly pretty alive, in my experience; my house seems to like me, though. I suppose yours likes you, too."

"Yours doesn't just like you; it protects you," she said.

"Suppose it does," I said, with a sudden rush of fondness for the old place. I had long ago forgotten to question exactly why it was that it was so hard for me to leave my house for the last few years; I was now convinced that it was a combination of the connection with Between that made me able to connect with the house and the wiles of Athelas, who hadn't wanted a live heirling running around Hobart to set off rumours that would get back to Zero's father. I had a lot of new memories that I hadn't wanted to delve into too deeply, and that was one of them: Athelas and his magnetic grey eyes holding me captive as he said, "It would be *very unwise* to leave the house..."

Something nudged against my shoulder, prodding me out of my memories, and I found that another piece of rubble was rolling its way up the broken wall and nudging itself into place like the piece that had just pushed past my shoulder to return to its place.

"Good job," I said to the wall, patting it gently. "Keep going."

It was going on more quickly now than it had been earlier, pieces visibly shifting through and up out of the rubble to crawl back into place in the wall or ceiling. A creepy little stream of disintegrated wall piecing itself back together.

At least that was something I wouldn't have to do—unlike the broken window that was still breathing dangerously cool air on us as we stood in the kitchen. I could, I supposed, wait until the kitchen table repaired itself enough and then try to stick it over the hole again like Zero had, but—

Hang on, though.

If the house could reknit itself, maybe it could reknit the window, too.

"Got an idea," I said to Morgana, grinning.

"It worries me when you say stuff like that while you're grinning," she said, but she followed me over to the kitchen window anyway, though she hung back a little bit when the breath of breeze became more ozone-heavy.

I leaned against the window frame much as I'd done last time JinYeong was on the other side of the window, avoiding the worst of the glass shards, and gave it a good pat, too.

"C'mon," I said encouragingly to it, ignoring the waiting, hungry dark outside. "You don't like being in pieces, and I'm pretty sure that you don't want anything from out there back in here, either."

It wasn't that I did it, exactly. It wasn't that I talked the house into doing it, exactly, either. It was a bit of both; a weird, sixth sense that seemed to extend my senses through the house and let me pull all the pieces together while they came together of their own accord as well.

I had the feeling that the house approved, so far as a house *could* approve, because if the rubble in the hall was gathering together at a good, steady stroll, the glass and splinters of the window skittered and scuttled together at a rapid, insect-like speed that had Morgana taking to the remaining kitchen stool with some haste, lifting her feet up and out of the way.

Glass formed and crystalized around the edges of the window just before the bumping, thumping noise began on the outside of the house, as if someone were thumping their fist against the wall in a steadily-increasing height.

"What's coming through the window?" asked Morgana, her eyes big. "Am I going to have to—what's coming, Pet?"

"Dunno," I said, resisting the urge to step back. I could help the house finish more quickly if I stayed where I was.

But that thumping kept coming, higher and higher, as the window glass scuttled back together, until I was caught a breath between staying where I was and ducking out of the way.

A shadow rose in the darkness, then Athelas' chair, worn and rather more battered than it had been a day or two ago, tumbled through the window with a sickening thud, and the window sealed itself up in a crackling of liquid glass swiftly hardening.

Morgana, over on her stool, gave way to an explosive few moments of giggling, and I said exasperatedly to the house, "I didn't ask you to bring back *that*!"

I left the chair where it was, though. Zero could deal with it when he got back—preferably without ruining another window.

IT WAS FAR TOO LATE the next afternoon before I heard the sound I had been listening vainly for since I woke up. Jin Yeong had returned early in the day for no other purpose, it seemed, than to make sure I was still okay; and having discovered that I was, to teach me how to do some kind of old-fashioned dance through the window. That had only been enough to distract me while he was there, and when he left, Morgana and I fed four very subdued lycanthropes and took turns to covertly wander down the back hall and listen at the door far too often.

I don't think either of us wanted to call out the other, so we just kept doing the same little dance until at last we heard the sound we'd been waiting for.

"What on *earth* is that?" demanded Daniel's voice, very close to the back door.

I took off for the back of the house with a gleeful laugh, Morgana close behind me.

Zero and Daniel were back safe!

I got to the door first and flung it open without checking

through the laundry window first, which was probably a bad idea. Luckily for me, it really was Zero and Daniel outside, because I didn't get a chance to say or see anything beyond the huge, leather-clad chest: Zero strode through the back door and folded me in a hug that pressed knife hilts into my cheek uncomfortably. I didn't like to wriggle; it was too nice to be the recipient of a hug instead of the giver, for once.

"You brought in a stray again," was the first thing Zero said to me when he let me go.

I followed his eyes, which had flickered toward the laundry door, and saw that Les was back and wearing a pair of very fine socks that were, I was pretty sure, Jin Yeong's socks.

"So did you," I said, jerking my chin toward the human teenager behind him. Sarah looked shaken but very determined, a sheen of Between to her that clung like a second skin and warned me not to touch her or get too close.

"Mine smells better," he said, and laughed a full-throated, glad laugh that made me realise he was almost dizzy with relief.

"S'pose you saw the scummy stuff on the side of the house," I said, as Daniel and Morgana took Sarah down to the living room. Maybe they wanted to give us some privacy—more likely, they wanted a bit of their own. "Had some trouble while you were gone."

"All over the back and side of the house," he said. "And as soon as I got back I could feel the window-seal was broken."

"I'm not dead," I pointed out. I didn't want to ruin his joyful relief by saying it, but I couldn't *not* add, "In fact, I'm very not dead despite meeting your dad earlier."

Zero went very still, but his eyes didn't freeze over and he didn't stride away, either. "So my father made it into the arena," he said.

"You don't sound surprised," I observed.

"I'm not. If I'd thought it was possible, I would have expected it."

"Athelas was with him," I added.

Zero said rather mechanically, "He's still with my father, then."

"You thought he would have gone off on his own when he's expecting payment from your dad? I don't reckon Athelas is going anywhere without whatever he was promised for doing this."

"I thought—" He stopped, a deep cleft between his brows, then said through his teeth, "I had hoped that he might have left, or have been run off. It would have been a sign that perhaps—"

"That perhaps he hadn't done it all? Or that he'd done it for a reason? You figured if he was in trouble with your dad, it would mean that he was still with us and just working the inside?"

"I thought—no, I hoped it was possible that he was there to get closer to my father in order to help us."

"Your face didn't look like it," I said. "Not then, not now."

"I would have believed it if I could," he said, with a faint rictus of contempt digging into one cheek. I wasn't sure if the contempt was for himself or Athelas. "It's good to know where we stand, at least. I would very much like to know how they got in here."

"Yeah, me too," I said. "Oh, by the way, there are bunyips out there."

"There are *what*?"

"Aussie thing," I said. "Maybe you don't know it—big, scaley, furry thing with three-foot claws and a tail that stabs people."

"It will be in my book," he said, but there was a faint curve to his lips again. "Don't try to condescend to me just because you met a behindkind animal before I did. I haven't forgotten that you're still bringing strays home, either."

"Technically, mine was already here," I pointed out. "And he also helped me to get away from your dad, so we should probably say thank you."

I'd already said thank you to Les, of course; I'd made him a whole pot of coffee, too—which was probably a mistake, in retrospect—and ignored him dancing on the kitchen island for a good couple of hours before I had to make him come down so that I could start getting lunch ready.

I gave him a couple of strawberries to play with later, after Zero and Sarah had sat down on the couch to debrief, hoping to distract him while I made dinner and listened in on the debriefing. His sudden descent from the kitchen bench gave Morgana enough space to edge around him safely and sit on one of the seats by the kitchen island without being hit by a flying arm or leg, so at least that was a success.

She was inclined to be curious about Sarah, so I filled her in while I chopped veggies and started up the rice cooker; and when the mince was simmering away, I resolutely grabbed the nearest, packaged brain from the fridge and brought it out in the hope that Morgana would be too invested in the conversation to go away despite what I was doing.

She saw what I was doing pretty quickly and wrinkled her nose. "Pet, do we have to do this tonight?" she said plaintively, giving up on her questions about Sarah more quickly than I'd feared.

"You said you were going to protect Daniel and the others," I reminded her.

"I am," she said. "Don't worry, if you're going to cook it, I'll try to eat it. Will it be the same if it's cooked sheep brain instead of raw behindkind brain, do you think?"

"Dunno," I said. "But I don't know where to find a morgue while we're trapped in here, and sheep's brain is about all there is for now unless you want to go hunting or try some leftovers."

She opened her mouth, and I added, "Don't worry, this is all yours: the others are getting mince. No brain for them."

Morgana giggled. "I don't think they'd mind, so long as it was meat," she said. "They don't even care if it's cooked or not: they can change into their wolf selves if the meat is raw—some of them even like that better."

"So what happened the other morning, anyway?" I asked.

Keep chopping, I told myself. Nice and casual, and don't tell her it's okay not to answer, just give her the space to not answer if she wants.

"What happened out there?" she countered, indicating the newly-fixed window. "You vanished through the window and were gone for four hours, then turned back up with Kevin and all over blood."

"Yeah, it could have gone better," I said. I hadn't done more than give her a bare-bones version of the night until I could tell Zero about it. Now that I had, I might as well tell Morgana. "Met up with Zero's dad and Athelas while I was out there."

She stiffened. "He's in here, too?"

"Yeah," I said. "So if you see him, run."

"I won't be running anywhere if I don't eat again soon," she said glumly.

"Well—"

"Yes, but I don't want to eat."

"All right; tell me about the morning," I said. "Before we came to get you."

"I heard the kids calling for help, first," she said, her eyes slightly unfocused. "They never call for help and they're dead, anyway. I didn't know what could be so bad that ghosts would be calling for help. Daniel ran up the stairs outside my room but he didn't hear me calling, and then Chelsea screamed."

"She was the one getting you coffee?"

"Yeah," said Morgana quietly. "She doesn't usually scream, either. I fell out of bed trying to get to her, and by then four of them were already in the kitchen and Chelsea was still screaming. I think they were pulling the blood out of her body or something, because one of them tried to pull me over in the same way, then reached out and grabbed me because I don't...I don't really have that."

"Good grief," I said. No wonder Chelsea had still looked so red around the face and eyes when I got there.

"I remember feeling so hot and *angry*, and I remember biting, too—I think I bit right through his ear and then—and then—"

"How'd it feel to walk again?" I asked her, because she was getting red and distressed around the cheeks again.

"I must have learned to walk once," she said vaguely, still caught up in her memories. "I don't think I have memories of actually *doing* it, though: it made me feel seasick and weird, and I had a bit of trouble staying upright, but there were enough... people to grab onto. Everything was a bit of a haze then because I was so angry. I made a bit of a mess of the kitchen, so I don't know how we're ever going to clean that up when this is all over."

"Yeah, I saw the mess you made," I said, slicing brain into delicate layers. "It was a good thing, too; reckon Chelsea and the others would have had a bit of trouble if you hadn't done it."

Morgana nodded, but she was a touch paler than she had been earlier as she watched me cut up brain, a faintly squeamish look on her face.

"It's probably better if you don't look at it," I said. "Why don't you keep an eye out for Jin Yeong instead? He usually comes back at around dinner time; let me know when he gets here, all right?"

Morgana nodded silently and turned her eyes on the living room, where two lycanthropes in wolf form were curled up together between the back of the spare chair and Zero's bedroom nook, and Zero's broad back moved occasionally as he leaned forward to take something from the coffee table.

I didn't notice the first time her hand reached out absently and took a slice of pink meat and slipped it into her mouth as if it was a snack, but I definitely noticed the second time.

Heck. Was that normal?

I opened my mouth to ask, but Daniel scowled a warning at me from the kitchen table and I shut my mouth again. It wasn't like I wanted to cook brain, and if she was going to eat it raw...

It wasn't until the chopping board was nearly empty that Morgana turned her head again and said, "There he is."

I caught a glimpse of JinYeong at the window in the living room just as Morgana caught sight of the chopping board, then the slices of brain, then her own hand.

"Oh no," she said, her voice tiny and horrified. "What did I do? Did I...did I *eat* that?"

"Yep," I said, biting back the addition of, "Nice and raw, too."

"But it isn't—I didn't—"

"How do you feel?" I asked her, since she seemed to be having trouble getting past the raw brains concept, herself. "Lively? Healthy?"

Her eyes met mine, and I didn't have to see the faint, almost iridescent ring of red around her irises to read the fascination there, though there was still a bit of horror. "I feel *really* good. As good as the first time, too; I was afraid I'd only get that kind of energy from eating straight from the...straight from the source."

"Red eyes look good on you," I said, shrugging one shoulder and putting down my knife. It was hard to know what else to say when your best friend is turning into a monster and it's the most healthy thing for her. Humans are meant to avoid monsters; they're not meant to approve of their friends turning into monsters.

Mind you, I was pretty used to monsters by now, I thought, meeting JinYeong's eyes and smiling involuntarily.

"You might as well go over," Morgana said resignedly. "You've been waiting for him all day, after all! I'll just sit here and try and pretend to not eat."

I couldn't help laughing at that, because her hand slipped out and pinched away another slice of pink brain as she said it. She didn't look at it as she put it in her mouth, but this time I was pretty sure she knew what she was doing, regardless. I left her to Daniel's watchful eyes, then washed my hands and crossed the room to go and greet JinYeong.

Something must have happened on the way over, because when I copped a full sight of him, his hair was more than fashionably askew and the tail end of his tie was only hanging on by a thread. There was also more than a bit of dirt on his left hip that looked like it continued around to the back—like someone had sent him flying onto his backside.

"You're looking a bit messy," I said, grinning. "What happened to you?"

He shrugged one shoulder, mouth pursed in what seemed to be mingled pride and amusement. Whatever had happened, he'd come out on top. More, it was something that had been useful to him.

He didn't try to talk too much this time, which was nice. It wasn't as though we could understand each other, anyway, and it was nice just to have him there. He hadn't brought along anyone else to try and get through the window, either, which made me wonder whether he'd given up, or had something else in mind instead.

He seemed content to lean on the windowsill there on the other side of the worlds and look me over to make sure everything was healing all right, and I was conscious of being glad that I'd finally taken the time to shower and clean up the mess earlier. I saw Jin Yeong gaze at the very nearly healed wall behind me, too, and smile. Then he caught sight of Athelas' slightly-more-battered chair and one brow shot up.

I shrugged and grinned. "Can't stop strays from getting in," I said.

He didn't understand, but he still looked amused. It would have been nice to have been able to explain to him that Tuatu was coming to him with a private network badge if another could be found—or even to explain that he needed to be findable for the detective—but he wouldn't have understood that, either.

My breath hitched on a sigh and I leaned against the window, perched on the arm of one of the kitchen chairs that someone had thoughtfully put there for me.

"You gunna stay there all night?" demanded Daniel, appearing in the living room from somewhere toward the back of the house.

"Mind your own business," I said mildly, throwing the seat-pillow from my chair at him. "Shouldn't you be having a bath or something? You lot smell flamin' terrible—been rolling in dead stuff out there?"

"Pet, there are *banshees* in the bathroom."

"They're fine so long as you don't antagonise 'em," I advised him, turning back to the silent shadow that was Jin Yeong. He was drawing now, which was interesting. It looked like it might be a person, but time would tell.

"I'm not taking a bath while the banshees watch!" Daniel said firmly.

"Put the tie frog outside the bathroom door; they love that thing. They might get a bit noisy, is all."

"I don't care if they do their haggis-and-dance celebration, so long as they're out of the bathroom," said Daniel, and went away again—probably upstairs to find the tie frog as I'd suggested.

My phone rang shortly after Jin Yeong grew irritated with his drawing and ripped off the page he'd been working on to start another. He saw me answer the phone and his eyes narrowed, but it was more of a thoughtful narrowing than an annoyed one: Jin Yeong wanted to know why I was able to use my phone but not able to use it to talk to him.

As soon as I picked up, Tuatu's voice said, "Pet! Why haven't we heard from you!"

"Been bearding a bunyip in its den," I said. "It was flamin' unpleasant, too. And Zero was out for a while, so—"

"He isn't back yet?"

"He got back just a while ago: we got Sarah. It just took a while longer to do it than we thought. She's fine, but we haven't got her parents. Apparently she isn't sure whether they're inside or out; they were on their way out of the house when everything went down. They weren't in the same room when everything happened, so you'll need to check on your side, too."

He let out an audible breath, and I heard a second whistle of air that passed across the phone receiver a second later.

I grinned. "Tell North I say hi. And that she owes Zero, because he was the one who got Sarah out. We'll try to get to her parents as soon as we can; apparently we're going out again tomorrow. Morgana needs to power up with a bit of brain, and—"

"Please never tell me what that means. We'll look for her parents as well, all right?"

"Fine," I said. "What'd you find out about the building and bit of land I asked you about?"

"It's only been a couple days, Pet."

"I know. Figured you're pretty resourceful, though; and if North was helping..."

"I found something," he said. There was a grin in his voice. "But I don't think it's anything you'd be interested in."

"I'm interested in everything," I said. "Chuck it at me."

"There was a wedding there—some sort of invite-only, star-studded thing in the twenties. Apparently the press tried to get in but couldn't. It was in the papers, but without photos—and some of the Hobart cops were moonlighting as security."

I sucked in a swift breath. "Any of those men known to be... special? Different?"

"Don't know," he said, with a shade of frustration in his voice. He must have spent a bit of time trying to run that idea down, himself. "It was a long time ago. The records were paper and we lost a lot of them in a fire fifty years ago."

"Flamin' typical," I muttered. "Any record of the marriage?"

I heard the satisfaction in his voice. "Yes. I managed to track it down with the help of your computer hacker friend—your other friend isn't answering his phone. The hacker is a bit jumpy, by the way. Are you sure he's trustworthy?"

"'Zul's always a bit jumpy," I said. "He's not comfortable working with the good guys."

"That doesn't make me feel any better, Pet."

"Nah, I mean he's not comfortable working with the good guys when the good guys are Zero and can potentially kill him if they don't like what he's doing. He also knows that the bad guys don't want him working for the good guys, so he's a bit insecure."

"I can understand that," Tuatu said. "He managed to find a few things, anyway; the marriage record was for a Miss Emily Simmons and Dr. Lukas Lin, and he was apparently a big deal in the 20s. She was a nobody, if what the papers said was true. Rich socialite marries poor nobody, that sort of story. I haven't been able to find much else for either of them, though; even your hacker hasn't been able to find much else."

"Oi, Tuatu," I said, my thoughts sharpening. "Did Abigail and her lot manage to get any of their...things to you? Any books?"

"Got a delivery the night before everything happened," he said. "And one of them—the little cricket bat kid—put a download on my phone. It's been laggy ever since."

"Yeah, it was a pretty big download," I said, delight growing in my chest. "Perfect! You've got some of their records, then!"

"Their—they downloaded some of their records onto my phone?"

"Yep! Reckon it'll come in pretty handy, too."

"It's also making my phone slower than a wet week."

"So buy a new phone!" I said cheerfully. "Anyway, check there: look for any mention of that Emily Simmons, in particular. I want to know how things went."

"I don't think it went very well," said Tuatu. "There's a death record for her just a few years later. That was one of the few things I could find."

My heart went cold. "Flamin' fae," I said savagely. "Reckon you can find out if there was a kid?"

"I can, but why? You think he killed her?"

"Don't know," I said. "But there's something important about that bit of ground that kept the—someone there for a flamin' long time. If he got married to a human, that would have done it: for cold-hearted people, fae spend a lot of time ruminating on the past and holding onto trauma. It just doesn't make sense if he was the one who killed her."

"I've heard that it's not too safe being close to behindkind in general and fae in particular," Tuatu said dryly. "Someone I know is always being attacked."

"Good point," I said. "Someone else might have done the deed. See if you can find out more about that Doctor Lukas, too, though, all right?"

"Will do. You any further toward getting out of your cage?"

"Nope, but we're not dead yet, so that's nice."

"How likely are you to get out soon?" he asked, carefully neutral. "North wants to know."

"Things getting messier out there?"

"A bit."

There was a heaviness of experience in those words that made my brows rise. Whatever was going on outside in Hobart, it was bad. Maybe it would be just as well if Jin Yeong stopped coming around to the house and started helping Tuatu instead.

And thinking of Jin Yeong...

"You manage to get one of those badges?" I asked.

"I'm working on it. If I get one, where am I supposed to take it? I haven't seen hide nor hair of the vampire since we were working together on the waterfront. I could have used his help."

"Just bring it to the house, I suppose," I said. Jin Yeong was coming back to the house twice a day at the moment, whether it was to drag another potential helper to assess the situation or to lean up against the window and make sure I knew he was *there*, and *warm*. "I'll have a word with him about helping out, all right?"

"I'd appreciate that," Tuatu said, and there was a repressed relief in his voice that worried me.

Heck, how bad was it out there?

"Look after yourself," I said, catching a flutter of movement in the window. "I gotta go now. I'll call again when we know about Sarah's parents."

I hung up without hearing his reply, because Jin Yeong was starting to make signs that he was getting ready to leave, and I didn't want to waste the time I had left with him. Unluckily for me, Jin Yeong was swift and decided; he had finished his drawing and now flipped it up against the window so I could see it.

I took a look at it and said in astonishment, "What the heck?"

He pointed at it wordlessly, more insistently this time.

"All right, all right, I'm looking," I said. It was a drawing of a faceless figure like you might see when a fashion designer sketches concepts into their sketchbook; the figure wore a pretty loud grey chequered suit with lines of yellow through the chequers. It was something I wouldn't have been surprised to see Jin Yeong wearing: just loud enough to appeal to him, and just fashionable enough to suit his dignity.

Jin Yeong waited just another moment or two, then flipped shut the notebook and tucked it into his pocket. He made the smallest of air-kisses in my direction, then turned on his toes before I could react and sauntered away.

"Flamin' typical," I said, pushing myself away from the window so I wouldn't find myself stuck there for the next hour.

Someone had thrown the chair-seat pillow back at me, and it was leaning drunkenly against the wall. I crouched to pick it up and after that it was easier to sit on the floor with my back against the wall, taking the cushion's place, one leg propped up and the other stretched out in front of me.

No one was trying to kill us, and none of the lycanthropes were trying to kill each other; all in all, there didn't seem to be much point getting up right now, so I sat gloomily where I was for a little while longer and watched Morgana absentmindedly eat slices of brain while watching the lycanthropes.

She wasn't watching them closely enough, because a moment later, Kevin kicked the chair next to me for what seemed like the sole purpose of making me glare at him and asked, "What are you moping for?"

I scrambled up off the floor, immediately defensive. "I'm not moping; I'm resting! Anyone cooking for you lot needs their rest. *And* I fought a flamin' bunyip yesterday, so—"

"Yeah? Then how come you get *tired* right after the vampire goes away every time?"

I glared at him. "I don't!"

Kevin looked around and then leaned closer, confidentially. "I'm saying this 'cos you saved me," he said. "So don't hit me. Do you even know how much your face lights up when that ankle biter is at the window? You look like Dylan when he gets a sniff of giblets."

"If you want dinner you'd better belt up now," I told him, scowling. "Jin Yeong isn't giblets and my face doesn't light up."

"All right," he said. "But I'm only shutting up because I want dinner. Don't forget that."

CHAPTER EIGHT

By the time dinner was ready most of the dining room wall had knitted itself back together, and the dining table was beginning to look like a table again, even if it was a bit sway-backed.

Zero threw a look at it and took his bowl of veggie-mince-and-rice down into the living room instead. The lycanthropes followed him, arranging themselves around the living room so as to leave the seats for Zero, Daniel, Morgana, Sarah and myself. No one seemed to want to sit on Athelas' chair, and I didn't blame them. Associations aside, it had a kind of black glimmer to it that was probably due to it being out in whatever the blackness was outside our dining room window.

When we were all more or less settled with our bowls, Daniel shot a look at Zero and asked, "Have you changed your mind?"

Sarah, her face immediately pinching, said, "You can't! As soon as you start playing the game, you have to keep playing!"

"I haven't changed my mind," Zero said flatly. "I told my father I wouldn't participate in the trials, and I won't be doing so. I haven't thrown my hat in the ring through my childhood, and I'm not about to do so now."

"Hang on," I said sharply, looking at Sarah. "What do you mean, you have to keep playing? Did you—"

She flushed. "When I was first taken Behind, they taught me how to fight. I agreed to compete in the trials, so there were already people outside the house, waiting to treat, when I got here. In order for the trials to end, I have to be either among the dead or triumphant: the trials won't end otherwise."

"Then it seems like a pretty bad idea for any of us to agree to compete," I said. "I mean, it sounds like the king is the sort to be waiting outside for whoever comes out *anyway*, but—"

"The king hasn't yet done anything illegal in this round," said Zero.

Daniel said gloomily, "True."

"Funny thing I noticed," I said, pushing my suddenly tasteless mince around my bowl with my spoon. "You lot keep saying how nice it is that the king is doing things all proper and legal this time, but out of all the people I've seen in this flamin' closed system that I didn't want to meet, do you know who I haven't seen?"

"The king," said Daniel, nodding without surprise. Seems like he'd been thinking about it, too.

"He gets it," I said, pointing at him. "If we all have to be in here to pick out the next king, how come he's not either in here or dead?"

"I'd prefer dead," said Daniel.

"Exactly!" I said triumphantly. "So why isn't he? How do we even get to grips with him like this? The only person from the outside that we've been able to get up close and personal with is your dad, Zero; and we don't really want to be getting up close and personal with him."

"My father has gone all in," Zero said. "If this gambit of his doesn't work, the king won't leave him alive once he's out of the trial arena. Anyone aligning themselves with my father will also face death or worse."

"Yeah, but to be able to do that, the king has to be alive," I said.

Sarah, slowly, said, "At what point does he die? The king?"

"Oooh!" said Morgana, her eyes widening. "That's a good point. When will he die? Shouldn't he already be dead, or dying? Daniel, you told me it's a natural cycle."

"What I'm wondering is, is this something he can run away from?" I said, while Daniel was still trying to swallow a mouthful of mince and rice before answering. "You lot say the king usually dies naturally or whatever; when he's coming to the end of his reign, the heirlings start showing up naturally. None of this lot of the heirling trials has happened naturally; Lord Sero was out there trying to kill every heirling he could get his hands on, and someone else was out there trying to keep as many alive as possible so they'd have a finger in the pie no matter which one came out on top. It was all conniving from both sides. So if this is supposed to be natural, which way around is it?"

"Does the coming death of the king force the heirlings out, or does the appearance of the heirlings bring about the end of the king," said Morgana, nodding.

I crossed my legs beneath me, warming to my question. "We know which one the king believes, 'cos he murdered all the other heirlings in the last we-don't-know-how-many cycles. He also didn't die, which makes it look more like heirlings are the deathknell of the king than the other way around."

"They're symbiotic," Zero said. "You can't have one without the other, but no one can tell which is the root and which is the fruit."

"Well, that's flamin' useful."

"Your point still stands," he added, surprising me. "The death of the king historically precedes the heirling trials; there will be a great many people wanting to know how the king's death will come about."

"Reckon the king will be wondering that himself," I said.

"What I want to know is, can we use that kind of advantage to make sure he's the one that carks it once we get out of here? Because he obviously isn't considered one of the heirlings: he would have been in here if he was. As far as I see it, we have to make sure that we stay alive long enough to get out of this system with whoever wins, and that the king is pushing up daisies before he gets around to murdering the heirling that wins out."

"The heirling that wins out is likely to try and kill us."

"Thanks, Eeyore," I said, glaring at Daniel. "Let's assume that we manage to survive—or at least hide out—until all the actual competing heirlings are dead—"

"—Except for Sarah," Morgana reminded me.

"Oh yeah, that's another problem."

"Thanks," said Sarah, but she looked a bit more cheerful anyway.

"So we assume that we all survive until that point," I began again, the glimmering of an idea in my mind. "Just hiding out in the house where no one can get at us, because the house is—"

"What's the good of staying in the house if the king's just going to be waiting for us once we get outside?" Daniel said morosely.

"Because we still don't die until we get out, you gloomy git," I told him. "And maybe we don't have to die then, either. Can't we... I don't know, bring him to judgement for meddling in the heirling selection and trials?"

"There's no way of bringing the king into any kind of judgement," Zero said. "Even if one of us was the champion and wanted to call him to single combat or restart a new trial with him joining the surviving heirlings, we'd have to know his name."

"That's all right," I said. "I'm working on that."

"You're—Excuse me, you're *what*?"

I stared at Zero. "I'm working on it! Got a few ideas about where we might be able to find his real name. That's one of the reasons I was trying to call Detective Tuatu in the first place."

Morgana, grinning, leaned against Daniel and seemed to settle in for the duration.

"How on *earth* do you think you're going to find the name of a *behindkind king* who has been living for centuries without being challenged by name by anyone Behind?" Zero asked incredulously. "Pet, I know you like to look at things from a positive point of view, but—"

"Fae always let their guard down when they're around humans," I told him. "You know you do."

"Not enough to give out their name freely to humans, willy nilly."

"You're the one who told me," I said, grinning. "You said that heirlings have to have at least a drop of human blood. They gotta have behindkind blood, too; but the human blood is non-negotiable. And the king owns that bit of land right in the middle of Hobart, so—"

"Behindkind "own" land everywhere," he said impatiently. "They glamour or trick humans into—"

"Don't think you understand," I said. "He properly *owns* it: family property that was passed down through generations for as long as Hobart's been around. In the human world, he has actual paperwork with an actual name on it. Tuatu's just been having a bit of trouble getting to it to have a gander at the name."

Zero stared at me, perplexed. "Why would the *King of Behind* own a piece of land in a small city centuries younger than he is?"

"Same reason as every other heirling ended up being an heirling, I reckon," I said, grinning. "He fell in love with a human for a while. You know, for people who are always boasting about how above emotions they are, fae are pretty flamin' impressionable when it comes to a pretty human girl or boy. He lived there for about twenty years, as far as Tuatu can tell."

"You can't tell me he gave her a real name!" Daniel said, in disbelief.

"'Course not!" I said. "But he gave *a* name to the woman he married, and he gave a name when he bought the land, too. If Ath —if Athelas is anything to go by, he'll probably have been playing games with those names."

Zero, a furrow between his brows, said, "Let's not discuss Athelas," and he said it with such harshness that no one else quite liked to say anything at all.

That was all right with me. I didn't know exactly what it was I was chasing, after all. I just knew that when it came to fae and names, and fae and humans, the fae didn't always behave as cleverly and emotionlessly as they liked other races to think. And I was pretty sure that that was where I'd find what I needed.

I couldn't sleep that night, but at least I wasn't the only one. It was just us girls upstairs: Sarah sitting up on the couch with her arms wrapped around her legs like she was afraid something would come after her any second—she probably was—and Morgana, tiny and dramatically white and black, beside her. Chelsea sat on the floor in front of the armchair where Chantelle was curled up in her human form as though she was still in her wolf form, trying to heal. We'd tried to turn the lights off, but that just left us looking at each other in the darkness and that wasn't much fun, either.

"You're worse than the lycanthropes when they're wolf, Pet," complained Morgana, at last. "What's bothering you?"

"Dunno," I said, grinning a bit. "What about you? Don't see you getting much sleep, either."

"I don't like it when Daniel goes out," she said, with an almost blistering simplicity. "I don't like him coming back home with wounds and bruises. I don't like having bad dreams about him while he's away."

"I don't like having dreams at all," Sarah said. "North taught me how to stop most of them, but some still get through. Sorry that you've got to go out again because of me, Pet. I told Zero that I'd go instead of Daniel."

"You don't have to be sorry about that," I said. "Of course we're going to make sure your parents are okay! That'll make two of us going out, anyway: reckon Zero won't stop me going out this time. I think he'd rather keep an eye on me at this point, and now that the kitchen window is fixed, it should be a lot safer in here."

"You still don't look comfortable," she said, too sharp despite her young age. She looked just a bit younger than Morgana looked —that is, about twelve to Morgana's professed sixteen—but both of them had far too much experience for the age they appeared to be: Morgana because she was actually something like a hundred years old, and Sarah because she'd been trapped Behind for a year or so. Spending that long Behind was enough to give anyone a wealth of experience—along with a wealth of grey hairs—that they'd much rather not have.

"I feel like it's a bad idea to go out again," I said slowly, giving voice to thoughts I didn't quite understand. "Not that it's a bad idea to make sure your parents are okay, but it feels like *stuff* is closing in on us, and I don't know what direction it's closing in on us from. I don't like it. I don't like that Zero's dad is in here, either."

"You've got a feeling of doom," Morgana said, propping her chin on the back of her hand. "That's understandable, I suppose. Maybe you'll feel better when you see Jin Yeong tomorrow—don't glare at me! You always perk up a bit after he comes to the window. You might as well admit you like the fact that he keeps coming here despite not being able to get in. Did you think he'd get tired of it and go away?"

"Vampires are very clingy," Sarah said, tucking her feet under Morgana's pillow. She looked as though she was feeling a bit safer, which was nice. "And he's only about seventy in vampire years, isn't he?"

"There are *vampire* years?"

"Vampire years, fae years—do you know that rock dusters don't actually age, they just ossify more and more until they stop moving?"

"What are vampire years?"

"Stop changing the subject," Morgana said, and I stuck my tongue out at her.

"Vampire years start from the date the vampire is turned," said Sarah. "They regress a lot at the start with all the hunger and feelings and stuff. Even after they get to the point where they can control the hunger, some of them never learn to control their feelings again; they're pretty clingy when they find someone they love. You're lucky he's managed to avoid biting you."

"He bites her a *lot*," Morgana offered.

Sarah stared at me, horrified. "He *feeds* on you?"

"He doesn't feed on me, he bites me," I said, hunching my shoulders. "Sometimes he kisses me. It's different."

"He *kisses* you?"

"Don't look at me like that!" I protested. "I get super speed and a lot more strength when he bites or kisses me!"

"You really are fully human, then!" Sarah said, awed. "Or at least, you aren't part fae; but there aren't too many races that can mix with humans and still look...well, human."

"What about you, then?" I asked, feeling a bit too warm about the cheeks and in need of a change of subject. "Aren't you fully human?"

"I don't think so," she said. "Not many of us heirlings are. You're about the only one I know for sure, and you've probably got a bit of something else back in the line. With me, we think it's mer: there are stories about my grandma and a mysterious man from the navy."

"It isn't just biting and kissing," Morgana said, *sotto voce*; and she sent an innocent look in my direction when I scowled at her.

"I thought you were like me," I said to Sarah, slightly disappointed. "Fully human. My three psy—I mean, Zero keeps saying that humans can't do the sort of stuff I can do."

"They can," said Sarah. "But it's not that usual, either. Humans have magic but we don't get taught how to use it."

"That sounds about right, too," I said gloomily. I'd once known how to use the magic I had, but my parents had made me forget. Now that I remembered again, there was still no one to teach me how to use it.

"What would you want to try and do, anyway?" asked Sarah. "Instead of going out again, I mean? If there's a way we can find out where my parents are—whether they're in here or out there—that's better than going out again while the arena's still so full of heirlings and hangers-on."

"I don't know that, either," I said. "I just...I feel like there's gotta be a better way of getting to your parents than running around in the maze out there. And I feel like something's going to come clawing through the windows at any stage. I need to understand why the house is acting the way it is."

Morgana, looking doubtful, asked, "Is that important right now?"

"Maybe," said Sarah, an unexpected ally. "Instinct is important when it comes to Between and Behind. Things usually bother you for a reason."

"Yeah, that's what I thought," I said, and got up to wander around the room.

The girls watched me for a little while, but they must have been tireder than they thought, because by the time I'd gone around the entirety of the upper house, Chelsea and Chantelle were fast asleep and Sarah had also fallen asleep on Morgana. Morgana wasn't asleep, but she seemed to be in a sort of trance state that I'd seen Zero in a time or two. The behindkind equivalent of power-napping, is how I think of it.

I left them to rest and went downstairs to check out the windows there, unsure exactly what I was looking for. Half of the lycanthropes were asleep in the living room, though Daniel was in the kitchen drinking coffee and looking worried. That was about as normal as Zero polishing his multiple knives and swords, so I left him to it and circled the living room.

I even went into the little alcove where Zero slept for the few hours per night that he sometimes slept and tried the window there, ignoring the odd looks from everyone camping out in the living room who was still awake. From there, I could see the front patio and the road but there was the same kind of distance between the window on my side and the window on the outside that I had felt when I tried to get through to JinYeong. Nothing quite matched up with the world outside, even if everything was as it ought to be in here. It was our own, smaller version of the heirling arena outside: self-contained, seemingly impervious from the outside, and running on its own rules.

I didn't see how I was supposed to fix the gap between the arena and the outside world, let alone our house and the outside world. It wasn't just that we were vibrating at a different rate as the outside world, it was as though we were trapped inside a bubble full of other bubbles that intersected in dangerous ways: the bubble of the heirling arena, stuffed to the brim with self-contained bubbles like my house.

I leaned my backside against the edge of Zero's desk, huffing out a breath, because there was nothing useful about that knowledge. It was just one more nail in our collective coffin, because unless we could find a way to convince the arena that the trials were over, it didn't seem likely that we would be able to get out. And for the arena to think the trials were over, at least Sarah would have to be either dead or triumphant.

I shoved my hands in my pockets, musing on the possibilities —or lack of them, more like—then took them out to push the books and piece of paper or two that I had nearly knocked off the desk back onto the desk. One of them fell on the floor anyway, fluttering down and away from me with the same kind of annoying aloofness as its fae owner.

Only it wasn't the same kind of creamy, heavy-weight paper that Zero's books and files were usually made up of—it was human paper. It could have been something from one of the files Zero and Athelas were always pinching from the police station, but it had an even thinner feel to it than regular weight paper.

Nope. It wasn't something from a file; it was a piece of paper from my *own* things. It was the photocopy of my great grandmother's driving license.

I couldn't help the deep stab of fear that made my fingers grip the paper tightly enough to put my finger through it. Why the *flaming heck* did Zero have the copy of my great grandmother's driving license that had gone missing from my room?

Had he had it since it went missing? Had Zero found it in the living room where I might have lost it, or had he actually come into my room to find and remove it? If so, why? How had he known it was there, and what to look for?

Could *Zero* have been the one Athelas was looking for—

Nope. Couldn't think like that. I wasn't going to start distrusting Zero just because Athelas had betrayed me.

So I stalked back out into the living room with my stomach moving in slow, heavy, sick lurches, and asked Daniel, "Where's Zero?"

"He's trying to clear away the banshees from the bathroom," he said. "Since *someone* didn't care about—hey! Where are you going?"

I ignored him and headed down the hall, skirting around the last few bits and pieces of rubble that were still rolling slowly and gently back toward their place in the wall. Zero was just coming out of the bathroom when I reached the door, and since a sleepy lycanthrope pushed past me to go to the toilet right at that moment, I grabbed Zero by the leather-clad arm and towed him toward the laundry room instead, where I had to stop the old mad bloke from digging through the sheets and send him tottering toward the door.

I shut the door behind him and said crisply to Zero, "What the *flaming heck* is this?"

He stared at me, then at the crumpled photocopy, and the complete confusion on his face settled the sickness of my stomach in an instant. Whatever it was, he expected me to know what I was asking.

"You took this out of my room," I said, trying to clarify for him. Now that I was certain this wasn't another betrayal, it was easier to take the time to try and find the right words to ask what I wanted to know. "You've worked with humans before—"

"Yes," he said shortly. "I told you. Back then I was young and idealistic."

Young and idealistic. That was pretty close to something Athelas had said to me that night—that night when I learned that there was someone he hadn't been able to bring himself to kill.

"Was she one of the ones you worked with?"

It would explain *so much* about why my parents had been the way they were—how they had known the things they had known.

Again, there was that confused, not-quite-believing look. "No, Pet," he said. "She was my nurse."

"But—" I started, stopped, and the memory I had stolen from Athelas barely a week ago played again in my mind, unprompted.

"She said *Father*," I said, with a bit of a buzz in my ears. "The nurse in Athelas' memories called your dad *father*. My great grandma. Your nurse."

"She was my sister," he said coolly. "I thought you knew! I thought you were keeping it quiet because you didn't want Athelas or Jin Yeong to know."

"Why would I do that? How the heck was I supposed to know who she was to you?"

"You had the picture!"

"Yeah, because she was *my* great grandmother!"

"You really didn't see what was on the USB, did you?"

"I'd be pretty flamin' insulted if you weren't suggesting that I was clever enough to out-bluff you," I said. "Considering you think I've been fibbing to you this entire time. Why'd you keep calling her your nurse, anyway?"

"She was my nurse."

"All right, all right, Mr. Precise! She was also your sister."

"I wasn't allowed to call her sister: I was only allowed to call her *nurse*. I don't think I was even supposed to know who she was, but that sort of thing gets out. My mother was already pregnant when my father stole her away from the human world; she gave birth a few years before she became pregnant with me. My sister looked after me until we lost her somewhere between 1920 and 1930; she escaped to the human world. When my father found her and brought her back in the early thirties she looked...much older. Ath—someone told me that age catches up quickly with humans who spend too long Behind, once they get back to the human world."

"She was the one he wouldn't kill," I said, looking away. Why hadn't Athelas killed her? Had—hang on. Athelas. Athelas had killed Zero's brother and refused to kill his nurse—my great grandmother—when Zero was ten?

I tumbled into protest. "Wait; no, no, no. You said—ages ago you said you were *ten* when your step-brother was killed. How were you ten in the 1930s? You were born somewhere near the turn of the century, you *said*—heck, I'm going mad. You can't have been ten!"

"By fae accounting, I was," he said coolly. "Until we're of age, we account roughly one fae year to every human four—both physically and mentally."

I stared at him for far too long, caught between laughter and bewilderment. "You lot age in *dog* years?"

Well, the opposite of dog years—but that would make humans the dogs, and I didn't want to put that idea in his head when fae were already too inclined to think of humans as slightly more clever animals.

"By the time we're of age, our development has sped up," Zero said, very stiffly. "Our years then become closer to human years. I gave the best age you would understand to make you understand why I...why I acted and reacted as I did."

"You didn't want me to think of you as being immature, so you faked your age?"

"I did not fake my age; it was as near a comparison as I could make!"

"You faked your age 'cos you didn't want me to think you'd acted like a kid when you were actually thirty-odd in human years," I said firmly. "When do you age out, anyway?"

"It's *coming of age*, and it happens after we pass beyond our first ten years. Any magic or special gift comes out at that time."

"Pretty sure that's just becoming a teenager, but whatever. So you age properly after that?"

"Our mental processes develop much more swiftly after that and we pass through puberty; our bodies still do not age like those of humans."

"You lot really need to stop telling humans we're inferior," I remarked. "At least we don't take forty-odd years to get past the age of ten developmentally."

Zero, his lips thinning with annoyance, looked as though he was about to say something, but another thought struck me.

"Heck, you were only around twenty by fae count when you met Jin Yeong? That was in the fifties, right?"

If that was right, although he'd been roughly fifty in human years, developmentally, he'd only have been twenty or so: just a bit older than me. It made me wonder how old he'd been when he met JiAh—and made me understand how things had become so messy with her.

"So you were in your twenties when you were going around with that human you found, too."

"I didn't—I didn't find a human and start going around with him! He was a human who came Behind to avenge his sister, and—"

"If you tell me he's a relative of ours too, I'm gunna roll my eyes so hard they fall out."

Zero took in a thin breath through his nose. "He was no relation to either of us."

"I suppose that's something. How did you end up being with him, anyway?"

"I met him when he stole away a human from my father. He came Behind to find his sister who was taken from the human world, but when he discovered that she was dead his mind turned to correcting the imbalance he saw in the worlds so that such a thing would never happen again. It was a futile task, but at that time I was ripe for such a task."

"I bet you saved a lot of people anyway."

I could have sworn there was moisture to his eyes when he laughed softly. "We saved...oh, *many*. But he also paid a high price for the lives he saved, and when it came to his life, I couldn't save it. A human like that saved so many lives, but I couldn't even save one human."

This time there was no confusing it: I saw the salt drop as it fell, just before Zero passed his hand over his face to brush away any others. I hung my arm around his neck and tightened it a bit; just enough to be nearly a hug but not enough to suggest that I was trying to comfort him because he was crying. I was pretty sure he wouldn't like that.

"I should have been able to save his life," he said, clearing his throat. He didn't try to pull away from my arm, though. "He was just a human, and I'm—"

"Big, strong fae," I said, nodding. "What happened?"

"We took on a job to save a couple of children; some unseelie canton Behind had taken them to soak up magic and drain them of their lives. We got in without a problem and found the children, but on the way out someone caught onto what was happening and locked down the entire canton. I got out with the children and he...he wasn't quite as quick."

I asked, "You couldn't get him out?" even though I knew it couldn't be that easy.

"I could have," said Zero, his voice weary. "I would have had to leave the children, but I could have done it. The canton had already sent guards after us and they were in clear sight, but they would have left him to recapture the children. He made me save the children instead of him. I would have dropped them and taken him, and he knew it—he could have been saved if he'd been able to trust me to save the other humans instead of him."

"What'd he do?"

"Ran away from the border like a madman to engage them before I could offer to treat with them."

"He just...fought? Didn't try to use Between?"

"No," said Zero. "He couldn't see or deal with Between in the way that you can."

"Flamin' heck," I said softly. "He kept up with you and fought alongside you when he couldn't even manipulate Between? How'd he get Behind in the first place?"

"He found someone who was willing to help him cross over for a price. Your—our human friends told me a little bit about that when I went to—"

He stopped, and I found that I knew exactly what it was he had been about to say.

"You asked 'em for information when you went there to ask Abigail for her help and to sign me over to them like a flamin' package."

I didn't say it harshly, because Zero was still crouched down on the tiles with his forearms propped on his thighs, and although I hadn't seen another tear he looked *tired*. I suppose everything had to come to a head after Athelas' betrayal, not to mention the pressure building on pressure as the world around us prepared for the heirling trials and a new king.

Zero faintly smiled, though he didn't quite look at me. "He would never tell me himself; he said it was no use looking back on things he couldn't return to. He said he was happy Behind, and I think he was."

"Sounds like he died doing what he wanted to be doing," I said. "And like he made his own choices."

"I know," said Zero. "But today—lately—it keeps occurring to me that if he'd been able to trust that I'd respect his wishes, he would still be alive."

"I wanna say yes on principle," I said, "but you don't actually know that. Anything might have happened between him trusting you not to toss the kids to save him and you both working together to get out."

"There would have been a chance, at least," Zero said.

"Is this you trying to break yourself of old habits?" I asked, and found that I was a bit teary myself. "Because they say practise makes perfect, and if you're gunna apologise to me—"

"I wasn't going to apologise," said Zero stiffly. "I am sorry about telling the humans that they could have you in exchange for help. I was trying to do everything I could think of to keep you safe—I knew this was coming and that I wouldn't be around forever."

I couldn't help laughing. "Old habits really do die hard."

"I'm *trying*," he said, and this time he looked at me properly. "I'm trying, so please be patient."

"Okay," I said, slightly shaken. Zero wasn't good at apologies and he certainly wasn't good at asking for help, and he had just done both. That was pretty important. "I'll bear it in mind."

"My sister was a kind person," he said, almost at random. "You would have liked her. She made life easier for everyone—even the people who didn't like her."

"That how she ended up Behind again?"

"I suspect so," he said. "If my father had threatened her family —and since you're in existence, she must have had one—she would have come back without fighting if he offered to kill someone in her stead."

"Yeah," I said gloomily. That made sense of the story mum had told me about great grandma Anne—she just left one day and never returned. "Hang on," I added, my eyes kindling. "This means you're my uncle, right? We're not just related, you're my uncle; I've got living family!"

"It's not—it isn't much to celebrate!" he said, half perplexment and half amusement. "It just means that you're allied by blood to one of the people who killed a matriarch of your family."

"No, it means I'm allowed to love you!" I said jubilantly.

"Allowed to—allowed—" Zero stopped, and then said, "Since when has who you're allowed to love or not stopped you loving them? As for the kamikaze hugs and the—"

"Yeah, but that was before I knew you were my uncle," I explained, edging around the real explanation. There was too much there that I couldn't say aloud. I was allowed to love him because now that I knew he didn't love me as a woman but as a niece, there was a brightness and buoyancy in my heart that I hadn't felt for some time. "Now I know you're my uncle, I'm allowed to do all that. You're half human, you should understand —it's a human thing."

I leant my full weight against him, linking my other arm around his neck for good measure and burying my face in his shoulder.

Zero, marginally less stiff around the shoulders than he would have been if I'd done something similar when we'd first met, sighed. "What are you doing?"

"Heck, you should know what a hug is by now! Haven't you been paying attention?"

"I didn't say you could hug me."

"I'm allowed to give my uncle a hug; that's what nieces do."

"You're not my niece; you're my great-great—"

"Well, then you're the one who should be hugging me, you old fossil! I'm allowed to love you now; you're my only uncle!"

"There's no need to abandon decorum in the house just because you've found out that we're related!"

"There was never any decorum in this house," I told him, clinging stubbornly around his neck. "And it's my house now, anyway; you're just here because you're family, so you should flamin' behave yourself."

I saw his mouth open to repudiate the assertion—watched the resigned expression that flashed across his face in profile a moment later. Zero had forgotten that the agreement he'd signed with me not so long ago no longer held for him any more than it did for Athelas—though for very different reasons.

"Yeah," I said. "You forgot that you're just a guest here now, didn't you? You better not go throwing any more vampires through the walls."

"Vampires," said Zero, as if snatching at straws. "That reminds me! We're going to have a discussion about vampires and dating, and the fact that you're far too young to be—"

"Nope," I said hastily, releasing him. Much to my relief, I could hear a scuffling outside the door that probably meant someone was out there, waiting uncomfortably for the right moment to knock on the door. "We're definitely not gunna talk about that."

"Pet—"

Then came the knock. It was a reluctant, tentative sort of knock, and when Zero said impatiently, "What?" someone cleared their throat.

"Dunno whether you want to know or not," said a lycanthrope voice apologetically, "but that vampire's glaring at everyone through the window again and we'd prefer if Pet came out to make him stop, please."

I escaped from the laundry room before Zero could call me

back. There was a time and a place for discussing dating, but I didn't think the laundry room at midnight before an expedition into Behind was that time. More than that, I didn't want to be in the position of defending my right to date Jin Yeong when I wasn't even sure I wanted to do it.

CHAPTER NINE

I woke up with a smile on my face the next day and the warmth of the knowledge that I had an uncle. Real family. Alive family. Family that was a bit too inclined to protect me against my wishes, but that was always there despite that.

The pleasant warmth of that remembrance lasted until it was apparent that Jin Yeong wasn't' going to appear at the window before we had to leave on our excursion to look for Sarah's parents. I'd already had a quick call from Tuatu that I had been hoping would tell us he and North had found the Palmers safe and sound outside the house, but had been to tell me that there was no sign of them instead. Neither North nor Tuatu had been able to get in the house yet, either.

Sarah didn't get any paler, but she did look sick. I suppose that's what happens when you fight your way out of Behind to get back to your parents, fight off fae who want to use you as a pawn in their efforts to secure the crown and are using your parents as collateral, and then find that neither you nor your parents have escaped them after all.

"Don't worry," I said. "We'll find 'em. We might not have lycanthrope noses this time, but I'm all right at getting through hedges and figuring out what's happening with Between. I can fight all right, too."

"I know," said Sarah, and surprised me by smiling. "There are lots of stories about you, did you know? When I first got here, the other heirlings who were trying to invade the house were already talking about The Pet."

"Heck, that's all I need," I said gloomily. "People out there who know who I am."

"At least they only know your job function," she said, and shivered. "It's worse when they know your name, even if you're a human. They can't exactly make you do things, but they make it really hard *not* to do things if you're tired or aren't paying attention."

"How come your house didn't protect you?" I asked, my attention still caught on the earlier part of her conversation. "They're usually pretty good about that, with heirlings. We thought you might be the harbinger for a while, but you do the same sort of things as me, so—"

"It's a new built house," she said. "Not much Between there—actually, that's something my parents tried really hard to stop getting in. They spent a lot of time trying to keep out anything that wasn't human. We even have a proper human saferoom that's made out of iron instead of steel."

"Heck," I said soberly. She wasn't wrong about the fact that the house was set up as a booby-trapped nightmare for fae. I'd been to Sarah's house briefly one night while I was trying to make sure Upper Management didn't get their hands on her, and I'd seen the lines of iron shavings that would have made life extremely hard for any fae that tried to breach the property, at least. That had been the night that Zero showed up as an enemy and Jin Yeong had fought almost to the death for me to get away.

That remembrance pinched a raw little nerve somewhere near my heart and made me glance over at the window, but there was no sign of Jin Yeong. I made myself look away from the window and asked Sarah, "Is it possible for your parents to have been hidden away by the house anyway?"

"I really don't think so," she said. "You don't understand, Pet—you and your house are outliers. I was talking with Morgana, and her house isn't anything like as lively as yours; it doesn't heal itself on command, either. We don't know anyone who has such a connection to their house."

"I know another person," I said. That brought with it the reminder that Athelas was the one who had knit that connection between myself and the house—and between Ralph and his house. "It's not a very happy story. We're closely connected to our houses because of what happened to our parents when we were kids."

"The houses aren't special," Zero said briefly, stopping in the living room with us for a moment. I couldn't help beaming at him, and the reluctant smile that answered warmed me. "The location and amount of access to Between is the important thing; some people draw more to them than others, and some areas draw more to them than others. Are you ready?"

"Ready," I said. I'd already pulled a couple of weapons out of Between, and Zero was prepared too, with his big double-handed sword strapped across his back. He had a sheath for his sword, but I didn't bother with mine—I had the feeling we'd need them nearly as soon as we stepped out of the house, especially if Zero's dad had gotten closer to finding out where we were by now.

"Ready," said Sarah. She didn't have a weapon, but I'd seen her manipulate Between, so I knew she was already prepared for that.

"You remember the way back to the house?" I asked her.

"It'll look different, anyway," Sarah said, with a hopeless little shrug. "We'll have to find our way back again."

"It won't be as difficult this time," Zero said, and I could have sworn he was being comforting despite his gruffness.

"Why will it be different and why won't it be as hard?" I asked, looking from one to the other.

"There are roughly two hundred houses out here," said Zero. He left us in the hall to look briefly through the laundry room louvres, then shouldered his way back into the hall and opened the back door. "There were yesterday, at any rate. As heirlings die, their points of entry seem to die off as well: there'll be far less this morning, and far less paths to take in the labyrinth. It's all about cutting off options until only two remain, facing each other. When there's only one option, one point of entry, the arena will open."

"So the king can swoop," I muttered. I let Sarah go ahead of me and followed along in the rear, stepping out into the scent of lemon myrtle and soft darkness once again. "And speaking of swooping, your dad was pretty close to the house already yesterday; if there are less paths to take and less options to choose from, he's gunna find us pretty flamin' quickly."

"I very much doubt my father will be able to get through the house's defences," Zero said dryly.

"Yeah, but are we gunna be able to get through him and *back* to the house?" I asked. "That's what I'm worried about."

"We'll face that when we get to it," said Zero. He didn't seem too worried, which would have been nice if he ever showed much emotion in general.

Sarah and Zero were both right about the labyrinth: as soon as we stepped from our backyard and into the hedges, I could feel and see the difference. Instead of the T-section that had formed from the opening of the labyrinth into the backyard, there was a single road leading to the right, running along the back of the yard and much further.

"Reckon Morgana's place vanished, too?" I asked. "We went that way to get there the other day."

"I don't know," he said, with a taciturnity that reminded me that if Morgana's house had disappeared, it was also likely that Sarah's house could disappear at any time, parents or no parents.

"I mean, ours didn't when we went off to get Morgana," I

mumbled, and Sarah looked a bit more comfortable when next I glanced at her.

The hedges seemed darker today, or maybe I had just got used to being on the inside of the hedges while chasing after the bunyip. Ridiculously, inside the hedges had been a little lighter than the outside was. Whatever the reason, it left me feeling oppressed and vaguely on edge, and I was actually starting to hate the smell of lemon myrtle, which lingered and followed us no matter where we went. Even a good hour's trek into the hedges I could still smell it, a visceral reminder that there was now nowhere safe in the labyrinth.

We had a brief skirmish with some very determined goblins who seemed to be fighting on behalf of an heirling who promptly ran away when he saw his goblins weren't a match for Zero alone, let alone Zero and a human fighter. I would have stopped fighting the goblins if I could, sick to the stomach, but they kept fighting for their leader regardless and I didn't have time to try and figure out how to capture them alive instead of killing them before they were all dead.

"You can't capture goblins," Zero said shortly, when that regret tumbled out into words.

"We could have tried," I said, wiping off my blades and trying not to look at all the bodies. "They're smaller than us."

"Goblins can't be captured," said Sarah, sheathing a little knife I'd had no idea she was carrying. "I mean, you can capture them, but they don't stay captured. I've seen them bite through their own wrists to kill themselves rather than remain in captivity. They're feral."

Zero gave her an approving nod and led the way forward once more, leaving me to bring up the rear again. I did so with slightly more cheer; it wasn't that the knowledge made me feel better about killing the goblins, it was more that knowing there had been no good choices made the fact that I'd had to choose *something* seem more generally, instead of specifically, horrible.

"Watch out for twin fae," I said to Zero softly as we turned into a new section of the labyrinth. Here it was slightly lighter in terms of visibility, but the hedge itself was darker; more, it was familiar. "They were setting up in one of these lanes for someone."

"They found someone," he said, turning back to look at me and then attending to the front again. His voice sounded pretty grim.

"Waiting for you, were they?" I asked, unsurprised. "Reckon they weren't too happy to find you, though."

"They were happy for a short while," he said. "They're distant cousins of mine; they've been training all their lives for this in some remote part of Between that borders the human world. From what they'd heard of my reputation, I gather they expected me to be more of an easy target."

I couldn't help grinning, and I saw the edge of Sarah's cheek crease with a brief smile, too.

"They thought you're a sissy because you wouldn't follow your father's footsteps," I guessed. "And they heard about you going around with the human and figured that clinched it."

"I suppose so," he said, turning into the next section of the L-bend we had been walking down.

I lost sight of Zero for a brief moment and trotted a bit to catch up with my eyes still on Sarah, unease kicking into gear in my stomach. I nearly walked into his broad back a bare step around the corner and stopped short just in time, relief singing through my veins.

For a second—just one second—I'd thought that I was about to lose him, too, and I didn't think I would be able to bear that. Stupid to think that I'd lose him in a second, between one hedge and another in the labyrinth, but that was what this place did: hid dangers and death around every turn, slaughter under every shadow.

"Walk a bit slower, can't you?" I said plaintively. I'd just gained an uncle last night; I didn't want to lose him today.

Then I caught sight of the reason we'd stopped.

It was a house. No, not a house—more of a mansion: white marble, art nouveau, and very, very big. It looked as though someone had picked it up and put it down very precisely in the middle of that wide lane to stop whoever might come along in their tracks. It extended fully across the path, a doorway arched invitingly right in the middle of the lane, and merged almost seamlessly with the hedge on either side, blurring slightly where the branches should have scratched against the marble walls. I had a feeling that it would be no use trying to push through between wall and hedge there. Goodness knew how big it really was. It was big enough to rise higher than the hedges, though, and that was pretty flamin' high.

"Heck," I said. "Who put that there?"

"It was always there," said Zero. "I told you: the pathways move as the arena grows smaller."

"Reckon we should go back and try to get around?"

"I don't think there is another way back," Sarah said, worrying me. Just like I'd been able to sense the way back home each time I'd been out in the arena, it was likely that she could sense the way to her own home.

I didn't like the idea of walking through someone else's home to get through the pathway, and said so.

"Neither do I," said Zero. "But it's our only way forward. Did you see a single turning on the way here?"

"Not since a bit after we left our house," I said, my heart sinking. "Call this a labyrinth, do they? Not much of a labyrinth if it only goes one way."

Zero didn't wait for me to finish complaining; he just walked up to the door and shoved at it. It opened straight away with barely a few shudders of damp or rust as it did so.

"That's heckin' suspicious," I called. "You sure you don't want me to try and do something to the hedges to get around this thing?"

Zero ignored that, too. Flamin' rude.

I huffed a sigh and trotted to catch up once again. Sarah waited for me at the archway but disappeared inside as soon as she knew I was coming. I supposed I couldn't blame her: I would have been doing whatever I needed to do if it were my parents, too.

"Reckon the house is still growing," I said as I caught up with them. "It's sorta eating up the hedges where it's growing. What do you reckon this bloke is doing to make it do that?"

"Killing or allying with a lot of heirlings," Zero said shortly. "Keep quiet and pay attention, Pet. Any heirlings who are still alive today will know how to use Between as well as their martial skills; they'll be more dangerous."

"Yes, boss," I said, looking around the room for any sign of trouble. There was no way I was going to trust a house that had its front door unlocked—not somewhere Behind, anyway. I gazed across the roundness of the hall and the massive staircase that flowed up and around both sides of the room in a glorious art nouveau sweep.

Then I looked up, and my heart jumped so physically that I very nearly gasped. JinYeong stood there at the head of the stairs, his dark eyes on me. I know he saw me; our eyes met and both of us stood perfectly still for that brief second.

Time seemed to start again, and I heard JinYeong say in Korean, as if despairing, "Ah, not again!" Then he turned and vanished back the way he'd come, the white marble hall above swallowing him as if he'd never existed.

"JinYeong!" I yelped, and dashed up the stairs after him. "Zero, it's JinYeong!"

"Pet, wait!" shouted Zero, but I was already in the hall above.

I heard them sprinting up the stairs behind me and length-ened my stride, glad to have safety at my back. That sense of safety lasted just long enough for me to dash after Jin Yeong's blue-suited figure into a darkened room that echoed its massiveness around me and for Zero and Sarah to catch up with me.

Then the doors shut behind us with finality as the room began to light up, revealing a thin double-line of mixed behindkind across the other side of the huge chamber, some with weapons and others without. They didn't look too impressive—if anything, they all looked scared—but I didn't like the fact that they were there, waiting.

"Welcome to my manor," said a carrying, tenor voice from behind that line of behindkind. A soft glow lit the space behind them for a few feet, leaving a gulf of darkness between them and the figure that now appeared in robes of white and gold, his arms outstretched in beneficent welcome. "I'm so glad you've come to play today!"

"Flamin' heck, it's another heirling," I said, disgruntled. "Was that really Jin Yeong I chased up here?"

"Who's to say?" said the man—or at least, he looked like a man. "Not everything about my house is real, but some things are. You can—" he added, snapping his fingers "—only guess, after all!"

For an instant, I saw Jin Yeong again, looking around wildly as if to work out his surroundings, then the man snapped his fingers again, and the brief vision was gone.

"You're a mimic," Zero said flatly.

The mimic clapped his hands. "Oh, well done you! You were much quicker than the last one I had here!"

"Let me guess," I said. "A mimic can make a version of something it wants you to see?"

Zero nodded. "A construct. It's not real, but it looks and sounds real." To the mimic, he said roughly, "Stop playing games before I come up there and make you stop."

"If you're not going to play the game, you're not allowed on the platform," the mimic said chidingly. "Only players get to enter the field of play. You'll see I have some protection, after all."

He gestured at the double line of mingled behindkind and lifted one shoulder far too smugly.

"What's this?" asked Zero. "Your army? They don't look up to much. It'll take me a moment to get through them to you, so you'd best stop throwing illusions around."

"No," the mimic said coolly. "These ones are cannon fodder."

I felt an icy touch of anger. "What?"

"They're heirlings we came across on our way. Instead of killing them, I had them swear fealty, and of course they all jumped at the offer. Everyone wants to live just a little longer, regardless of the circumstances. They all think that if they can get just a little bit more time, they'll be able to escape later."

"And you send 'em in to fight and die instead of you."

"Only with people like you," he said. "You can kill them, if you want. You'll have to kill them if you want to get to me, in fact. But I think you're the sort who don't like killing innocents."

"I'll kill anyone who tries to kill me or my friends," said Zero. "It would be stupid of you to assume otherwise."

The behindkind looked surprised, then shrugged. "I'd heard otherwise about you, Lord Sero. I was told you'd gone soft. You can—"

"Better than being soft in the head," I told him, rolling my eyes. "Look, are you going to keep talking forever, or can someone else get a word in edgewise?"

"I *beg* your pardon?" he said stiffly.

"You sounded just like his dad," I said, jerking a thumb at Zero. "That's not a compliment, by the way. Okay, so you made a bargain with this lot that you'd spare their lives if they swore fealty to you, right?"

"I have already explained to you the terms of the agreement!" said the mimic, aggrieved. "If they swear fealty to me, they live! If they don't, they die!"

"Okay, so what happens if you die?"

"Then they're free, I suppose," he said. "I don't bother myself with unlikely possibilities. You came here in pursuit of your friend —would you like to speak with him?"

The showy little git clapped his hands and the expanse of darkness just beyond the double line of heirlings between us and him lit up like a stage. On that stage, blinking in the sudden influx of light, was Jin Yeong—but it wasn't *just* Jin Yeong. To be exact, it was four Jin Yeongs. Each of them looked at me unwaveringly once they had grown used to the brightness of the light; each of them was the very image of Jin Yeong.

"Oh, didn't I tell you?" the mimic said sweetly. "I can only work from real life. I can't create a construct unless I've seen the original. Your vampire friend used a door he shouldn't have been able to access and sneaked into the arena last night. He's been wandering the manor since then, trying to find his way out. It gave me a lot of time to study him; I've been practising ever since I heard I might get a chance to meet you both."

I had to fight hard not to exhale all the fear and worry I'd had since Jin Yeong hadn't appeared outside the windows this morning.

"I was told a little story about him and you," added the mimic. Grand and expansive, he said, "I'll give you the chance to save your friend. If you win and choose the right vampire, you and your friends may walk out of here with my good wishes. If you do not, you must swear fealty to me."

"Your guardians aren't very strong," Zero said, looking over the children between him and us. "They're children—I would kill them in a few moments."

"Yes," he said. "But it'll take you those few moments to get through them—and by then I'll be long gone. Good luck finding me before I find you—just when you think you're safe, the closest of your allies will stab you in the back, and you'll discover that it was me all along."

"Fine," said Sarah. "We'll just leave, then. You can't stop us getting out."

"You'll never find your way out of my demesne—I am the key by which the doors of this establishment are opened," he said triumphantly. "At each turning there is another turning, and at each—"

"Yeah, yeah, there's another turning, we get it."

"And *then*," he added, swelling with outrage, "just when you think you're safe—"

"Here we go again," I muttered.

"—my allies will return and you will be taken prisoner regardless!"

"*Hyeong*," said one of the Jin Yeongs, his voice uncertain. "You wouldn't leave me here?"

Zero spared him only the briefest look before he asked the mimic, "Who is your ally, then?"

"You should know," the mimic said mockingly. "He carries the same name as you."

"We can't wait for my father," Zero said, his hand rising to the grip of his sword. "Nor can we leave Jin Yeong here."

I stared at him. "You want to just kill these kids?"

"They won't let us pass them, and if we let him go—"

Sarah said, "It's true," her voice hard and sharp. "And they'll try to kill us next time if we leave them alive, too."

"I'm not killing kids," I said.

"You'll have to if you want to get to your friend," the mimic said happily. "It won't do you any good, either: you'll never find me again once I'm out of sight, anyway. I could be anyone you know."

"No, you couldn't," I said, without bothering to hide the contempt in my voice. "You don't have the depth to be anything but a deflated balloon puffed up with someone else's air."

I let my eyes flick contemptuously across the four Jin Yeongs who stood just out of reach and added, "Your constructs aren't even that good. I already know which ones aren't Jin Yeong."

"Then accept my challenge," he said.

"Fine," I said. "I accept. If I lose, I swear fealty to you. If I win, I leave here with *all* of my friends and you release your minions from their oaths."

"Done!" he said at once. "Come through!"

"*Pet*," Zero said, through his teeth.

"I told you," I said to him, almost dizzy with fury. "I am *not* gunna kill kids! If they come back and fight me later, I'll get them then! I'm not going to cut through 'em as if they're grass just so I can get to that slimy little git. For once in your life, trust me to make the right decision so that we can save *everyone*."

"They'll just kill you afterwards," he said, pleadingly.

"Maybe," I said. "But I'll deal with that then."

As I approached, the heirlings parted to let me through as with a single mind, and I saw the blankness of fear in their eyes. None of these kids knew how to fight—none of them even knew how to hold the weapons in their hands. I was pretty sure some of them still thought they were trapped in some kind of nightmare.

"One of them is your friend," called the mimic. "Choose well, and I'll let you leave with him. Choose badly, and all of these little heirlings will have to sacrifice themselves to secure my escape. You said my constructs were pitiful—let's see if you can tell them apart from the reality."

"Yeah, all right, all right," I said. "I've got the idea. How long have I got?"

"Five minutes," he said. "They'll each have a chance to address you up to three times, but I won't allow anything else. I'll gag the real vampire if I have to."

I heard Zero shift behind me as I climbed the stairs toward the four Jin Yeongs, and didn't have to look at him to know that he had drawn his sword. I ignored it, because there was nothing I could do to stop him if he refused to trust me this time. All I could do was hope that he would wait and trust me.

The silence stretched out behind me as I climbed the stairs and right up until I stepped onto the uppermost step, shredding my nerves with the idea that it couldn't continue. But it did continue, and I began to really trust for the first time that Zero was going to allow me to do as I'd decided.

Now that I was up here, I wasn't feeling quite so assured of that decision, but there was nothing else for it but to keep going. I'd already gone too far to stop now. It wasn't just that each of the four on the stage looked exactly like JinYeong; each of them had an actual presence in the room—took up space, bent the air around them, created warmth.

"All right," I said to those far-too-real JinYeongs, and drew in a breath that was nearly audibly shaky. "Convince me."

As if he had been waiting for the command, the second cocked his head with exactly JinYeong's command, and said, "*Petteu*, come to me!"

Number One just said softly, "*Naya.*"

I let my eyes run over each one of them in turn as they called out to me. Number Two had called me Pet; Number Four hadn't used *banmal* with me. Number Three—well, Number Three was wearing an orange tie. I might have believed it to be JinYeong if it had been a jewel-orange, but it was neon orange.

I passed down the line of JinYeongs, ignoring the cold gaze of the mimic on the platform behind, until I came to Number One. Then I stopped; just near enough to embrace him, but far enough to leave a small space between us.

"*Aljana?*" he said, one hand slipping around the back of my neck while his thumb caressed my ear. "*Nal aljyo?*"

"I know you," I said, smiling up at him. Then I pulled all the pretty pieces of Between from the walls around us and forged them into a long, wicked-sharp silver knife within my fingers; and with that knife I stabbed upward and right into his heart.

"If you want to make me think you're JinYeong, you're gunna have to try a bit flamin' harder," I said, my fingers white around the braided grip and dripping with blue blood that stained the honey-coloured topaz protruding below the bottom curve of my fist as well.

I let his body fall to the ground, my blade slipping free, and the body changed before it hit the marble platform, the other Jin Yeongs vanishing around it. Even the mimic who had seemed to be standing on the platform above us melted away until there was nothing but the single body—too tall and broad to be Jin Yeong, his blood too blue.

"You said the other heirlings would know how to use Between," I said, turning back to Zero, who was staring at me and the body with the glazed sort of horror I'd only seen once before in his eyes. "You didn't think any of them were Jin Yeong, right?"

"No," he said, his voice barely a whisper and his eyes still stricken. He dropped to his haunches, raking his hands over his short white hair, and exhaled into the floor beneath him.

"Liar," I said. I dropped the bloody knife and ran lightly back down the stairs and through the line of heirlings. They didn't try to stop me—in fact, they seemed to draw back from me—and by the time I got back to Sarah and Zero, a faint shuffling had begun in the ranks. One weapon hit the ground and was hastily retrieved, but its owner took it and bolted for the door.

I kept a wary eye on the others as I stood by Zero's kneeling form, but it didn't take long after the first one broke rank for the others to start leaving in ones and twos, each gripping their weapon and avoiding looking in our general direction. I didn't blame them; blood had begun to trickle down the stairs toward them, and for all I knew, it was the first death they'd seen.

"Liar," I said to Zero again, leaning against his shoulder and draping my arm around his neck as I watched them go. "It's all right to take a moment when you think someone you love has died. It's all right to need a moment when someone you love betrays you, too."

"There aren't any moments left," he said. "There's too much happening."

"You don't have time to not take a moment, then," I said. "You either take a moment now, or collapse later. Your choice. We haven't got anywhere we need to be right now. Just hunker down there and breathe for a while, all right?"

He didn't say yes, but he didn't say no, either—nor did he get up. He just crouched there, leaning on his knees and staring at the marble while I leaned against him to give him time to recover and tried to feel what I could feel of Between around me in the room.

Most of what I felt was nothingness: a vast, empty space pretending to be something it wasn't, and devoid of any life that wasn't in the room we were in. No JinYeong, then, I thought mechanically, trying to avoid the thought that suggested there could be a lifeless JinYeong somewhere out in that nothingness.

"I can't feel anything," said Sarah. She glanced at Zero and asked, "Is he going to be all right?"

"Yeah, just give him a minute," I advised. "I can't sense anything, either. It feels like we're in one of those rooms for 3D computer games; we could walk anywhere and feel like we're getting somewhere, but we've been walking on the spot the whole time."

Sarah made a face. "Thanks. That's a really comforting thought."

"Sorry," I said. "Don't worry about it; we'll get out all right."

I took a bit of a walk around the room to see what I could see, stopping briefly at a corner that had a funny little clock hanging on the wall in a soft swirl of wall that seamlessly folded in on itself and almost on the clock.

"Got one of you at home," I told the clock, then left it where it was and moved on.

I took my time around the room, enjoying the artistry of it all while it was still there, and seeing the silverish filigree of each of the constructs still slowly wafting apart with each moment after its caster's death. I probably took a good half hour to wander around the room while Zero silently dealt with his emotions, and when it looked like he might be about to stand up, I headed back toward him.

I bumped his leg with my knee as he stood and said, "You know I wouldn't actually kill Jin Yeong, right?"

"Of course," he said, and this time his voice was certain.

"I would have told you if I could do it without giving the game away," I said. "But I knew I'd only have a second to get the beggar before he changed into something else once he knew I knew he was one of the Jin Yeongs. Figured it was better to get him as quickly and painlessly as possible, or he'd find a way to use those poor kids against us again."

His huge hand reached out and enclosed mine, cool and clammy. "Thank you," he said.

"That's what I wanted to say," I told him.

"No," he said, and this time he took both of my hands and looked at me properly. "Thank you for allowing us to save everyone."

"Well, what else are nieces for?" I said, grinning at him. "C'mon, we'd better try to get out of here."

"What of Jin Yeong?" he asked, rising. "The mimic might have spoken the truth when it said it works from the original."

"If he's here in the house, we'll never be able to find him," I said. "And I don't think he is here: the mimic wouldn't have run the risk of impersonating him if he was still here for us to find. Reckon he left a while ago; he was probably looking for us."

"Don't expect him to turn up at the house," Zero said, and he very carefully didn't point out that it was most likely that Jin Yeong was already dead.

"Nah, he's probably up to something else," I said, because I didn't want to say *dead* either. I refused to believe it: Jin Yeong had had a plan last time I saw him at the window, and he wouldn't have failed so easily at it.

I threw a last look around the cavernous room and noticed

the gleam of silver that was still somehow present in the centre of the platform up above.

"Oi," I said. "The knife hasn't gone anywhere."

"It must prefer being a knife to being separated pieces of Between," Zero said.

"Looks like it. Reckon I should bring it along? Seems a pity to leave it here."

More than that, it seemed a pity to let it stay here to be picked up and used by someone else. It wasn't that I particularly wanted my own weapon that didn't have to be drawn out of Between; it was more that I didn't like creating something that obviously enjoyed existing, then leaving it for someone else to use.

Maybe I was the jealous sort.

I was already trotting up the stairs to get it when Zero said, "Bring it. See if it will come with you. Better yet, see if it's still around tomorrow after you take it back to the house."

"I'm more worried about if *we'll* be around tomorrow," I said over my shoulder; but I said it cheerfully, and I *felt* cheerful. You know, for someone who had just killed another person and had had her hopes shattered again. "You reckon Jin Yeong is actually in the arena, though, right?"

"I think Jin Yeong is very determined," said Zero. "And I think we didn't see him at the windows this morning."

"You reckon he's dead or in here," I translated, picking up the knife and darting back down the stairs and toward the door. "Okay, that's good. He's in here, then."

"I didn't say that," Zero said, starting after me. "Pet! I didn't say that!"

"Not to worry," I told him, grinning over my shoulder. "I did."

I kept a grim hold of that thought, too, because if Jin Yeong wasn't in here, then he was out in the human world and hadn't come to the window that morning for an unknown reason. But if he was in here, how had he got in, and why hadn't we seen him? Worse, where was he now?

THERE WEREN'T EXACTLY turns after turns like the mimic had told us, but the doorways and staircases definitely didn't lead back to where they should have, and we'd been walking around in irritatingly clean marble halls for quite some time before we had to stop and take stock.

"Well, we're on the bottom level again, anyway," I pointed out. "That's good, isn't it?"

"Only if we can find a doorway out," said Zero, his voice lingering in the hall as he stepped into the next room. Sarah and I followed him, still not too keen about being out of sight of each other for long.

"He said he was the key," I remarked. "Maybe we should have dragged his body around with us."

It was a bit late for that now; I doubted we'd be able to find the same level again, let alone the same room we'd left his body in.

"Wait," said Zero, stiffening. He looked around the room we were in, and I saw the utter irritation that swept over his face for one second before he strode over to the nearest wall.

"That's a wall," I told him. "Dunno if you've got some snow blindness going on or what, but that's definitely a wall."

Zero sniffed a short laugh, and then he just...walked through the wall.

"Heck," I said into the silence that he left behind him. "The flamin' *house* was mimicked as well."

"I would never have thought of that," Sarah said, her eyes wide.

"'Course you would," I said. "But that's the good thing about going around Behind with friends; there's always someone else to think of it first so you don't have to waste time."

"There aren't any friends, Behind," she said sadly.

"That's just what they want you to think," I told her. "It's a lie they tell you so it's easier to manipulate you."

"I'm sorry," she said.

I didn't have to ask what she was sorry about: I still remembered her young-yet-old voice agreeing with Zero that it was best to kill the heirlings.

"Heck," I said. "If I'd been stuck Behind for a year and had to claw my way out, I probably would have thought the same. I was lucky enough to go Behind with friends whenever I had to go. That's why I said that you should always go Behind with a few friends, if you can. Then there's always someone to be strong when the other person isn't. It's easier to be strong enough to do the right thing when there's someone there to support you."

"You didn't have much support back in there," she said.

"I dunno," I said, thinking back to the silence as I had climbed stairs toward four JinYeongs. "There was enough. C'mon; we better go through before he thinks he has to come back after us. He'd never let us live it down."

CHAPTER TEN

There was a dead kind of silence to Sarah's house. It wasn't until we'd been in it for a few minutes that I understood why that was. I'd been so used to seeing Between about anywhere I went that the complete absence of it felt almost like death.

Once I came to that realisation, another came with it. The soft luminescence that muddled the floor beneath me in what seemed to be set paths wasn't just a dirty floor: it was the traces of the humans who had lived in the house, painted in what must have been human magic leaking through the very soles of their feet to sink into the carpet and tiles.

More, I could tell that the tracks were recent: maybe only a day or two old. I knew that because the fresh tracks Sarah was leaving as she stepped through the door were brighter by far, new and strong, while the ones by the door she must have left by yesterday were glowing softer.

"Did you blokes search the house while you were here?" I asked, following the strongest adult tracks across the room and toward the next room. I thought they might go upstairs, but they didn't. They led across the lower floor instead, and toward the back of a room that should have been deeper than it was.

"Of course," Zero said. "We looked in every room."

"They were here," I said, frowning, still following those tracks. I probably wouldn't have been able to follow them if it were my house or Ralph's house, but the complete lack of Between and fae magic around the place made it easier to see the faint traces of human magic. "Looks like your parents have a bit of the touch for magic, too."

"They used to joke about it," said Sarah, her face momentarily softer. "Mum's knack for turning channels at just the right time— Dad with his plants. The jokes stopped pretty quickly after I started being able to...do stuff."

"Makes it easier for me to see where they were around the house," I explained. Of Zero, I asked, "Can't you see it?"

He shook his head, frowning. "Behind doesn't acknowledge the existence of human magic: we have no way of being able to verify or recognise it. I can see a pattern on the floor, no more."

"I can only see the really strong bits," said Sarah. "I'm better with Between than magic. What are you seeing?"

"Tracks," I said. "I can see where your parents walked last. Here."

They followed me across the room, and we stopped at the wall beside a nice bit of furniture that was just a bit too big to be a hallstand with a softly weeping fern on each side of it that brushed against the wall.

"What's here?" I asked. "It's not just a wall, is it?"

"It's the saferoom," Sarah said, her voice hushed. "They went in there?"

"Reckon so."

"I don't understand," she said. "They wouldn't have gone in there without me. They didn't even call out to me, and they *would* have if they thought we were in danger!"

"They could have been lured in," Zero said.

"Someone lured them into the saferoom while I was still in the house?" Sarah said, her voice catching. "That doesn't make sense. They would never have trusted someone in the house who wasn't...wasn't...me."

"You reckon someone's been playing silly beggars with your face again?"

"I suppose so," she said bitterly. "I'm the only one they would have trusted."

"It wouldn't be the first time that parents were beguiled by someone with the appearance of their child," Zero said, surprising me with the kindness of his intent in saying it. "Can you open it?"

By way of answering, Sarah took down first one and then the other of the ferns, and the section of wall between the corner and the hallstand sank back an inch and slid silently sideways.

"Flamin' heck!" I said, impressed. I'd never seen a saferoom before. I tried to tap the touchpad on the door, but my hand seemed to skitter sideways without quite being able to touch it. When I tried to put a hand on the door itself, the same thing happened.

"It's iron," Zero said. "As soon as the door closed, it would have been separated from the arena. If it were outside the house I suppose it would be back in the human world by now: there's no more hope of getting into that room than there is of us getting out of the arena before all the terms are met."

Sarah gave a very small sniff that I realised was her version of a sob; quiet, private and self-contained, and I put my arm around her shoulders without really thinking about it. She went stiff for a brief moment and then her head turned into my shoulder.

And then, over that head of golden hair, on the wall beside that iron door that I couldn't touch here in the arena, I saw two palm prints glowing like a beacon on the wall where the fern had covered just a minute before.

I grinned, fierce and sharp. The Palmers must have stood there for a long time with their hands pressed against the wall to leave enough of a mark; they knew that much about magic, at least.

"They weren't fooled," I said to Sarah. "They left you a note: look."

Sarah stared at the softly luminescent message for a few moments before her face crumpled again, whether in relief or disappointment, I wasn't sure.

"Reckon they knew it wasn't you," I said. "Reckon they were trying to get it away from you so you'd be safe: they would have thought that North would be there to keep you safe. That's why they went into the saferoom with whatever it was that was wearing your face this time."

"If they did so, they should return to the human world when the arena realises that this house's heirling has abandoned it for another house," Zero said. He sounded relieved. "There's nothing more we can do here. At the very least, they'll return to the human world when the house does."

"What about whatever went in there with them?" I asked.

"If it's fae, it's dead," he said. "If another sort of behindkind, it will be at least severely weakened. None of our world care for the complete suffocation of iron."

"Looks like North will be able to take care of them after all," I said. "Have they got food in there, Sarah?"

"Canned and vacuum-sealed, and bottles of water," she said.

"I mean, it's not like it's a successful rescue attempt," I said. "But only because they rescued themselves. I like this kind of rescue attempt."

"I wish I could tell them someone's coming for them," Sarah said, her brow furrowing. It was sometimes hard to remember that she was only twelve, but today wasn't one of those times. "They must be so scared!"

"Reckon they'll be happy enough to know that you're safe," I said.

And Zero, perhaps emptied of all of the comforting things he was able to say in one day, said only, "If there's nothing to be done here, we should leave."

. . .

I would have preferred not to go back into the mimic's house again, but it was still our only way home through the labyrinth. At least this time we knew how to get through it.

It was still chilling to walk back into the curving whiteness despite that, and the fact that the entrance hall was still as big as it had been when we first entered it worried me.

"The house should have shrunk, shouldn't it?" I asked. "Since we killed the mimic, I mean?"

"There was originally a lot of Between to it," Zero said. "There still is: it may take some time."

"Okay, that's understandable," I said. "But then why is my kitchen island right there?"

Zero stared in the direction of my pointing finger, and Sarah said in an awed voice, "It really is your kitchen island!"

"Yeah," I said. "And I want to know why. My clock was in here before, too, but I thought they just had a similar one, so I didn't pay too much attention."

"The stairs are yours, too," Sarah pointed out. "They're not in the right place, but—"

"They are if you untwist the curl of the room," said Zero. "Pet, are you doing this?"

"Beggared if I know," I said simply. Something like that had happened once before when I'd gone to another semi-sentient house; my house had followed me there and very nearly taken over the place. I hadn't been sure whether it had been protecting me or just trying to follow me; I still wasn't sure.

"You're a good house," I said to the countertop, patting it fondly. "You fix yourself up when I ask you to, and whenever I run into trouble in another house, you try and come to get me out."

"Pet," said Zero, his voice almost flat with shock. "Keep talking."

"Saw that, did you?" I asked, unable to stop the grin from

spreading over my face, much like the floor beneath us was spreading with kitchen tiles that definitely didn't match the marble of the mimic's floors. "You're a very good house that knows where to find me when I get stuck in another house, so we might as well see how far we can go and take over this joint!"

There was a surge of kitchen tile that ran across the floor and flowed down into a couple of steps and carpet; chairs grew from the floor and walls sprouted upward around us, melding with the sweep of the room. The staircase unwound itself, grew a bannister, and became darker and straighter. I could feel the hum of it now: the strength and elasticity of my house glomming onto this one and gumming up the idea of space and volume in the trial arena to swallow space as well as the house.

I reached out to that hum—reached out to it with the whole of myself and pulled.

I'm not sure what moved: us, or the house. Maybe neither did move. *Something* definitely moved, though, and I was inclined to think it was the trial arena itself. It wasn't too easy to think right then, though; whatever I'd done to help the house, it had left me in a fog of tiredness as strong as it was sudden.

Morgana's voice said, "Pet! You're back!" and there were suddenly other people in the room again.

"Yeah," I said vaguely, and sat down wearily with my back against the dining room wall while Zero and Sarah stared around the room with as much astonishment as the lycanthropes were looking at us. "Found a shortcut. Reckon life's gunna get a bit easier from here on in."

"I think the arena just got smaller," said Sarah, her voice barely a whisper.

I leaned my head against the wall, too light-headed to hold it up myself. "Yeah? Well, that'll be a bonus if it has. Someone wanna go and check? 'Cos I don't think I can get up right now."

Someone did go and check—someone even went and got me a

coffee—but by that time I wasn't awake enough to understand anything but coffee, so I drank it and went to sleep.

I was awakened from that sleep abruptly once more when someone asked crankily, "Where's that flamin' vampire?"

"He hasn't been here for the last two mornings," said Morgana's voice. "Is that really the first thing you want to know after you've appeared out of thin air, made the trial arena halve in size, and skulled two cups of coffee before passing out?"

"Any coffee?" I asked, and this time I recognised my own voice.

"Give her coffee," said Zero's voice. "She deserves it."

"Too flamin' right," I muttered, struggling to open my gummy eyes.

"I know she does," Morgana's voice said coldly and with dignity. "I already made some. If you're not concerned by the fact that she's asking for the vampire first when she wakes up, I—"

"I tell you that Zero's my uncle?" I asked her, finally blinking enough to be able to see more than a gritty slit of the room—just in time to grin maliciously at Morgana's open-mouthed expression. "No? It was news to me, too. Found out just t'other day."

"We'll have a discussion about the vampire when life becomes more assured," said Zero, his voice glacial.

Morgana gazed from Zero to me and back again, then did it once more, her mouth still open. "Wait, you're her uncle and you're not okay with her dating the vampire? Why? That's confusing to people!"

"Vampires are a high-risk love interest," Zero said. "And there are no guarantees about life expectancy in other ways."

"I'm not discussing love interests or life expectancy," I said. "I'm gunna discuss coffee and some breakfast, and that's it. You said Jin Yeong didn't come back this morning—what about last night?"

"Not a sign of him, sorry," she said. "But there was a skeleton sitting on our back patio last night instead—Zero let him in."

So *that* was the faint edge of blue I could sense about the room.

"That you, Ralph?" I asked.

"Your house *squashed* me," said a thin, cross little voice that I knew well. "It squashed my house, too, and now I have nowhere to go."

"Want some coffee?" I asked him, sitting up a bit groggily. Sure enough, there was the faintly blue figure of a small boy in knee britches and suspenders, his slightly-too-long and curling hair primly concealed beneath a cap.

"I'm not allowed to drink coffee," he said querulously. "Mother says—"

"Don't start that again," Sarah interrupted. "You can have milk if you don't want coffee, but not too much; we've only got enough to last us the next couple days, with the way everyone drinks tea and coffee in this house."

"Looks like you're settling in well," I said, grinning, as someone pushed a hot cup of coffee into my hands. Now that I was a bit more awake, I could see a few more people around the room. I couldn't help glancing briefly over at the window, too, even though I already knew it would be empty. "Just as mungery as ever. What are you doing over here?"

"I told you," he said coldly. "Your house *squashed* me and my house."

"Right. Well, that's good news, anyway," I told him, taking another sip of coffee. My brain was starting to buzz comfortably now, but I had the feeling it had been doing that while I was asleep, too.

"You're probably going to need more coffee," Morgana said. "You're not making any sense."

I bit back an argumentative rejoinder that she was the one who needed more coffee if she didn't understand, and said, "Never mind. You sure the arena halved?"

"That's what Zero said, and it feels smaller to me, too. Why?"

"Just got an idea about how we're going to get outta here, that's all."

Her face lit up. "What is it?"

"Can't tell you—I'd have to kill you."

"I'm already dead."

"See?"

"Pet—"

"All right, all right," I said, grinning, before Ralph could speak the very emphatic words that were on his lips (probably a querulous "*I* am already dead too!"). "But—"

"Oi, Pet!" yelled someone from upstairs, before I could finish. "The vampire's back! And he's in the backyard this time!"

My eyes met Zero's with a shock of relief; he looked pretty stunned for a bloke who rarely shows emotion. We rose at the same time, me slopping coffee over my jeans and Zero sending the couch shifting backward by a good foot and nearly tumbling Morgana off it.

We headed for the back door at the same time, too, the others behind us.

"Check out the window," Zero said to me. "Make sure there's no one else behind him."

I jogged into the laundry and jumped up on the bench there to get a good look out the window, cracking the louvres a bit. Lemon myrtle wafted through the panes of glass, and I saw Jin Yeong.

His eyes met mine, dark and welcoming, and I saw his mouth open.

"*Petteu*," he said. "I have come home."

"Hang on!" I yelled. "Zero! *Don't open the door*!"

Zero wasn't listening; I heard his hand close around the doorknob and the very slight rattle as it turned, and fairly hurled myself off the bench and around the doorjamb, tumbling into the hall.

I kicked the door shut before it could open more than a

fingers-width, nearly squashing Zero's fingers in the process. Then I slapped a palm against the door and suggested to the house without words that it was a good idea to stay *very* closed before Zero had time to open his mouth.

"Okay, so you remember the mimic?" I asked him, as the outrage slowly faded from his face. "The one that was making little JinYeongs back in the hedges? Reckon your dad found another one, cos that's definitely not JinYeong."

Zero's fingers twitched, as if he was forcibly restraining himself from reaching out again and opening the door. He asked, "Are you sure?"

"A hundred percent," I said. "JinYeong doesn't call me Pet. He hasn't for ages now."

"He knows better than to call your name while we're in here," Zero said warningly.

"Yeah, but he doesn't call me Pet, either. Not since—not since—"

Not since he'd done it to make a point in front of Zero's dad. Definitely not since he'd kissed me. Now that I came to think of it, there were a lot of milestones that I'd somehow missed—no wonder JinYeong had been so frustrated with me for not realising that he'd fallen in love with me.

"You think my father is behind this? Why?"

"'Cos the mimic yesterday said they were allies," I said. "And he said *our* allies. I'm gunna guess that mimics come in matched pairs?"

Zero huffed out a short sigh. "I suppose they must; I've not had much to do with them. My father certainly would have taken the other as collateral for the continued partnership with the mimics if so."

"*Petteu,*" murmured JinYeong's voice from just outside the door. "Will you not let me in? It was so hard to get to you!"

I kicked the door, and someone or something yelped. "Get lost, you face-swapping little creep!"

"Ah, *Petteu*!"

I went back to the laundry window and cracked the louvres open once again. "Oi!" I yelled. "Lord Sero! You might as well come out, because I'm not letting your little Jin Yeong mimic in!"

It was probably a bit much to expect Lord Sero to come out at once, but it was pretty unpleasant to have a projection of Jin Yeong's face and body standing there in the meantime, trying to pretend that it really was Jin Yeong.

Mind you, the mimic didn't know how to do Jin Yeong's expressions at all: now that I could see him trying to be soulful it was obvious that this was just a soulless mimic construct. The real Jin Yeong fairly oozed soul without even trying.

And that was the thing that wouldn't stop worrying away at the back of my mind, because the mimic *didn't* know how to do expressions very well. How did it know Jin Yeong's face so well but not have a good grip on his expressions? Where *was* Jin Yeong, and exactly how lively—or worse, otherwise—was he?

Slightly to my surprise, Lord Sero actually came out of the hedges. Maybe he was starting to know when I wasn't bluffing—a mixed blessing.

"Still shouting at people from your windows, I see," he said caustically. "Humans are such uncivilised creatures!"

"Uncivilised, yeah, but we're the ones inside the house," I pointed out. "We aren't camping out and making ourselves unpleasant outside other peoples' houses like a flamin' crusader army."

"Stop talking to my father, Pet," Zero called, his voice annoyed. "No good will come of it."

Lord Sero stiffened, and he called, "My son, come out and speak with me, fae to fae."

"Don't reckon he wants to talk to you," I told him. "He doesn't even want me to talk to you."

"I never thought I would live to see the day when my son would hide behind humans to escape his responsibilities."

"Hate to sound like a broken record," I told him, as Zero pushed through Morgana and the others at the door and came to stand behind me. "But you're missing the point again. We're in here and you're out there. That means we make the rules about who we're going to talk with and who we're not going to talk with."

"You're not going to talk to your own compatriots, either, it would seem," he said, indicating the constructed Jin Yeong that was still scratching at the door to be let in.

"You must think I'm an idiot," I said. "That thing isn't Jin Yeong, and if you think I'm gunna hold back from blasting it so far Behind that it wakes up back-to-front just because it has Jin Yeong's annoying little face, I've got some news for you."

A very slight frown came to his face. "How did you know it's a constructed appearance?"

"Because I'm not an idiot," I told him. "And because I'm not an idiot, I'm also not going to tell you exactly how I know it's not Jin Yeong. You'd just come back and try with a better version—we know you've got a mimic on your side."

I didn't miss the deadly look that Lord Sero shot at the small, unimpressive woman beside him, or the way that she shivered in the cool air. I did very nearly miss the movement with which he stabbed her in the throat, swift and short; the smallest of protests tumbled over my lips when I saw the blue blood, and my eyes went to the Jin Yeong construct.

It shouldn't have hurt to see him crumble and disappear—I'd stabbed a version of Jin Yeong myself, after all—but it still somehow hurt to see that hope disappear, even though I'd only had a moment or two to believe it.

"Good job showing us what a fantastic ally you are," I said to Lord Sero, giving him the double thumbs up. "That'll be sure to change our minds."

"Son," said Lord Sero, ignoring me and fixing his attention on

Zero. "You can't be serious! You'll ally yourself with another heirling and refuse to take part in the selection?"

"No," Zero said, his eyes flickering toward a doorway that was filled with heirlings. Morgana, Sarah, and Ralph gazed back at him, a mixture of emotions on their faces. "I've allied myself with four other heirlings and I'm refusing to take part in the selection."

"Look at you, learning how to be sarcastic," I congratulated him, patting his shoulder. "Oi, you lot; go jump in the lake. We're staying in the house and we're not coming out."

Lord Sero didn't need to know that we weren't coming out because we didn't need to come out. It didn't matter what reason he gave to our decision; he just knew we weren't coming out, so let him stew on that and not think too much about other stuff that he shouldn't be thinking about. I'd rather he was taken by surprise when we made a break for the outside world.

"I'm disappointed," said Lord Sero icily. "I had thought I'd taught you better than this; I see that I shall have to administer another lesson."

"When your kids are a hundred something, it's probably time to cut the apron strings, even if a fae century isn't the same as a human one," I told him.

Ignoring me, he said to Zero, "When I return you'll regret not listening to reason. I'm not so old that I can't bring you to heel when I need to do so."

"You bring pets to heel, not sons," I told him. "And I'm not the sort of pet that comes to heel, so you should probably concentrate on your butler."

Lord Sero's icy eyes were instantly on me, and I wondered exactly what point I'd scored.

Testing the waters, I said, "Oi. Where is your fae butler, anyway? You get sick of him or something?"

For a moment longer, I held his almost painful gaze, then Lord Sero looked back at Zero.

"You'd be well advised to bring your own pets to heel," he said, and swept away.

"Always nice to have a family reunion," I said, shutting the louvres and making sure the arm mechanism that closed them clicked shut properly. "What d'you reckon he's gunna try and do?"

"I don't know," Zero said briefly. "But you can be sure it will be something to give as much pain as possible. If he thought we still cared for Athelas, no doubt he'd bring him back here to peel him apart piece by piece until we let him in. It's a good thing he can't really get to Jin Yeong from in here."

I nearly asked, "What, you'd cave in for Jin Yeong?" but stopped myself in time, because I'd seen Zero nearly burn a revenant to death for snatching Jin Yeong away. It hadn't stopped him being prepared to sever ties with Jin Yeong when we got stuck in here, but if I looked at that from a Zero point of view, no doubt he'd been trying to do what was best for Jin Yeong in his own, emotionally constipated sort of way.

"Are you sure he can't get to Jin Yeong?" I asked instead. Ever since meeting the first mimic, I'd been on edge, the thought that someone could have Jin Yeong shut away and was just waiting to make use of him, turning over and over in my mind. I knew that I'd be able to tell if it was really Jin Yeong, but it didn't stop me feeling worried about him.

"If my father could have got Jin Yeong in here, he would never have bothered with something as chancy as a construct," said Zero. "Even if he didn't expect a human to be able to tell the difference, he should have expected me to do so. The fact that he didn't bring the real Jin Yeong means he couldn't do so."

"Well, that's a relief, I suppose," I said. "What do you reckon he's going to do, then?"

"He's probably going to try and find anyone in this twisty-turny nightmare of a bubble who means anything to us, and bring them back to hurt us," Daniel said, from the doorway. I hadn't noticed the other three disappearing, but now the door was full of gloomy lycanthrope. "Any friend, or acquaintance, or family."

"Good thing we don't have many friends then, I suppose!" I said cheerfully. "And pretty much every acquaintance of ours in here has tried to kill us, so that helps."

"Lady, I have never tried to kill you!" said Les anxiously, tugging at my sleeve. I didn't know where he'd come from, but it was nice to know he hadn't disappeared into the dirty laundry. "But when there is no bubble tea, what can a human do?"

"Not to worry," I told him. "I didn't mean you; you came in with us, anyway. We didn't meet you by chance."

"I doubt my father has any idea of who we care about—nor would he have any idea that a lasting alliance could form between heirlings, much less friendship. There is no one with whom he can threaten us."

"Good thing he doesn't know you still care about Athelas then," I said less cheerfully, echoing my own earlier words.

"I don't—I don't still care about Athelas!"

"Yeah you do," I said shortly. "If I still do when he killed my parents, there's no way you're not gunna still care. You wouldn't have thrown his chair through the window if you hadn't cared."

"Then let us say I don't want to care!" he snapped.

"All right, we don't want to care, but apparently we do, so it's a good thing your dad doesn't—"

"Pet, do we *have* to talk about it now?"

Daniel gave us both a bit of a weird look and said, "Everyone's waiting in the living room to discuss how we're going to get out of here because Morgana says you have an idea."

It took me a moment of looking blankly at the nearly empty doorway to realise that everyone had left while Zero and I were bickering.

Daniel's grin was irritating. "Are you finished?"

"Yes," said Zero with an insulting haste, and made a beeline for the door.

"Oi!" I called out, slipping back to the floor. "Wait for me! I haven't finished yet!"

Luckily for Zero, someone had made me another cup of coffee when I caught up with him in the living room, and that made me feel a lot more mellow as I sat down in my usual chair. There were also a lot of people sitting on the other chairs and the floor, looking at me with varying expressions of interest, eagerness, and bright inquisitiveness. The coffee made me mellow enough not to mind the lycanthrope gaze and kindly enough not to pursue the matter with Zero.

"First of all," I said. "I reckon Lord Sero managed to make a doorway into the arena. He probably has someone who technically could be an heirling but isn't, or technically is but doesn't count, and used them to get through by tickling the arena presets. He couldn't have gotten into the arena any other way—he couldn't have got into the arena after it started up without something like that."

If the lycanthropes could have pricked up their ears in human form, that was what they would have done.

One of them sat up straighter, grinning. "So what are we gunna do? Find the door and get out there?"

"Nope," I said, with a dark, fierce grin. "Reckon I know a better way. We're not going outside again."

"How come you mentioned the door, then?" protested Kyle. "If it's not important."

I narrowed my eyes at him. "It's important to *me*."

"Jin Yeong came through in the same manner," said Zero.

"Bingo," I said. "The mimics have observed him well enough to mimic him, so he's in here somewhere. We also know he only just got in during the last couple days, so the arena is still open."

"How come we aren't going to one of the doors, then?" asked Morgana, frowning. "Either Lord Sero's or Jin Yeong's? Do you think the doors are guarded?"

"The doors will be one-way," said Zero. "My father would

never leave a way for me to escape—or the other heirlings. He wants an end to this situation."

"That's what I reckon," I agreed. "So we're not going to go for a door. I just mentioned it because there are probably quite a few of Lord Sero's men in here by now using the same method, and we're going to have to account for them. What *we're* gunna do is try to grow the house."

"We're what?"

"We're going to grow the house," I repeated. "There's no point in going out there for people to take pot shots at us when we can just get the house to grow a bit more and put up with the usual sort of things Between throws at us."

"Won't they be able to get into the house eventually anyway?"

Surprising me, Zero said, "They haven't managed yet; Pet has a better grip on the house than I would have expected. Short of the king himself, I doubt there's anyone from the trials who will be able to get in here."

"We might get a few more banshees and maybe a bit of trouble when we're actually travelling through it, but I reckon that'll be it," I said, much gratified by this sign of trust. "That's pretty normal from Between, though. So long as it's Between and not Behind, we'll be fine."

"Only until the banshees start singing," muttered Daniel, but he didn't look too worried. I think he just likes to be morose to remind everyone that things can go horribly wrong.

"How does growing the house get us out of here?" asked Sarah. She was sitting cross-legged beside Ralph, who was leaning against her and pretending that he wasn't sucking his thumb. "We'll eventually get to be as big as we can get, and that'll be that. We'd also have to displace or consume the other people in the arena, because if we end up pushing against the outside of the bubble—"

"I'm not too sure about the other people," I said. "Actually, I'm not too sure about any of it, so it'll be a complete gamble either way. But we know that when an heirling is out of the running, their house vanishes and their supporters are taken out, too. There aren't going to be too many people left out there that aren't Lord Sero's blokes by now, and if we grow over the next couple of days, we should be able to experiment with what'll happen."

Daniel shot me a look that was on the verge of grumpy. "Yes, but how does taking over the arena get us out of it?"

"You know how I said this is just an idea?" I said.

Zero stifled a sigh. "You don't know exactly how it's going to get us out of here."

"Yeah. But I do know it'll make the arena smaller," I said, clearing my throat. "One way or another. We've just gotta make sure there are as few heirlings left in the arena as possible—and make sure all of 'em are in houses."

"We're working on a wing and a prayer?" Daniel said incredulously. "Pet—"

"Life as usual, then, isn't it?" I said happily.

CHAPTER ELEVEN

That night, I dreamed I was a house. Huge and serene and *moving*, I reached out to the stretchy world around me and pulled it into myself. The world grew smaller and another house drew near, but it was a small house, easily digestible. I took it into myself, shrinking the world even more, and felt a slight tickle from somewhere in the upper floor that might have been indigestion if I was still just a human.

Then, something sharp and smelly grabbed the small part of me that was my human shoulders and shook me awake, roaring in my face with an entire face full of razor sharp teeth. Half asleep, and more house than person, I had only a dazed moment to think, *Ah heck, this mongrel's gunna rip my face off* before someone snarled and the creature was ripped away from me.

A small, dainty shadow dripping blood crouched over the creature as I struggled to sit up and get off the couch, and for a moment grew luminescent with the blue flame that was burning up another of the crawlers and the skeleton that straddled it.

Morgana! I kicked and wriggled against the lethargy of being a house and not a person, struggling to get to her, and Morgana's head snapped up, glittering in blood and gore.

"Stay on the *couch*!" she snarled, her eyes entirely red, "and let us protect you! Look after the house!"

I stayed on the couch, sinking back into the haze of being house and person together, and heard Zero's voice rumble, "Get the night crawlers. I have the dustbunnies and I've secured the door."

Then I was dreaming again, or a house again, and human words didn't mean the things they should have meant. All that mattered was settling into the new space I'd taken and making it my own.

I might really have thought I'd dreamed it all if Zero hadn't been hunched in the doorway of JinYeong's bedroom the next morning when I woke up. Someone had cleaned the room while I slept, but there was still the distinct, lingering musk that the night crawlers had brought with them when they invaded, even if all of the blood had gone.

"Thanks for cleaning up the mess," I mumbled to everyone in the kitchen when I went down to make breakfast.

"Sit down," Morgana said. "No, stop trying to get into the kitchen and just sit down! You and the house took over about a quarter of the arena last night, Zero says. And I'm already making breakfast, so—"

"I can smell burning."

"Mind your own business," she said firmly, and two lycanthropes nudged me toward one of the stools at the kitchen island. "Drink your coffee."

"Oh," I said, looking down stupidly at the mug. "There's coffee there."

"I didn't spit in it," said Ralph, who was sitting in the stool next to mine.

If I'd been more awake I might have been a bit more worried, too. I wasn't, so I just sipped my coffee and woke up by degrees as the kitchen grew smokier and Morgana buzzed around like a little fire demon. Still, it was nice not to have to cook, even if we were going to have charcoal for breakfast.

Lord Sero was outside in the backyard again by breakfast time. Already tired from my night time exertions, cranky from the complete lack of Jin Yeong anywhere, and sick with worry at the thought of what that meant, I just scowled out of the new dining room window when one of the lycanthropes came to tell me.

"Lord Sero can flamin' stay out there as long as he likes," I said grumpily. "I'm gunna be making renovations to the place, so it's probably gunna get a bit uncomfortable out there. He'll move away when he starts to get the idea."

I wasn't as confident as I sounded, but I was definitely stroppy enough to be mean-spirited about my attempt. I reckon the house was feeling a bit malicious, too, because when I settled myself in Mum and Dad's room with a good view over the backyard and experimentally *pushed* at the Between in the back wall, the entire house grew creepingly and carefully—in fits and starts that seemed to coincide exactly with when Lord Sero wasn't looking.

It didn't feel exactly like it was me doing it; like yesterday, it felt as though the house was responding to what I wanted it to do —someone cooperating with me while our interests aligned. It didn't feel remotely like it had while I slept last night. But at least something was happening.

I'm not sure Lord Sero got the idea, but he did glare at the house with narrowed eyes as soon as the house started creeping up on him and his men, and when there were only a few feet left of space between the house wall and the labyrinth hedge, he gave a swift, short command that had everyone on their feet and into the hedges before I could see what would happen if the wall touched them.

"Good riddance," said Morgana, from beside me. She wasn't sitting down, but she didn't sit down a lot these days; she seemed to prefer to stand or bounce on her toes with a kind of nervous energy. "I suppose he'll be back, but at least that's given him something to worry about."

"That's the plan," I said, feeling more cheerful. I liked the idea of worrying Lord Sero without giving him any idea of what exactly we were doing. It helped that I wasn't one hundred percent sure of what I was doing, myself. I was just trying to get better acquainted with my house and what we could do together. "We'll probably get a few more visitors now that Sarah's here in the house being an active heirling, but at least we can get rid of them without going outside."

"It's funny," Morgana said slowly. "I used to feel safe indoors, and now I'd just like to get out. It's better that we can't get out right now, though, I suppose; I just don't like Lord Sero *being* out there."

I glanced across at her. "Why? He can't get to us."

"I just can't figure out why he wanted someone actually *in* the house," she said. "He could have just threatened to kill Jin Yeong in front of you if he wanted to get you or Zero to give yourselves up to him, but he tried to get the construct to sneak in, instead."

"That must be what's been bothering Zero," I said. "I suppose it depends on whether Lord Sero knows that Sarah's in the house —she's the only one of us who's agreed to fight in the trials. I can see him wanting to have her killed—or wanting the rest of us heirlings killed—but I don't see how he can have expected the mimic's construct to kill all of us."

"Exactly," Morgana said darkly. "It's been bothering me. I can't think of anything else but that Lord Sero was trying to get to one of us—either you or Zero. But I can't see Zero wandering off with Jin Yeong to be walked into something dangerous, and it's not like you would have gone anywhere with him alone, either."

"Yeah, nah," I said mechanically, with the sudden, terrifying thought stuck in my mind that I *would* have gone with Jin Yeong if I'd actually thought it was Jin Yeong. At this point, if I could have seen that he was alive and uninjured and *here*, I probably would have followed him out of the back door and into the labyrinth without questioning it.

"Good thing the mimics didn't do a great job at pretending to be Jin Yeong, I suppose," I said, for the sake of saying something to cover how terribly vulnerable I felt. "Well, now that they're both dead we shouldn't have to worry about any more fakes—and their house should vanish along with all the people they brought with them originally. I wonder if the heirlings they had under oath will vanish, too? It's not like they agreed to challenge the throne, so maybe the arena will count them as NPCs along with the people who were brought in with the actual heirlings. They aren't anywhere in the house now, so they must have gone somewhere."

"Must be nice to be an NPC," said Morgana. "They get the chance of disappearing with the house once their fighter is gone or has joined up with another group. Us heirlings have to fight, die, or form alliances—and then probably die anyway. I hope they got out."

"If they got out, they'll probably still have to fight or die later when the trials are over," Zero said from behind us. "How much did you take in, Pet?"

"Reckon it was a good twenty metres," I told him, turning my gaze away from the window and over to him.

"Tired?"

"Nope. I didn't do anything like as much as I did the first time; I don't even know if I was the one doing it. I should be good for a fair bit more, yet."

"Did my father notice?"

"Oh yeah, he noticed, all right," I said in satisfaction. "Don't reckon he knew what was happening, but he noticed it was happening."

"Was it wise to do it while he was out there?"

"How the flamin' heck do you manage to do a dad voice when you're only my uncle? That's flamin' terrifying!"

"I'm not your uncle," Zero said repressively. "I'm your great great uncle."

"Then you definitely shouldn't be able to do the dad voice. I'm pretty sure your father knows exactly what's happening everywhere in the arena at this point, so I didn't reckon it'd make much difference if I did it in front of him. He doesn't know it's me doing it—he just found out he had a bit less space than he thought. The arena's been getting smaller since this morning by itself."

"I noticed," he said.

"The hedges have gotten darker, too; did you notice?" said Morgana. "I can smell blood whenever someone opens a window."

Zero's eyes fastened on her straight away. "Nobody should be opening windows."

"That's Les' fault," I said. "He keeps creeping in and out, and the lycanthropes like to cheer him on as he runs for the house if someone's chasing him. He's done it twice since this morning."

"This is why you shouldn't bring strays home," Zero said coldly, and left the room.

He probably wanted to go and make sure Les was still in the house—or out of it, so long as that condition stopped being a variable.

"What's the hinky old bloke doing out there, anyway?" Morgana asked. "He always looks a bit battered when he gets back, so whatever he's going out for, he's paying for it."

"Dunno," I said. "He won't tell me. Hopefully he'll get caught in one of the houses that's been recently vacated and get taken back to the human world before someone gets to him."

"Do you think Sarah's parents have made it back yet?"

"I'll ring Tuatu and check in a couple minutes," I said. "Sarah hasn't asked, but I can tell she wants to."

More quietly, she asked, "What do you think happened to my parents when my house disappeared from the arena? I couldn't get into their room before I left, and neither of them answered when I said goodbye."

I hesitated, because I didn't know how much I could say without upsetting her. It wasn't so much that I was worried about an annoyed zombie in the house—it was more that she'd already gone through so much that I didn't like to put anything else on her. I was unfortunately *very* well aware of exactly what Morgana's parents were, and had done, and if they'd disappeared altogether when the house went back to the human world, that would be the best outcome I could hope for. Athelas, in his own twisty way, had made sure that all of the parents who bargained for their lives with the lives of their children ended up losing far more than they gained. Heck, it had probably been cathartic for him.

That didn't help me know what to say to the small zombie who no longer had to subsist unknowingly on the shadows left of her parents because she was now eating the diet that could keep her as more than just a shadow herself. It also didn't help that I was pretty sure they'd crumbled away to the nasty residue they already were at heart the moment Morgana switched over to a more...solid diet.

"Don't you reckon it'd be nice for them to get some rest?" I asked instead. "They've been around for as long as you have, but they're only shadows. Reckon it gets tiring being stretched as thin as that. Most parents would be glad to know their kid is up and about and safe—reckon they'd be glad not to be stuck in that room any more."

"Was it true?" she asked suddenly. "What the nightmare— what Athelas said? My parents agreed to let him kill me to save their own lives? Don't answer that," she added, before I could think up a good answer. "I suppose that'd be like asking you what you'd do if he came back begging for forgiveness. You were pretty close to him for a while."

"That was when I didn't know he'd murdered my parents," I said sharply. "I wouldn't just forgive him if he came back, even if he was sorry. He killed my parents—he killed yours, too; and Ralph's. Even Abigail and— That's not something you can just pass over. I'm going to make sure that he pays for it all. Him and Lord Sero."

"Still," she said. "I can't decide whether I hate him or them more."

"Yeah," I said, because there wasn't much else I could say. Bumping my leg up against hers, I added, "I reckon your parents are gone," and didn't try to say anything else. I had the feeling that she knew everything else I wanted to say, anyway.

FOR THE NEXT two days we pretty much just battened down the hatches. We knew Lord Sero was out there in the labyrinth, and he knew we were in the house, but there wasn't much point in worrying too much about it, because he couldn't get in.

Mind you, he was probably comforting himself with the fact that we couldn't get out either—without the knowledge that we didn't actually need or want to get out.

I was too busy stretching my abilities with the house to worry about Lord Sero, anyway. It seemed like every time I went upstairs there was a little bit less of the arena as heirlings and their houses disappeared, eating up patches of labyrinth with them; the pieces I took over were much smaller by comparison and far less likely to be occupied by anything I wouldn't want getting into the house if that was likely to happen.

I spent a lot of time climbing stairs over those couple of days, splitting my time between the kitchen and the window that overlooked the backyard upstairs, where the lycanthropes could usually be counted on to be grouped. From there, they could report on the houses that were disappearing, as well as offer a running commentary on visitors trying to enter our house.

The first day it was mostly fae and a few behindkind types I didn't recognise; the second day, we even had a minotaur. I don't think mighty minotaur heirlings are used to being jeered at by a window full of lycanthropes. They definitely don't like it, I can tell you that for sure. Obviously, that fact only encouraged the lycanthropes into a further excess of jeering, and the minotaur stomped back into the labyrinth with whatever tatters of dignity it still had left after a good hour of trying to batter down our back door.

I'm not sure any of the heirlings in the arena knew what to do with other heirlings who refused to leave their house and fight, either. None of them reacted to jeering lycanthropes any better than the minotaur had, and none of them seemed inclined to hang around and try to get us out.

That suited us pretty well: none of us that were heirlings particularly wanted to start fighting other heirlings when it could suggest to someone that we were challenging the throne, and Sarah had parents to get back to safely—not to mention a small, obstinate skeleton who seemed to have adopted her. She wasn't interested in challenging the throne.

On the third morning, I came downstairs to find that Les was out of the house again. I knew it because a very self-right-eous little skeleton sitting at the kitchen island told me so as soon as I got into the kitchen and before I had a chance to get my coffee.

"The smelly man left the house," he said. His chin grew more mulish as he saw my eyebrows rise. "You *told* us we can't leave the house. He *left* the house last night and took the spoons with him."

"She probably already knows," Sarah said. "Eat your cereal."

"He doesn't need to eat," I said, wandering around the two of them to put the kettle on.

"I know, but he likes it."

"Beggar me, he really did take the spoons," I muttered to myself, hovering over the open utensil drawer. "What do you reckon he took them for?"

"Depends on if they're silver or stainless steel," she said.

"Fair," I said, and shook the coffee into my cup. I could stir with a knife.

I was halfway through my coffee when I heard shouting from Mum and Dad's room. The lycanthropes were cheering from the windows, and that meant one of two things: an heirling fight had tumbled out of the hedges, or Les was back.

Given that Les had gone out earlier, I was pretty sure I knew which one it was.

"That'll be him back again," I said gloomily, and put my coffee down to go to the laundry. There was always someone to open the door for Les as he ran, but we all knew better than to just open the door without checking first.

Sarah and Ralph followed me more slowly; I heard them in the hallway as I opened the louvres in the laundry. Everyone else was probably upstairs to see the action.

Through the slitted louvres I saw Les; he was worse for the wear and staggering across the distance between the closest labyrinth entrance and the house, shoulders hunched as though he was running home during swooping season. I couldn't see what was pursuing him, so I nearly jumped down from the bench and went to open the door.

That was when the first harpy landed.

Heck. I nearly hadn't seen them. I hadn't seen *anything* that flew here in the labyrinth—not apart from actual birds.

I wasn't close enough: none of us were close enough. The old bloke wasn't going to make it to the house before those beaks snapped him up, either. I heard the shriek of the harpies, cutting through the outraged howls from the lycanthropes, and saw a beak slash down toward Les.

"The heck you don't!" I snapped.

Then I stood up, the weight of the house settling on my shoulders like an old, familiar cloak, and extended myself, or the house, or maybe both, to swallow Les and exclude the harpies.

Everything stretched, fluttered, then grew firm. The banshees set up a wail and began to gibber from the walls—or, more likely, the washing machine—as everything quivered once more, and stopped.

We were back to normal. Only this time, the house was somehow bigger.

And we were one person richer again.

Sarah, her eyes wide, said from the doorway, "Your house ate him!"

"No worries, he'll be fine," I said cheerfully.

Actually, I felt a little bit heady and dizzy: for a brief moment I had been as near to being connected with the house in all its huge, powerful peacefulness as it was possible to be, and it had been so easy to work with it to do what I needed it to do. As if it had been waiting for me—waiting for this day. That day in the mimic's house hadn't felt like this—so connected and capable. Even last night, half asleep and halfway between human and house, hadn't felt so absolutely and mindfully connected. Right now, I knew exactly where every person was in my house, just like I knew where every part of my body was.

"He's here in the laundry with the banshees; reckon someone better get him before they get in the plumbing and cross over to—"

There was a loud *clash!* and Daniel gave an agonised yell from the toilet. "Someone get these banshees *out* of the loo!"

I grinned. "Sounds like the banshees have been scared out of the laundry."

Someone erupted from the space between the sink and the washing machine, bawling, "Lady, lady, lady!" and I found myself crash-tackled by a hug in bristly beard, holey t-shirt, and a significant amount of body odour.

"Ow!" I said, trying not to fall over. I was used to giving kamikaze hugs, not receiving them. "You don't have to be so flamin' energetic! It wasn't like I was gunna leave you out there to die."

"Are there going to be harpies in here as well?" asked Morgana, over Sarah's shoulder, her black-lined eyes very wide. "Because I don't like harpies, and—"

"Nope," I said, fending off another hug from Les. "The house just sorta...covered over them—or maybe sent 'em out of the arena altogether. You know how Ralph said our house ate his, and then it wasn't there anymore?"

"If you managed to send them out of the arena by taking up the space they were taking, do you reckon you could do the same for the banshees?" snarled Daniel, emerging from the hallway. "They've been booby-trapping the loo again!"

"Looks like you and JinYeong agree on something," I said to him, grinning. "That's exactly my point, though—we've sent the harpies out of the arena! It wasn't just Ralph's house and the mimic's house we took over. We took over actual space in the arena. I reckon Ralph only got out into our backyard because he knew us and knew the way. He's good with instinct like that."

"You're all over blood," Sarah said, wrinkling her nose at me. "Maybe you should go and change before you tell us all of this."

"Blood," echoed Ralph. "It's gross."

"Blood is life," Les told them, waggling his beard.

"Oi," I said to him. Whatever he'd been up to out there, he'd managed to accumulate a fair bit of blood while he was doing it. "You gotta stop going out so much. We can't keep rescuing you, and we've got our own plans—you're gunna wreck what we're doing."

Zero, who had approached as silently as ever but not as unnoticed as ever due to my currently very connected situation, said, "You know how to get us out of the trials."

He sounded mildly proud, and that was kinda nice.

"Yep!" I said. "I thought I had a handle on it earlier, but now I'm sure."

"Very well," he said. "I can get us out of the house; the rest I leave to you."

"Nope," I said. "We're not going to try and get out of the house *or* the trials. We're going to make our house take over the trials until there's no more space for the trials and only space for the house. I just found out that I can kick other heirlings and not just NPCs out of the arena if they're in the space I take over with the house!"

Morgana gazed avidly at me. "You're going to make the house *eat the trials?*"

"See!" I said, pointing at her. "She understands me! What's wrong with you lot?"

"It's a ridiculous plan," said Zero, his eyes very blue. He was the closest to what I would have called *merry* that I'd ever seen him—the brightest I'd seen him since Athelas tried to kill me. "But a few days ago I saw you call your house to you, and just now I saw you command the house to swallow a human, so I'm willing to listen."

"Houses can't eat trials," the old mad bloke said. "But you should try it, lady."

"Of course I'm gunna try," I told him bluntly. "People have been telling me that I can't do stuff I can do for the last year. If I'd stopped trying before now, I'd probably be dead."

"What will happen to all the other heirlings?" asked Morgana. "We don't want them in the house after we've tried so hard to keep them out!"

"That's the good bit about harpies not being in the house," I told her happily. "When I nabbed Les, I pushed out the harpies at the same time; the house could feel 'em, and so could I. They're not in the arena anymore."

"Reckon most of the heirlings that weren't imprisoned are dead, anyway," Daniel said. "There are a lot less hedges out there, and I only saw two rooftops out there this morning. I can see the entirety of the labyrinth when I look out the back windows upstairs."

"The houses that are left are getting closer," I agreed,

nodding. "And it's not exactly that my house will eat the trials, it'll just fill up the arena so that it thinks there's only one house and one option left. I reckon that'll be enough to tickle the presets and connect us with the real world again."

"Should we wait for the arena to get smaller?" asked Daniel. "There are probably a few heirlings out and about, besides houses we can see."

"Nope," I said. "Reckon I'd better do it as soon as I can. I've just gotta call Tuatu so he can go check on Ralph's house and make sure it did go back when we swallowed it. Once we know that for sure, we can try and take over the place. He can give us an update on Sarah's house, too; it hadn't made it back last time I called."

It was nice to have a bit of breakfast while we waited for Tuatu to call back about Ralph's house. I was too keyed up to feel exactly hungry, but I definitely wanted to do something with my hands, and the others needed to eat.

I ended up eating more than I'd expected to by the time the phone rang again, too. I put it on the table in front of me, speakerphone on.

"Pet? You're all set; North just got into the house and she said everything is as it should be. You going to be getting out of there?"

"Some time today, I reckon," I said. At Sarah's wild flailing with a butter knife, I added, "Make sure you and North are at the Palmers' place first to check on them; we'll be all right here, but they might need a hand getting out of their safe room, and they might have a body with 'em."

"Stick close to Zero," he said. "And come back alive."

"That's the plan," I said, sticking my tongue out at Zero, who had looked up with a *That's what I'm always saying!* sort of expression on his face. "See you on the outside a bit later, all right?"

"See you then," he said.

I heard the *beep beep* as he hung up, and then someone said over the speakerphone, "It's that interference again. Want me to sort it out?"

"Just leave it alone," said another. "We've got too much to do, and the old twister will be coming by again soon."

"He was meant to be around—"

"I know. Leave it alone."

An unpleasantly sick feeling stole into my stomach once again. It was Ezri's voice; Abigail's, too.

"Turn it off," Zero said, his voice emotionless. His face wasn't emotionless, though; his brows cleft deep with a stricken line and his eyes dark and hooded with pain.

"It's just feedback," I said, swallowing. I turned off the speakerphone and pressed the phone against my leg to muffle the sound. "Don't listen. They're talking about stuff that happened before...before they died. Tuatu said he's been hearing it, too."

"Put the chip somewhere else, then," Zero said harshly.

"It's the last call we should need to make," I said. "Don't worry about it. I'll keep the phone on silent."

There wasn't another peep from the phone, but it seemed to have gotten to everyone a bit; the lycanthropes went back upstairs to look out the window, taking Morgana and Sarah—and by extension, Ralph—to see how much of the arena was left. That left Zero and me with Les, and I was pretty sure Les was just there to sneak out as many forks as he could from the drawers.

"Will it matter where the others are?" Zero asked.

"Nah," I told him. "Let 'em look out the window. It might be better than being in here to watch everything get a bit weird."

"You're expecting it to be *weird?*"

"Don't see how it couldn't be," I said, feeling a bit more cheerful. It was always fun to watch Zero being pushed out of his comfort zone.

"The dipstick is back!" yelled someone from upstairs, just as I settled myself at the kitchen island with a fresh cup of coffee to see what I could do.

Zero's brows rose. The lycanthropes' delight with finding new and worse names for his father was something that he didn't seem to be able to get used to. I suppose that's what happens if you're brought up by a bloke that horrible.

"Bet you wish it was Jin Yeong instead," I said, unable to help myself.

His eyes went slightly bluer, which was nice to see. Despite that, he said, "It's to no good purpose if it really is my father."

"Never thought it would be," I said, and got up to see what was going on, leaving my coffee behind. "The fun your dad brings with him every time we meet him—oi! Should I be calling him great-great granddad or something? He'd flamin' hate that. Maybe I'll do it."

I was unceremoniously seized by the back of the neck and hauled back to meet Zero's warning gaze.

"Pet," he said. "If you even *try* to—"

"Yeah, yeah," I said, grinning. "If I call him great-great grandad, you'll chuck me out the window and let me say it to his face."

"Close enough," said Zero, and let me go.

He followed close behind me on the stairs, too, but let me go ahead at the window—probably because he could see right over me. The first thing I noticed wasn't that there was a group of behindkind in what was left of my backyard; it was the fact that there was now so little left of the arena as a whole that I could literally see the front of what must be Lord Sero's mansion—he'd brought a whole *mansion* in with him?—through the gap in the hedges. There was no more labyrinth, just a gap between the last remaining hedge and our two houses.

And it had to be Lord Sero's mansion, because he was right outside my house with a group of behindkind—though for what purpose, I didn't know. I didn't like that I didn't know, either. But as I scanned the behindkind on the lawn below, something else interesting caught my eye.

"That's weird," I said, frowning.

Zero, his eyes running over the group in an attempt to make out exactly what the threat was, didn't look at me. He did ask, "What is?"

"That suit," I told him, pointing with my chin at a bloke fairly far back in the part of the group that seemed to be inspecting the base of the hedges that now led into what was left of our backyard. "It's flamin' weird."

I had noticed his suit because it was the suit Jin Yeong had drawn for me the other day—nothing like as well-fitting on this behindkind as it would have been on Jin Yeong—and now my heart quickened. Had Jin Yeong known this fae would be getting in, and planted something on him? Or did this fae have a message for me—was he an ally, someone who would fight for us quietly when we needed him?

That did make Zero look at me: a long, wondering look of confusion. "Why is it weird?"

"'Cos I already knew that someone was gunna be wearing it," I said. "Reckon Jin Yeong is giving us a sign."

Beside me, Daniel asked sceptically, "What sign?"

"Dunno," I said. "But he drew that suit pattern for me a couple days ago, before he vanished. He was planning something and this bloke has something to do with it. We should try to have a word with him if we can."

"Pet," said Zero, in a tone that was the verbal equivalent of someone pinching the bridge of their nose. "Are you suggesting that we should go out into the open to meet with my father?"

"Not exactly," I hedged. "Just that if we *gotta*, I reckon the bloke in that yellow-and-grey chequered suit will be able to help us out. And that maybe it'd be a good idea to try and talk with him if we can."

"What if he was warning you about a bloke in a yellow-and-grey chequered suit?"

"Shut up, Daniel," I said, grinning. I went to push open the window, prepared to be as cheeky as possible to Lord Sero since Zero had vetoed calling him great-great granddad, but Zero's huge hand covered mine.

"He's not here to talk," he said.

My eyes flicked back to the world beyond the window, and I saw with surprise that Lord Sero, having come and seen, was prepared to leave the conquering for another time. As I watched, he turned on his heel and marched back toward the hedges, his minions trailing behind him.

"Heck, that's not good!" I said. If my heart had lifted briefly a moment before, it was now beating a bit too quickly from consternation. "What'd he come here for if he's just going to turn around and leave? Is he going for psychology, or what?"

"Whatever it is, it's nothing good," Zero said quietly. "Make sure the house is as secure as you know how to make it, Pet. We should try to enact your plan as quickly as possible."

We went downstairs first, leaving the others standing at the window to watch the last of Lord Sero's men turn back into the hedges, and I couldn't help saying the other thing that had been on my mind for the last few days as we walked back down the stairs.

"Athelas isn't with your dad anymore."

"I noticed," said Zero, his brows cleft with a faint, sorrowful line. "That will have no good reason behind it, too."

Shaken, I said, "You reckon your dad killed him? Why?"

"No reason I can think of that makes sense," he said. "My father has everything he could possibly want, barring me, and all of that is due to Athelas."

"Yeah," I said. "That's what I thought."

Not that it should matter if Athelas was alive or dead; not that there should be a preference toward alive rather than dead. But it didn't make sense for Athelas to be dead—not when he'd done everything Zero's dad wanted him to do and more.

"We're not gunna let them win," I said. "Not Athelas—not your dad."

"We'll see about that," said Zero, cautious to the last. "My father seems to be planning something, and I wouldn't put it past him to have realised some of what's happening with the arena. We'll have to make sure we're ready to fight when you begin your work with the house—and you will have to harden your mind to complete your work even if your friends are dying around you."

"Yeah," I said again. "But there's also a really good chance that everything will go right for once—and we've got our secret weapon if something does go wrong."

Zero threw me a fond, exasperated sort of a look. "Is that your yellow-and-grey chequered suit?"

"Yep," I said, grinning. "Hey, I don't tell you how to guess what strokes someone's gunna make in a fight—don't try to tell me that Jin Yeong wasn't giving us a sign."

"What Jin Yeong hopes to do and what Jin Yeong accomplishes are often two different things," said Zero, but he said that a bit fondly, too.

The others came down a few minutes later. Apparently they'd come to the same conclusion as Zero: that it might come down to a fight if things didn't go according to plan, and that obviously I was going to be too busy to fight.

"I'm not having you fight in my kitchen again," I told them. "You can take up the living room; move a couple chairs or something. I'll sit up here in the kitchen with Zero."

"Do we have to do that now, though?" asked Morgana.

"What, take over Lord Sero's house?"

"You said you were going to take over the arena, but there's only one house left. Wouldn't it be better to try and fight Lord Sero and then get out when he's dead?"

"Only if you want to be king," I told her. "We don't know how he got into the arena, either; he must still have an heirling with him. We'd have to find out who they are and kill them, too. I don't much like that idea; anyone he's got is probably a prisoner."

Morgana winced. "Right. I don't want to be king or kill someone."

"Exactly," I agreed. "Right. I don't know about you lot, but I'm about ready to go. You might as well get out your weapons if you reckon you're gunna have to fight."

Only Sarah and Zero started checking automatically for weapons; I suppose that's how it goes when you're in a house full of lycanthropes, zombies, and revenants. Everyone has built-in weapons.

It left me feeling a confused mix of security and guilt as I settled myself on the kitchen floor, cross-legged. I didn't want people to fight and die for me, but if the last couple of times working with the house were any indicator, I probably wouldn't be aware enough to defend myself if things went wrong and somehow or other Lord Sero managed to get into the house despite me.

The house must have been ready, because as soon as I sat down, my connection strengthened. Just as I'd done once when very high on vampire spit, I saw the running threads and particles that made up the house—and maybe reality itself—and felt myself sinking down into that reality.

"Just make sure you lot don't die," I said to the group in the living room, before it was too late to say anything.

"Good grief, you two are exactly alike," Morgana said, flicking her eyes from me to Zero. "Anyone would know you're related!"

"Oi!" I said hazily, sinking deeper until I wasn't sure if I was floorboard or flesh. "*You* were telling me that—"

"I just don't know why you're always complaining about being taken care of when you're always trying to take care of other people," she said hastily. "All right, all right, let's get started."

At least, I think that's what she said. By then, words didn't mean a lot and all I could process were strands of Between and reality. In a bright, line-drawn transparency, I saw every edge and piece of the house, then right through the house and to the hedges, which were very nearly the same. My eyes followed right on to the mansion we faced, all brilliantly sharp and hard like diamond—or ice.

I think my body mumbled, "Here we go," but there was no space for words where I was. I was a house that creaked and grew and breathed, and I was feeling cramped. It was time to stretch out a bit.

I ate the lawn and hedges without a second thought—expanded into them and consumed them as though they were nothing. They became a part of me and disseminated into the woodwork, the life signs that had remained in them vanishing in a moment. Human me would have worried that I had killed them. House me knew that those signs of life hadn't been snuffed out, they had merely been pushed out because there was no longer room for them.

I was a house that lived and grew, and there was a stone house in my way. Cold and white and hard, it let me settle all around it, soaking up all of the space that there was to soak up, then rebuffed me as I tried to swallow it, too.

It thought it was stone and not house, but I knew it was a house.

I lunged—*we* lunged—and hit rock with such suddenness and force that I was thrown back into my body in a shower of dust, my connection with the house shattered and nearly broken.

My whole, human body ached as if I really had hit rock face first, and someone supported me from behind while sharply questioning me. The questions didn't make any sense, but that was more because there was too much dust and hurt and confusion around me than because I was still a house that didn't understand singular words.

The dust cleared a bit as I struggled to breathe, looking around wildly, and I caught a glimpse of the living room again.

Only instead of it being my living room, it was a room somewhere else. A room of marble and cold and dust, with grass for floor and stony flowers growing up its pillars and a lot of wide, vast windows. I'd seen those windows from the outside—from my own windows, in fact.

More worrying still, the room was full of behindkind of varying sizes and types, each of them staring at us with expressions that ranged from startled to snarling, and right down to plain hungry. Then, through a sudden parting in the crowd, I saw Lord Sero himself.

"Pet!" Zero said sharply, and this time I understood the meaning of it. "What happened?"

I tried to suck in a second breath and seemed to choke on stone dust. I coughed like an asthmatic smoker for a full minute before I managed to drag in enough breath to wheeze, "You know how my house has been eating all the others?"

"Yes?"

"Well, your dad's house bit back."

CHAPTER TWELVE

"Can they hear us?" I panted, gazing at that expanse of marble and grass that was far too full of behindkind and separated from us only by thin air, dust, and the edges of the kitchen-dining room walls. I had my answer before Zero's negative sounded, because I could see their mouths moving without being able to hear a sound. "Ah heck, reckon I've merged the houses instead of taking over. What did they thread through this marble to make it so flamin' hardy!"

Zero growled, "Keep trying to take over the house. I don't want to be here longer than I have to be."

I was already trying, my eyes on Lord Sero and all of his men. It was the equivalent of trying to force myself through a straw instead of a tunnel, and just when I thought I had found a weak spot, it closed in on itself, pulling tight. In fact, everything seemed to pull tight to one spot—a spot that drew my eyes as well as all of the connecting points of the room.

Lord Sero, in fact.

"I'm trying," I said, trying not to worry him by saying exactly what I *could* see. "I can't feel where the others are, though, and I don't like that. They should have been with us."

"We don't even have the living room," he said. "They're here somewhere: try again."

"I am," I said shortly, after another brief, vain effort. "It's like it's tethered here—like your dad is the tent peg holding it in place."

"Will it help if you're in the same room as the tent peg?"

"Don't know," I said, sending a worried look up at him. "Reckon we'll have to find out?"

"It won't hurt to see," he said. "We can always retreat if need be."

"We don't know that," I said, grabbing for his trouser leg as he started for the couple of steps down into the other house. "Oi! We don't know that! Stop! I'm not having my uncle die to test out a theory!"

"You might need a weapon at some stage," he said, gently removing my hand from his trouser leg and pulling me up to stand beside him. "My father doesn't know you can pull weapons from Between, so make the most of that surprise when you do it: show them what a niece of mine is capable of. Get the heirling sword if you can—that will throw them off and give us a few seconds more."

"What are you gunna grab, then?" I asked. He had his sword on him, but he hadn't drawn it, and that worried me.

"My father, if necessary," said Zero, and stepped down into where our living room ought to have been.

"Flamin' heck!" I grumbled, and followed him. I didn't want to see if being in the same room as his father would make things easier, but if we were gunna die, we might as well die together.

Lord Sero watched us with an almost hungry expression, right until we stepped down onto marble instead of carpet.

I don't think they expected the involuntary smile that curved my mouth—or the laugh that escaped my lips a moment later. But I couldn't help it. The minute we stepped down from the kitchen and into Lord Sero's vast room, delight coiled through my stomach and fairly sparkled to the tips of my fingers.

Because curling through the air, fragrant and insidious as always, was the italicised scent of JinYeong's cologne—the one thing that had been missing from the first mimic's almost perfect version JinYeong; the most important thing Lord Sero's second mimic had also forgotten. Heck, for all I knew, mimics didn't know about scent. Maybe they only concentrated on the visible.

I couldn't see him, but JinYeong was here. Somewhere in this vast marble hall, JinYeong was waiting for his moment to show himself.

"You think this is a joke?" asked Lord Sero incredulously. "For a human you are ludicrously unaware of the perennial precariousness of your situation."

"For a bloke who sheds flowers everywhere he goes no matter the season, you're the last person who should be sneering at perennial faults," I pointed out. "You shouldn't have been so flamin' precious with your house if you didn't want people in your hall; I would have booted you out of the arena without bothering you if you hadn't made it so flamin' hard."

A few of the fae around Lord Sero tried very hard not to look at each other, while the behindkind in the yellow-and-grey suit clicked his teeth together in what could have been annoyance but seemed to be amusement. More importantly, he did it as if he were used to having teeth a fair bit longer and sharper than he actually had—and as if the action had been disillusioning in the extreme. Then he caught my eyes and very deliberately winked at me.

Flaming heck. JinYeong hadn't sent us the man in the yellow-and-grey chequered suit; he *was* the man in the yellow-and-grey chequered suit. How the heck had he managed to get into the arena wearing someone else's face and body?

I didn't dare to let my eyes linger, but I looked him over quickly, desperate for something that would confirm the madness of the idea. He was taller than JinYeong, with a five o'clock shadow and skin that was far too white for the blue-black of his hair, and his eyes were startlingly green. Pretty much a carbon copy of every far-too-pretty fae I'd seen, with all of the beauty of JinYeong and exactly zero of his warmth.

I met those green eyes fleetingly once more, and he smirked at me. The face was completely wrong, but that smirk was pure JinYeong: self-assured, pleased with himself, and utterly smug.

"Flamin' heck," I muttered, and Zero looked down at me. At him, I said, "Tell you later. Just don't forget what I said about that secret weapon."

We had enough problems to be going on with; I didn't want to give JinYeong's game away by speaking too loudly. Through the marble of the house I could barely feel where the others were—I couldn't hope that Lord Sero was similarly ignorant, and I definitely couldn't hope that he wouldn't use them as leverage if he was able to take them prisoner.

"I would ask why you've invaded my demesne, but it makes very little difference. You're in my power now and I certainly won't be allowing you to leave."

"You know that we can fight, right?" I inquired. There was a merry brightness in my blood that I usually only got from vampire spit, and it was very hard not to grin outright. "We're not just gunna give ourselves up to you."

"Bold words," Sero said, smiling without humour. "I know that your other little friends are somewhere around my receiving room: I've already dispatched people to deal with them."

"Yeah?" I said. "You know there's a zombie with 'em? Don't reckon your blokes will have a fun time trying to take 'em prisoner. I'm also pretty sure that you've been losing a lot of muscle lately as the arena shrinks."

"Yes, I gathered you'd been busy reducing the arena," he said. "And I was aware that once you'd taken care of whatever was left out there, you'd turn your eyes on my demesne. I made sure I was ready for you—you really ought not to think I'm so stupid."

"The arena shrinks itself," I said, trying to pay enough attention to Lord Sero while at the same time feeling out the room and the great house for any way to push on with our plan. "I just helped it along a bit."

"It was very useful of you," he said pleasantly. "And gave me the time I needed to make arrangements I might not otherwise have been able to make."

"Glad to help," I told him flippantly, sick to my stomach. I really hadn't expected him to know what I was doing, much less to be ready for it.

"Moreover, I have more than enough staff to deal with the assorted rabble in my receiving room. Let us come to some agreement, son: your other heirling friends are going to have to die, but everything else is negotiable. I'm not unreasonable."

"We're not here to negotiate," said Zero, at last. "We won't be here for long, either."

There was a great and absolute iciness to him that seemed fragile rather than hard. It worried me. I wondered, for the first time, if this house was somewhere he knew well rather than just a house that Lord Sero had commandeered.

"This estate is bound to me," Lord Sero said. "You'll find it hard to get through the house without going through me. I'll give you all non-essential members back once I've killed the heirlings if you give up now, my son."

"Got a counteroffer," I told him, once more briefly meeting and then avoiding the eyes of the yellow chequered fae-who-was-Jin Yeong. "We'll take all of our people and Zero's just gunna come with us. How's that suit you?"

"I will not argue with household chattel!" said Lord Sero, his voice tight. He turned his eyes back on his son. "The others go nowhere until I have the heirling sword in hand, the Pet in custody, and you by my side. I'm willing to be gracious and grant you a small concession—nothing more! Take the offer while you can."

"We'll accept no offers from you," Zero said. "Pet?"

"Working on it," I said.

"I told you," Lord Sero said coldly. "This house is bound to me; nothing you can do will make a difference. If you won't come gently, all of your friends will die and you'll likely be hurt."

"You can try to get our friends," I said. "But I told you: we've got a zombie, and she's pretty annoyed already. Even if you kill us, it still won't get you the heirling sword."

"I'm not going to kill my son, you absolute buffoon," said Lord Sero, in snarling exasperation. "He will take the throne with the aid of the sword. You are the one who will die, after your human friends."

"Yeah, see that's the problem," I said. "Your son doesn't know where the heirling sword is. I'm the one who does. So if you kill me and the others, it's hooroo to the sword and hooroo to the throne."

I saw Zero's incredulous gaze in my peripheral and turned my head to explain cheerfully, "I took it and hid it while you were washing off the blood the other day. Put it somewhere nice and safe where I can get it later."

Zero smiled for the first time since we'd entered the house. "Good Pet," he said. To his father, he said, "I stand with the Pet. If you want either of us, you'll have to fight, and I think you'll find that our friends aren't so likely to fall easily, either."

Lord Sero drew in a deep breath through his nose. It was so similar to what I'd seen Zero do time and time again, that it threw me for a moment. "Let us try to come to an understanding," he said to me. "You're always kicking and scratching—there's no need. I'll even allow some further concessions: all you have to do is swear fealty to my son. All of the other heirlings and yourself: swear allegiance and there's no need for us to fight."

"Sorry, what?"

"A simple choice," he said, smiling down at me with dark, shadow-etched lips. "Continue to support my son as you've been doing all along—merely make that service official. Swear fealty to my son and I won't kill your friends. They'll have to swear to it as well, but they won't die."

"I wish you'd flamin' make up your mind!" I said bitterly. If Athelas had always been hard to understand, it was because he deliberately made himself opaque and spoke in riddles to hide himself. Lord Sero was almost impossible to understand because he changed his mind at what seemed like a breath of wind, and for no reason that I could tell. Within the last few months he had tried to recruit me, then kill me, tried to recruit me again, and then had gone back to wanting me dead.

Now we were back to recruitment again?

"You need to get a grip on yourself," I advised him. "No one likes to work for a bloke who changes his mind every few days."

What I really needed to do was try and make my house keep eating Lord Sero's house; if we kept talking for long enough, that would probably give me the time to urge things along. I shot a quick look at Zero and he met my eyes briefly.

"He's your dad," I said to him, shrugging. "You talk to him."

That was as much of a hint as I could give him. If only I could give the house a bit of a hurry-up...

"I already signed a contract with the Pet," Zero said coldly. "I don't need my father's help to arrange my household."

Hazily, with the part of my brain that wasn't involved in trying to move the house along, it tickled me to realise that Zero hadn't said he *had* a contract with me, but that he'd *signed* one with me.

"I could beg to differ, but instead, I'll command. Take up the family mantle and do your duty by your canton!"

"I gave that up years ago when I took the gold with the Enforcers," Zero said.

I risked pushing at the slow-as-molasses movement of my

house, hoping to bring carpet down into the grass and make the room more living room than marble chamber.

Lord Sero said sharply, "You cannot give up a birthright nor your responsibilities—and *stop meddling with the flow of my manor, human!*"

"Didn't reckon you'd notice, actually," I said, since it was no good trying to pretend now that I hadn't been doing anything. The carpet had grown a few inches from the bottom of the stairs and into the grass floor, so he probably would have seen it, even if he couldn't feel it.

"You may be the master of your own home, but you are not the master here," he said. "And I think the time has come for you to be separated from my son, at least momentarily."

I didn't understand what he'd said quickly enough; in the instant between the words and the realisation that Lord Sero too could influence his house, the floor reefed itself apart and stole Zero away from me.

I managed to slow it down—to mitigate the distance Lord Sero created between us—but I was too late to the work, and Zero was on the far side of the hall with his father and the entire mob of behindkind between us before I could do more than stop myself from hitting the wall.

"One of you, attend to the human," commanded Lord Sero, turning his shoulder on me. "I wish to converse with my son. Hurt it if the need arises."

The behindkind in the yellow chequered suit strode forward lazily and started across the hall, smirking again.

"Pet, get *back* to the house!" thundered Zero.

If it hadn't been the fae in the chequered suit walking toward me, I probably would have obeyed him. As it was, that fae sauntered the whole way toward me, his cologne wafting before him like a welcoming party, and I stayed where I was, the desire to laugh rising in me again.

Instead of laughing, I waited until he was right in front of me, then I grabbed him by the ears with a gurgle of laughter, breathing in far too much scent, and kissed him. His arms folded around me straight away, tight and familiar, and when I let him go and he released me just a hesitation later, the face that looked down at me was Jin Yeong's own face instead of a pale fae face with green eyes.

"I missed you!" I said, my hands slipping away from his ears and to his cheeks instead, trying to pretend that there wasn't a wet warmth in my eyes. "You better have a flamin' good excuse for disappearing!"

Jin Yeong gave the faintest of sighs and said, "I would verrry much like to kiss you again right now but I think there is no time."

"Good point," I said, as Lord Sero's voice cracked open the air with all the efficacy of a whip.

"It's the vampire! Take them, you fools!"

"I really hope this isn't your best suit," I said to Jin Yeong, with a laugh caught in my throat. "Because it's a flamin' bad fit!"

"I will not regret it if this one is ruined," he said, his eyes dark and liquid and laughing. "I am already repaid."

We turned to face the forward surge of behindkind, Jin Yeong unbuttoning his suit jacket and me reaching through the livening froth of reality that was Between to do something I'd never done before.

This time, instead of reaching for a real thing and drawing it through Between to make it into a weapon, I reached right for the weapon itself: the heirling sword, propped up in the built-in wardrobe in my parents' room.

It came out, too. I'm not sure I expected it to—I'm flaming sure no one else expected anything of the sort, either. Next to me, Jin Yeong gave an incredulous laugh; ahead of us, the tumble of behindkind wavered and stopped. Behind them, Lord Sero stared at me with eyes that could have been shards of glass.

Welp. If I didn't die in the fight, he definitely had plans for me that I wasn't going to like. It was no use worrying about that now, though; Jin Yeong and I had to survive long enough to join Zero, who needed to survive long enough to get to us. I was pretty sure we'd be okay if we could just join together and fight.

"Heads up!" I called to Zero. Then I threw the sword at him, hilt first, trusting in his long reach and the fact that the sword wanted to be with him to get it there in one piece. It fluttered in the air, yellow and fabricky, then cool, blue steel as the hilt met Zero's ready hand.

Behindkind drew back around him, wary and dark-eyed, and I saw the flash of satisfaction in Lord Sero's eyes as they ran over his son.

I sniffed and reached more leisurely for two nearby candlesticks that turned seamlessly into twin swords. Lord Sero was very much mistaken if he thought that Zero handling the sword meant that he was taking up the mantle of challenger. Zero handled the heirling sword just as if it were any other sword—a means of fighting his enemies. Maybe that's why it had kept coming to him when he wasn't even slightly interested in becoming king.

I felt the brush of Jin Yeong's arm against mine as he stepped forward to draw even with me, and looked across at him to find that his eyes, so bright and familiar in expression, were waiting to meet mine.

Those eyes said, *Shall we?*

"Might as well," I said aloud. "Otherwise they'll start thinking they can get away with crashing heirling trials all over the place. Oi."

His eyes met mine once again.

"If we make it through this, I'll date you. Only to see how it goes, though. Reckon we can get to Zero without getting killed?"

He shrugged one shoulder, but his eyes were glowing. "There is half a chance. *Hyeong* will provide the other half, I think."

"Oh well, that's better than I figured," I said; and, creating just enough space between us that I wouldn't accidentally cut him, I swept my swords up into a crossed defence to meet the first attack. A wiry, muscly behindkind who looked part-man and part-tree sliced down with such energy that I had to spin away from the blow instead of blocking it. JinYeong lunged past me and directly at the throat nearest, and that fae went tumbling backwards into the oncoming behindkind, gushing blood. I cut and thrust, ducked and parried, and tried to keep even with him, aware in the flurry of battle that if we became separated, our chances would drop considerably.

I could no longer see Zero above the hulking figures that surrounded Lord Sero, but I saw the blue glow of the heirling sword in the twilight softness of the background of white marble, a beacon to show us the way to press toward. The constant, arterial spray of blood beside me that was JinYeong pushed forward, slowed, pushed forward. Watching me, waiting for me.

I couldn't see movement at the great entryway through the crowd, but there must have been a flurry there, because the sound of growling rose until it was a frenzied snarl above the noise of the fight: the lycanthropes, joining the fight. My heart jumped in hope, and for a few moments the fight seemed to turn in our favour, the pressing from the right and left reduced by the number of us fighting. Half of our attackers had turned to fight off the new attackers from the rear, and Zero was pushing in from the side. Now I could fight and press straight ahead instead of always having to watch my flank, and JinYeong seemed to surge forward at my side.

I hadn't expected Lord Sero to take part in the fight. He never had while I'd known him, and it never occurred to me until he was right there in front of me that he could possibly be so much annoyed by me, or just determined to see me actually dead, that he joined the fight himself.

JinYeong saw; tried to get to me. I caught a fractured glimpse of him just as a rock duster swatted him sideways and into the wall, then a hand big enough to circle my throat completely was throttling me from behind and fairly shaking the swords from my hands.

"Enough!" said Lord Sero, his voice sending ice through my veins and down into the ground. It froze the grass and sent frosty flowers springing up and spreading in a sweeping crackle of ice that slicked the ground and grew to form a wall of stylized white roses around the two of us and all of the nearest behindkind with him, opaque and beautiful.

Through those roses, I saw Zero on one knee with Daniel beside him in wolf form and Morgana's slightly misty figure all white and red, crouched over a prone body. I looked wildly around for JinYeong and saw him at last behind the wall of ice, several feet away from the others, a crumpled mass of yellow-and-grey suit. He dragged himself up, blood cascading down the left side of his face from a jagged tear that tore his forehead apart from the eyebrow and down toward his ear, and fell over again only a step closer to the icy wall.

I struggled furiously to pull away, but the hand around my neck tightened remorselessly and lifted me into the air, then hurled me at the ground. I hit frozen grass with a sickening crack, though I couldn't tell if the crack was from my head or my ribs, which seemed to stab me in the side that stuck to the icy ground.

I couldn't breathe, but I wasn't sure if it was because I was wounded or because everything hurt so much. Lord Sero grabbed me by the hoodie and dragged me to my feet, and by then I was breathing by pure instinct. Everything *hurt*, and when he shook me it seemed as if my entire body spasmed in pain.

"Be *still*," he snarled down at me, as if I could control the pain.

"Maybe. Stop shaking. Me then," I groaned.

Distantly, I heard the roar of Zero's voice, and his fists against the wall of ice.

"Another movement and your pet dies," Lord Sero said to his son, shaking me again. "You will give yourselves up."

There was only a moment of silence before I saw Zero throw

away the heirling sword. Sarah did the same with her weapon, and the lycanthropes sat, whining.

"Don't you flamin' give yourselves up!" I yelled, sick with pain and outrage. "You flamin' keep fighting!"

Lord Sero smiled down at me with savage amusement in his eyes. "It's amazing how simple things become when one finds the right pressure point. You have a talent for becoming precious to people, it would seem—and now the people who are most precious to you will die."

"Let me go," I said, through my teeth. "You're gunna flamin' regret it if you don't!"

"I very much doubt it," he said. To the others behind the ice wall, he called, "I'm going to take apart this little pet of yours piece by piece until you swear fealty to my son. I may even take a few more pieces off after you do, so think hard about how long the Pet can endure and how many functioning parts a human can lose before life becomes unviable."

I couldn't hear anything from behind the ice wall, but it was obvious they could hear us: a furious froth of movement boiled against the ice as soon as Lord Sero started talking, dark around the edges with pain and lack of breath. I saw a fractured moment of Jin Yeong's snarling face and Morgana's red eyes, and rolled my eyes back up to meet Lord Sero's amused eyes.

"Reckon you're gunna be sorry if you don't let me go," I said, slurring a little. "'Cos one of the things about people loving you is that they'll do a lot for you, and I don't reckon I could stop 'em if they get out."

"We'll begin with your ears," he said disdainfully, ignoring me. "You don't use them, so consider it a kindness in me to take the appendages you aren't using first."

"Take my ears off and my friend is gunna take your face off," I spat at him. "She's flamin' hungry these days and you're not gunna like it if you make her angry."

He laughed at me, reaching out to pinch my ear between his

forefinger and thumb, and I bit his wrist. I bit flamin' *hard* and tasted blood—and as I tasted that blood I knew in an electrifying moment of clarity that what I had just done couldn't be taken back.

I could have stopped then, but I bit harder instead. It must have hurt, but Sero only laughed again and contemptuously shook me off. I hit the ground hard and lost the last of my breath in pain as my rib was jolted again.

"Human until the end," he said, sneering down at me. "When you're powerless, all you can do is turn savage and die snarling."

I don't think he expected me to grin with bloody teeth, and I'm flamin' sure he didn't expect the laugh that came out, as bloody and wicked as any of Jin Yeong's chuckles.

"Don't reckon you understand, mate," I said. "I mean, I'm savage, yeah—savage enough to bite you. But that's not the important thing about me right now."

"The important thing about you right now is that you're precious to my son," he said. "And you are no less precious to me thereby. Son—"

As he spoke, he turned to pace back toward Zero. He tried to turn, anyway; there was a weakness in that turn that had him grabbing at the shoulder of the nearest behindkind, and he only got a few steps away before I called after him.

"Wanna know what the important thing is?"

He staggered as he turned back around too, and I could have sworn that there was fear in his cold blue eyes. "What did you do to me, you feral?"

"The important thing about me today is that I told the vampire I'd go out with him," I said, still grinning that bloody grin at him. "Kissed him, too, which is probably more important."

"Your revolting display is of no interest to me whatsoever," said Lord Sero, looking ill. "Vampires may kiss humans once in a while, but in the end they have only one desire: to bite and to consume."

"Maybe when they think about them as food," I agreed, staggering to my feet. "But my vampire doesn't think of me as food, and you're missing the point. You're not feeling too well, are you?"

Through his teeth, he repeated, "What did you *do* to me, you *feral?*"

"Now, if he'd bitten me, you'd be fine," I said, swaying with my feet sinking in grass instead of crackling against it. Ice was melting. "All that saliva would've gone straight to my bloodstream. But the thing about kissing is that saliva gets a bit mixed, and I'm pretty sure you've got a bit of vampire spit doing loop-de-loops in your blood now, too."

He stared at me in disgusted outrage. "How *dare* you infect me with that vampire filth!"

"That's the funny thing about you lot," I said, gasping a bit as my injured side went into muscle spasms. "You're more outraged about being contaminated than you are about potentially dying."

"I refuse to die for such a reason," he ground out.

"Don't reckon you've got much choice," I told him, grinning another bloody grin at him.

"If I am to die, so are you, *human!*" he spat. "I don't know exactly what mix you are, but—"

"You'd think so, wouldn't you?" I said. "But vampire spit doesn't do that to me—heard you gotta be fae for it to work like that."

He stared at me, still clinging to the shoulder of the bloke he'd grabbed, and said thickly, "You must have fae blood—there's no other strain of behindkind that would have left you looking so human and yet carrying the abilities you carry."

"Nope," I said. "I don't know about being an heirling through and through, but I'm pretty flamin' sure I'm human through and through. I've been taking in vampire spit for the last year; I'm pretty well adjusted now."

Lord Sero's face worked, and he released his hold on the behindkind to stagger toward me, his sword rising with difficulty.

His minions let him come, and that surprised me until I realised that he hadn't given them any other orders.

He raised that sword properly, but as if in a trance, and made as if to attack.

"Nope," I said again, batting it away. "I'm not going to let you stab me just because I'm a lowly human and you're a powerful fae."

"You've all but killed me," he said. "You little fool, you've all but killed me. I can do so much for you if you'll only swear fealty —you don't even have the mental capacity to realise how much power you could have behind you."

"Know what the funny thing is?" I asked, groaning through another wave of spasms from the muscles around my broken rib. "You're gunna die from an infection from an unconnected, stupid little human like the unimportant piece of garbage that you are, instead of a glorious death somewhere that your family can spin and make sound good."

Even though he'd talked of death, I wasn't sure he quite believed it yet. But as he grew weaker, it seemed that I grew stronger—or maybe it was just that it was easier to connect with the house. As his strength waned, I saw the connections of the house again: the connections of his house and mine, slowly but surely fusing together. We hadn't stopped in the sudden, screeching halt I thought we had: my house had still been gently, slowly, taking over. And now I began to see how everything connected again.

Lord Sero was a lightbulb—connected to the grassy floor, all the threads of his house flowed through him. More importantly, I saw the poison of Jin Yeong's spit coursing through his body, a black filigree among the glittering blue connections of the house.

He dropped to one knee, shoulders sagging. "Wait!" he panted. "Wait! I swear fealty! I swear fealty to you! I and mine are yours to command; all you have to do is save me. You can't face the king alone, but if you have my backing you'll yet live to see the change and for centuries after."

For once, I was nearly stunned into silence. At last, I croaked, "What?"

"*I. Swear. Fealty*," he ground out. "I will be your man, and you will have at your back *countless* resources—in your hands *countless* weapons. Heal me."

I didn't want to be king—I *desperately* didn't want to be king. But for a moment I could see a potential future that didn't involve my sudden and painful death. I didn't have to be the king: with the amount of power Lord Sero harnessed at my control, I could make sure that everything was put right in the world Behind and Between—including finding the right behindkind to be king. From there, I could make sure everything was put right in the human world as well. I would have the power to change things I couldn't change as a human. I could support a decent candidate, and I wouldn't be alone in it; I'd have the actual ability to make sure that the chosen heirling made it safely to the throne.

I would have the power to do everything that needed to be done to protect my friends and my small family. I would be able to see next year and the year after with what remained of that family. I could even think about properly dating without the possibility of being hunted down while out for something to eat. More than that, I would be able to take something evil and spoiled and turn it into something by which good could be done.

I could defeat the King Behind and rout the entire Behind legal system while being supported by a good half of the system itself.

I drew in a deep, shuddering breath, terrified at the strength of my desire to accept that offer. To be able to live, and love, and die when I ought to die instead of dying young while trying to fix problems that were too big to fix alone, alone.

I could even see how I could heal Lord Sero—like the house, which was running with Between that circled right around and into him, Lord Sero himself was flowing with Between. If I fed the poison that was running in his veins into the house and then severed him from it, it would be like plucking a flower before it could die from a good dose of weed killer.

"You've got no idea how much I wish I could accept your oath," I said, still shaken by the strength of that desire and with an aching heart for all that I was giving up. Across the room and through a film of icy flowers, I could see Jin Yeong, still bleeding from the forehead but on his feet and pressing against the ice. It wasn't like a relationship with him would ever have been normal, anyway, even if we weren't worried about dying any day we left the house.

"You can accept it—you must! You won't live without it."

"Yeah," I said, with a sigh caught in my throat. Jin Yeong's eyes were on me, dark and liquid, unwavering. "Maybe. But at least I'll die as a human without building on someone else's corrupted empire. I've never much liked walking over bodies, and it's probably a bit late to start getting used to it now."

"You have no choice," he said through his teeth. "You must accept the oath. I am yours to command and preserve."

"Nope," I said. "That's one thing I do know about oaths of fealty. They don't have to be accepted. You can sit there and die while your men watch and try to decide whether or not they're going to stay with you."

I don't know if it was a plea or if he just couldn't hold himself up any longer; Lord Sero's bent knee dropped to the grass beside the other and he slumped forward, supported by the palms of his hands.

"Save me," he said, his voice a husk of what it had once been: the brittle shell of a flower about to be tossed into pieces on the breeze. "You won't live without my support."

"It's already too late," I told him. I could see the poison lighting up his entire body now. A moment ago I could have saved him. Now, to my relief, I couldn't. That awful, sticky, heart-wrenching temptation was gone as if it had never been, unable to be called back. I would never again have the chance to handle that kind of power. "I don't accept your oath of fealty. Moulder away into the ground where your corruption might be able to do a bit of good."

A moment later, a thin crack tinkled across the surface of the ice wall around us. I couldn't help the quick, conscious look I sent at that crack, and in the brief moment it took me to look back at Lord Sero, he was face down on the grass, ice flowers dying around him. By contrast, the thin crack in the wall of ice grew fatter and stretched further, supplementing the truth that the dead flowers had already told me.

"Heck," I said, dropping back another step.

Lord Sero was dead.

I half expected his remaining behindkind to kill me before the ice could melt and let in Jin Yeong and Zero with their flanking of lycanthropes and zombie. I mean, yeah, Lord Sero was dead and the minions didn't technically have to do what he said anymore, but I wouldn't have been surprised if they had.

To help them think twice about it, I said hazily, "Got more spit where that came from. I kissed the vampire for a pretty long time: haven't seen him in a while. You really want to risk it?"

They mustn't have wanted to risk it. Either that, or they were glad that Sero was dead; it took only the next crack of the failing ice wall to send them on their way, running, galloping, or pattering out of the hall and toward the nearest exit.

I barely saw them go because I was using up too much energy just to keep standing. Sero senior had hit pretty hard, and I still wasn't sure I hadn't lost a tooth. I had definitely broken a rib or two: it felt like someone had crumpled up my right lung like a paper bag, and every breath was murder to take. Funny that I hadn't noticed that particular problem before. There had been pain with each breath, but at least I'd been able to breathe properly. Hopefully I wasn't going to die now that we'd just got ourselves into a more stable sort of position.

There was a final crack and the hurrying of footsteps, then I was enveloped in vampire cologne and vampire arms from behind at much the same time. I leaned back into the welcome strength, still struggling to breath, and saw Zero's face somewhere above me.

"What did you think you were doing?" he demanded.

"Killed your dad," I said. I added, "I'm not sorry."

"Nobody's sorry," he said. "Sit down, Pet."

"Nah," I mumbled. "No time to rest."

"We're not in a hurry," he said impatiently. "JinYeong, lower her to the ground."

I leaned my head tiredly against JinYeong's cheek and asked him hazily, "Wanna change your mind? You can get someone out there who's a heck of a lot less feral and a heck of a lot more beautiful."

"I am already beautiful," he said. "What do I need with someone beautiful?"

"JinYeong, confine your energy to the situation at hand," said Zero, his voice a threatening rumble.

"I am attending to it," said JinYeong. He wrapped his arms around me a little bit more firmly and I let him do it. It felt warm and comforting, and besides, I was pretty sure you were allowed to hug the person who'd said they were going to date you. Unfortunately, the action pressed my broken ribs a bit too hard into the arms that were wrapped around me.

I gasped an *ouch* and JinYeong nuzzled into my neck, then bit me gently. The bright fizz of electricity that bite sent through my veins slipped icily into my ribs and made an unpleasant sort of flutter in there in my lung.

"Oh, that's weird," I said, but there was already less pain in my side. More vampire spit meant faster healing—at least for me.

"You're telling us," Daniel said sourly, appearing around one side of Zero as the surge of energy from Jin Yeong's bite strengthened me enough to let me stand alone.

"Everyone alive?" I asked. It was hard to pay attention to the threads in the house and the faces in front of me at the same time, and there was a fuzz of life down somewhere in the bowels of the house that was niggling at me, too.

"All good," said Morgana. "We had a bit of trouble before we came to find you, but that's all taken care of. I can smell blood somewhere else in the house, though."

"Figured you might have had a bit of fun," I said. Her face was bloodier than Jin Yeong's ever had been, and I didn't like to think about what was staining her black dress darker up near the neck. "But yeah—reckon there are prisoners somewhere further down in the house. We might want to go check on them."

"That will be the dungeon," said Zero, unsurprised.

"Lord Sero brought a *dungeon* with him? Flamin' heck! He likes to go everywhere prepared, doesn't he!"

"Apparently not enough," said Zero. He was far too happy for someone who had apparently just inherited a lot of baggage he probably hadn't wanted to inherit. "But I suppose I can't blame him for that; you can't really fully prepare for a pet."

"At least I'm toilet trained," I said, with some asperity. To Jin Yeong, I said, "Oi. You're warned: Pets are trouble."

"You are not my pet," he murmured in my ear. "You are my Ruth and I will not be warned."

Zero cleared his throat loudly and asked, "What about the house?"

"It's still connecting up with this one, nice and slow," I said, shifting away very slightly from Jin Yeong with the sudden realisation that I tended to blush when someone murmured in my ear while embracing me. "We'll have time for a bit of a poke around before I make sure everything lines up properly. Now that your dad is dead, I shouldn't have too many problems."

Jin Yeong let me move away, but moved to stand beside me instead, his arm brushing against mine.

"How'd you get in, anyway?" I asked him.

"I knew that *Hyeong*'s father would have his finger in the pie. I thought I would find the pie if I found the finger."

"That sounds flamin' weird, but okay," I said.

"Where was the finger?" inquired Daniel, grinning.

"Lord Sero owns many manors," Jin Yeong said. "I visited many before I found a way in."

"You sneaked into Lord Sero's *house?*"

Jin Yeong, looking almost insufferably smug, said, "I went into *many*. I am very good at sneaking. Also, I have a friend who is *verrry* good at making new faces for people."

"I notice that it didn't last too long," I pointed out.

"I became emotional," he said, shrugging one shoulder and sending a glimmering smile in my direction. "I lost my grip on the spell."

"Want us to leave you here to flirt while we check out the dungeon?" asked Daniel. He was enjoying himself far too much.

"No!" I said, at the same time that Jin Yeong said, "*Ne*."

Still, he followed me when I joined the others.

Although I was the one who could feel every line and connection in the house, it was Zero who led the way to the dungeon, solidifying my suspicion that he knew this manor much better than he'd let slip.

I was glad of his leading when we were in the lower floors: there was a darkness and dankness to the air that was more than just physical dark and damp, and I didn't seem to be able to stop shivering. Even with the light that Zero snapped into place with a click of his fingers, there was gloominess and a feeling of moisture so present that they seemed to seep into my bones.

"Nice place," I muttered, as we made our way lower still.

At last we reached a floor where there was a single corridor, formed from impenetrable marble on one side and iron bars on the other. When we reached the end of it, there was a single door in the barred wall that opened from hinges and had no lock: iron, I was pretty sure. It opened for me, but Zero gave it a wide berth, and the second door, set in more bars of silver, made the lycanthropes whine as they passed through it.

"Look at me, being all human and helpful," I couldn't help saying.

Zero pushed ahead of me and Jin Yeong stayed at my side: I think they were too worried about me being captured again to do anything else. But there was nothing for them to worry about, after all. My sight might have shown me a fuzz of life down here, but the behindkind we found in that awful room were only *barely* alive: a collection of perhaps twenty diverse behindkind sprawled on the wet marble floor in their own blood and mess.

All of them looked up as we came in, and I heard snarling from the back though I didn't think any of the behindkind in here had the wherewithal to make good on that threat.

"All right, you lot," I said, before any of the lycanthropes could start growling in response. "This whole house is going to go back into the human world, or the world Behind—wherever it came from. You can either waste time trying to make trouble here, or get out of the house before it goes back to wherever it was Lord Sero pinched it from. I'm pretty sure there'll be a few of his men back there where it came from, so if you want to escape, now is the time."

A blue girl with gills and a tail rasped, "You're not going to kill us?"

"Nope. You get out of here in the next fifteen minutes, and you'll just go back to wherever it was that you came from before you were taken for the trials. Just make sure you're out of the house if you want to be safe."

"Are you sure you want to do this?" Zero asked. He asked it loudly, too; he wanted them all to hear him. "They'll likely come back and try to kill you later."

"We won't," said the blue girl, dragging in a breath. "I promise I won't!"

"They're not trying to kill me right now," I said. "Can't go slaughtering people who aren't trying to kill me right now. They're only half alive as it is."

"You may not have the chance later," he said.

Jin Yeong sent him a reproachful look. "Do not try to turn her into a killer, *Hyeong*," he said. "She already gave you her answer."

"I'm not about to turn into behindkind," I said shortly, though I wasn't sure whether I was offering reassurance to Jin Yeong or showing disapproval to Zero. "Let 'em go; half of 'em can't even stand up straight."

"Very well," he said, and I didn't think he was disappointed. Resigned, maybe, but not disappointed. To the motley lot in the room, he said, "You'd be wise not to wait for the king to come along and take survey of the trials when you get out; I suggest running fast and far."

I hadn't thought that more than one or two of them would be able to stand, but at the mention of the king, there was a panicked stir around the room as heirlings and attendants shuffled, lurched, and lunged to their feet, tentacles, or paws, and made for the door as expeditiously as they could.

"We should leave while we can, too," Zero said, watching the melee with cautious eyes. Maybe he was still expecting some of them to attack us. "If you think you can take over the whole house this time, that is."

I nodded, but I couldn't help sending a lingering gaze around the room. It wasn't that I sensed anything with the human, magic side of myself, and it wasn't exactly that the bit of me that understood how Between worked had noticed anything, either. Rather than either of those, it was my simple human nose that was trying to tell me something.

I smelt blood—a particular kind of blood. And there was none of that kind of blood to be seen in the room, though there was enough of behindkind blood there in general. A few bodies, still, too. The whole place was messed up, and I shouldn't have been able to smell the blood through Jin Yeong's cologne, either.

"Wait," I said slowly, and sent a look around the room once more.

No; not the whole place. There was an empty corner that wasn't messy or bloody. Just an empty corner, and when I stepped across the room, flanked by the silent shadow that was Jin Yeong on one side and the hugeness of Zero on the other, it didn't become any less suspiciously empty.

I stared at it for a while, then gave a short laugh. It wasn't an empty corner. It was a corner that was trying very hard to convince people that it was empty.

"You might as well drop the act," I said into that corner. "You're gunna lose control when you lose consciousness, anyway. Might as well come out and say hello."

The suggestion of emptiness didn't immediately disappear; it faded away slowly, sinking into a gloom in which it was clear enough to see a supine figure wallowing in the darkness of the blue blood around it.

Zero stayed where he was, his hands reflexively clenching into fists, so I was the first one to step over into the corner and verify what we all already knew.

"Well now," said Athelas, smiling up at me with blue, bloody lips, "isn't this a pleasant surprise!"

CHAPTER THIRTEEN

"Flamin' heck," I said mechanically.

Jin Yeong's right hand closed around my left just as I grabbed at Zero's leather sleeve with my right. Zero's lunge forward dragged us both forward regardless, boots skating across moss and mould.

"Stop!" I snapped at Zero, straining uselessly at his sleeve. "Stop and think!"

"You're the one always telling me to tap into my feelings," he said, low and furious. "Why do you want me to stop and think now?"

"*Hyeong*, there are questions to ask," said Jin Yeong. "There are many things that need to be made clear."

"Oh, I think everything is clear enough, don't you?" enquired Athelas, laughing gently with what sounded like lungs full of blood. "Such a charming way to meet again!"

The lycanthropes and the other girls gave us space, Ralph clinging to Sarah but avidly observing. There was no way Zero could be allowed to take revenge right now. Ralph might not be technically alive, but he was still a child and still very capable of taking things in.

"You'd better bring him with us," I said, my skin as cold as my voice. I found that I couldn't bear to look at Athelas, so I looked at Zero instead. "JinYeong is right: there are some questions we need to ask him, and I don't reckon we'll get any answers by handing him over to anyone just yet."

"I wasn't thinking of handing him over to the investigators," Zero said, his voice chilling me still further.

"We won't get answers from him if he's dead, either," I reminded him. "Bring him along alive; it's time for us to go home."

Zero finally looked at me properly. "As easily as that? What changed?"

"Your dad died," I said. "And the houses have kept on merging the whole time—it's our ceiling in here, now. All we have to do is open the door and walk right out. Nobody has to die right now— we can figure it out later."

"I make no promises," said Zero, but I thought the rather murderous expression had faded from his eyes.

It wasn't quite as easy as that, of course: the closed system would try to stop us if it could, but by now the arena was more house than closed system. Lord Sero's manor was no longer his: even the dungeon around us, all mouldy and damp, had a very house-y sort of ceiling to it and had gotten a whole lot smaller. It was *my* house, now. And not only was it used to doing what I wanted it to do, it *liked* doing what I wanted it to do.

"Get a good hold of Athelas," I said to Zero. "We're taking over the house, and I'm not sure if everything is going to be in exactly the same place when I finish."

"Fascinating!" murmured Athelas. He was leaking a lot of blood from a lot of places, so I wasn't sure if he was trying to needle me or if his mind was only half aware of what was going on and he really was fascinated by what was happening.

Zero, his face turned away from his former butler, tightened his grip enough to make Athelas whiten, but didn't look at him.

His voice barely a thread, Athelas added, "So delightful to take part in this unexpected family reunion! I really did expect you to kill me at once."

"There's time yet," said Daniel.

Morgana, distinctly red about the eyes, added, "You might have killed me once, but if you try to do the same to Pet, you ought to know that I'm *very* fast and *very* hungry these days."

"And yet, here you are alive," Athelas said, and coughed up too much blue blood to be healthy. "Did you ever manage to stop feeding on your parents, little zombie? They've been feeding on you for so long in return that I doubt they outlasted your exodus."

"Ignore the old man," Jin Yeong murmured in my ear. "When he begins to talk so much, there is a reason."

His voice pulled me away from the confusion of thoughts that whirled and bit at the edges of my mind, hurting my heart. "I don't have time to listen to you," I said to Athelas. "And Jin Yeong is right: we need to be acting, not talking."

"Mosquito," said Athelas to Jin Yeong in a fond sort of a way, and fainted.

"Everyone needs to be close to me," I told them. "That means you, Ralph! I'm not going to be fetching you from the walls or a painting, so stay with Sarah and try not to turn rooms sideways."

Ralph, looking sulky, muttered something about the house not *liking* him and he wanted his *own house* and Sarah said unsympathetically, "Shut up, you little horror. Your own house probably kicked you out because it didn't like you."

"I am a *revenant*!" said Ralph in icy fury, his skeleton glowing blue and immediately doing away with any appearance of a normal little boy. "How dare you call me a horror!"

"Revenants are horrors," she told him, unimpressed by the display. "Eat your biscuit. I know you have one in your pocket."

"I don't *eat things*, I am *dead*."

"Liar. You just don't need to eat things," she said. "Pet is going to do something with the house, and everyone will feel a lot safer if you're already doing something with your bony little hands."

To everyone's surprise, Ralph took the biscuit out of his pocket and flickered once or twice until he was a little boy again instead of a skeleton.

I cleared my throat and added, "It'll probably be best if we all get out of the house and into the front yard as quickly as we can when we get back, too."

"We'll run like the wind," said Chelsea dryly. "I've had enough of vibrating time and space, thanks very much! What do we do now?"

"Stand there and keep quiet," I told her, feeling the manor quiver around me as it joined to my own house. "The house is nearly big enough, and I reckon it won't take long for the arena to perceive it as the winner. When it does, that door should synch up with the human world again."

"Should?" queried Zero, his brows rising.

"Well, that's the theory," I said. "Shut up, Daniel."

"He didn't say anything!" Morgana said reproachfully.

"He looked at me. Here we go: everyone into the hall behind me, *now*!"

I felt with a deep, absolute solidarity the moment when my house grew so vast that it pressed up against the outer bubble of the heirling arena; the moment when the arena acknowledged one house, one choice, one possibility. The moment when the dungeon around us grew carpet and became my living room once again, crowding us closer together.

The house seemed to buzz around me until I felt that buzzing right into my teeth, then settled on its base and just...stopped.

"Now!" I said, heading down the hall and toward the front door.

I reached for the door handle, and we *did* walk out the front door, just like I'd said. The door opened for me with barely a hitch, and I swept it against the wall, stepping out into sunshine with JinYeong close behind and the others between me and Zero.

I had a suspicion that he might try to stay behind in the house, so I let the lycanthropes exclaim about the sunshine and breeze and reality of the human world while I stepped aside on the patio and waited for Zero to step out with his prisoner.

Zero hesitated in the hallway as Ralph came out hand in hand with Sarah, wary of the sunlight and inclined to cling to her as if she really was his big sister.

"You're so dirty!" I heard her say as she passed. "When was the last time you had a bath!"

"I don't *bathe*, I am a *revenant*!"

"Well, you're a revenant who stinks," she retorted, her voice fading as she tugged him out into the yard.

"Go on without me, Pet," said Zero, his face deep in shadows. "I'll follow along later."

"*Hyeong*," said JinYeong. "Come out. It's no good staying in there."

"You gotta come out as well," I told Zero, bright and firm. I didn't want him to know I saw and knew the shadows on his face; or that Athelas had already woken again, the same shadow in his grey eyes. "I want to make sure everything has arrived in the human world properly before we go back into the house."

"No need on my account!" whispered Athelas. "My lord and I have some matters to discuss."

I didn't wait for Zero to reply again; I reached out and grabbed the sleeve of his leather jacket, and he came along with me as if he had been weighted toward the front and only needed the smallest of extra weight to draw him forward.

Forward, through the hall, over the doorstep and out onto the patio—and as he came through, the whole house shook once more.

"Quick!" I said. "Get off the patio!"

It was only the four of us still on it, and we got off just in time.

There was a feeling of immense weight, then vibration, and something heavy and not-quite-right lifted away from the house and sucked itself back into Behind with a devastating power that seemed as though it could have taken us with it if we weren't solid in a completely different way to it.

Morgana said in a shaken voice, "That was a bit too close for comfort, Pet!"

"Yeah," I said, drawing in a breath. I was going to have to tell her my name at some stage—probably once we were past people threatening me with the use of it. "I mean, maybe it wouldn't have sucked us in if we were still on the patio, but I didn't really want to take the chance."

"Well done, Pet!" said Athelas, in a bare thread of a voice. "You really are stepping into your birthright!"

"Nobody flamin' *asked* you!" I said fiercely. He had no business bringing such an expression to Zero's face as he had back in the hallway. "So belt up!"

"She hits pretty hard," said one of the lycanthropes confidentially to him. "I'd shut up if I were you."

"You shut up, too, Darren!"

"I'm *Dylan*."

"Both of you flamin' shut up!"

"That's rude," said Darren. "I wasn't doing anything."

"I know," I said. "Sorry. But can we *please* stop talking to the prisoner!"

"Oh, is that what I am?" Athelas said with a whisper of a laugh, gazing up at Zero, who wouldn't meet his eyes. "I could have sworn I was *dead meat*, as the colloquial goes, but I'm sure you know what you're talking about!"

"Put the old man back inside," said Jin Yeong, nudging his shoulder against mine. "He is bothersome out here."

"I assure you that there's little likelihood I'll be less bothersome inside," said Athelas. He must have been starting to heal at last, because his grey eyes looked sharper now that we were outside.

"Look, half of us already want to kill you, so you should probably shut up," Daniel said.

I didn't miss the worried look he shot at Morgana, or the way she was clinging to his arm. It nearly made me laugh, because as she had threatened earlier, zombie Morgana could take Athelas on and possibly even win.

Maybe Athelas was just seeing how many of us he could needle. He said in his politest steward's voice, "I shouldn't like to deprive you of the pleasure of your ire."

"I'll find a place for him inside," Zero said.

"How delightful," said Athelas. He hadn't struggled since Zero had him in his grip; neither did he struggle now.

"A couple of you go with him," Daniel said to the lycanthropes, and three of them split away from the group sniffing around the yard to jog back toward the house. "We'll wait out here for North. Sarah said she'll probably be around as soon as she verifies that the Palmer house is free again—with the parents, with any luck!"

"I don't need a babysitter," said Zero, his voice a threatening rumble.

"Didn't say you did," said Daniel, but his eyes met mine briefly and I saw understanding there. "But we don't know if there were behindkind things pushing into the house while it was settling back here. I assume you don't want to lose your prisoner because you're fighting off weird behindkind."

Zero hesitated for the briefest moment, and in that moment I saw both regret and amusement flicker across Athelas' face.

"Don't get comfortable," I told him. "Zero isn't the one you should be worried about. A few of us heirlings are going to have a lot of questions for you."

"How delightful!" he said again. "Will you turn torturer?"

"Don't reckon I need to," I said. "Reckon there's enough in

your head to do that for both of us: I took memories from you before, and I'll do it again if I have to."

For the first time, I felt as though I'd scored an actual hit instead of just amusing Athelas in that twisted way he seemed to enjoy things: his eyes dropped, the amusement utterly vanishing from them, and I saw the slight, bitter smile that passed briefly across his lips.

"How fitting!" was what I thought he said, but Zero was already dragging him back up onto the patio and into the house by then, three lycanthropes bounding after him with far too much energy given the events of the last few days.

I felt my phone buzz in my pocket, and when I pulled it out a small fizz of delight curled in my stomach: I had reception bars! I had real, human reception bars, and Tuatu was calling.

"Oi," I said by way of answering. "You and North better get over here: we're out and I reckon Sarah's gunna want to see her parents as soon as she can. You might want to see how they feel about skeletons too, because she seems to have adopted one."

"Pet—"

"They seem like nice people, so they'll probably adopt him too," I added. Jin Yeong grinned and settled his shoulders against one of the patio beams, eyes liquid with malicious enjoyment. "He doesn't take much to look after, either; just a bit of electricity and water to play with, and make sure you don't let him trap visitors in the walls."

"Pet, the Palmers are *not* going to want to adopt a skeleton and—"

"He's only a small one!"

"I'm not discussing skeletons over the phone," Tuatu said firmly. "*Are you all right, Pet?*"

"Oh," I said, surprised. "Yeah, of course. Talking to you, aren't I? Sarah's in really good nick, too, so—"

"I wasn't asking about Sarah," he said. "I already know she's okay. I wanted to make sure that you're not leaking blood or missing any important body parts."

I sniffed a bit, unexpectedly overcome, and Jin Yeong stiffened.

"Oi, Tuatu," I said.

"What?"

"I love you."

He gave a long-suffering sigh. "I love you, too, Pet. Please try not to die or disappear before we get there, all right?"

"All right," I said, and hung up to a narrow-eyed Jin Yeong.

He shot a molten look at my phone and said, "You told that human you love him."

"He's basically my older brother at this point," I argued. "Of course I love him!"

"Also you told *Hyeong* that you love him."

"He's my uncle! I'm supposed to tell him I love him!"

"Only I was not told that you love me," he said moodily.

"That's because I don't love you like a brother or an uncle," I said. "I already said I'll date you, but you're going to have to wait for a little while before I give you any other *I love you*. Unless you *want* a sisterly—"

"I will wait!" he said hastily. "I will not be an uncle or a brother to you!"

"Oi!" said a lycanthrope. "Reckon you two can stop canoodling for long enough to find out why this bloke is looking into our yard?"

"Did you just say *canoodle?*" demanded Morgana.

"What did I tell you?" I said to Kevin. "Your vocabulary is from at least five decades ago and—oh heck, that's all we need!"

It wasn't just a bloke looking into our yard: it was a golden, shaggy-haired man with slightly stooped shoulders and a pleasant, golden retriever type of look to him.

"Get away from the fence!" I said sharply to the others, and strode down the path toward the gate. He couldn't see any of us— couldn't hear us, if I was correct—but as soon as I spoke to him directly, he would be able to. "Sarah and Ralph—get back inside where you won't be seen. Morgana—"

"I'm staying," she said. "Until North and Tuatu get here, anyway. You might need the backup."

"Me too," said Daniel, when I turned to him.

I didn't bother to appeal to the other lycanthropes or JinYeong, who was a warm presence at my side. I just waited until Sarah and Ralph were out of sight, then I stopped short of the gate and addressed the King of Behind.

"Coming to mop up the mess?"

His eyes sharpened on me at once, then flickered across to JinYeong's face and the small group behind us.

"Something of the sort," he said. "But possibly not in the way that you're expecting. I'm...a little surprised to see so many of you crowded here. And yet, when I think about it, it's not so surprising."

"You're gunna be a bit more surprised when other heirlings pop out of the woodwork again," I advised him. "We're not the only ones who came out."

He studied me for a while as though perplexed. "That's not possible," he said. "Not unless every one of them swore fealty to you. They swore fealty to you? I think you'll regret that."

"Nope," I said. "I don't want people swearing fealty to me so that I don't kill them. That's your bag."

"Not at all," he said pleasantly. "I prefer to clean up loose ends completely. Those swearing fealty always find the fealty burdensome after a certain amount of years, or service. It's far better to make a clean cut with things."

"Don't reckon you've managed that this time," I said. "Thought you were a bit cleverer than this: it isn't much good for you if an heirling is chosen, is it?"

"No good at all," he said. "I wasn't responsible for this round of the heirling trials—if I had been, I would have made sure to be in a position to observe the proceedings."

"You mean participate, don't you?" I said, glad to have that particular suspicion confirmed.

"I'm certain Lord Sero had that thought, at least," he said, without answering directly.

"You reckon Lord Sero knew it was coming and got himself into a good position to be in the arena."

"You don't? I would have thought you'd have seen him in there."

"You're not wrong about that," I admitted. I didn't want to give away too much, because I didn't know what was important. "He made a bit of a nuisance of himself."

The king gazed at me for some time, then at Jin Yeong, who snarled very slightly and silently to display his canines. I saw the amusement spring to his eyes. He said, "I see. I think I'd like to speak with Lord Sero."

"Sorry," I said. "He's dead. We left his body in there somewhere, so you can go talk to that, if you want to, but it might be a bit squashed, if it even still exists."

Cautiously, he asked, "Did—did you let the vampire kill him?"

"S'pose you could say that," I said, pinching Jin Yeong's fingers as he opened his mouth to—presumably—rectify the incorrect part of the king's assumption.

"It seems as though Lord Sero made a mistake by not arranging for the two of you to be separated."

"He tried," I said. "Didn't work out real well for him."

"I see," said the king again. The amusement was more pronounced now. "Unfortunate from a purely informational point of view, of course, but he has been a...thorn in my side for quite some time now."

"Ah," said Jin Yeong, suddenly and softly, for my ears only. "There is a story here."

"*Kuroegae*," I said, and caught the immediate delight in his dark eyes. Before he could do anything ridiculously hasty, like kiss me in front of the king, I said, "Don't get carried away. There's no need for everyone to understand what we're saying, that's all."

"You should certainly be separated," said the king. There was no amusement in his face now; instead of an affable, golden-haired puppy, he looked like a shaggy, age-cragged, stony version of himself.

Now, more than wondering exactly what Lord Sero had had on the king to make it too difficult to kill him, I was wondering what we were going to do to stop him killing us if he could get into the yard.

He probably knew what I was thinking, because he let the underside of his face show for just an instant longer before he went back to looking like his usual, puppy-dog self. He said pleasantly, "If speaking with Lord Sero is impossible I would like to speak with the steward. I'm quite certain that one is still alive, by hook or by crook."

"Yeah, can't do that, either," I said.

"Um, Pet?" said Daniel, shuffling a bit closer. "Are you sure about that? We don't want him, do we?"

"I don't see what use you could have for him," the king said. "Nor is he your subject. He is mine—and so is every person in your vicinity."

JinYeong gave a small, contemptuous *tch!* of laughter. "I have no king," he said.

"I mean, technically you're not my king, either," Daniel said to him. "We're not proper behindkind and we don't have the same rights, either. But Pet—what's the use of keeping Athelas? You know how sick it makes Morgana, and it's not like he didn't—"

"I don't like giving stuff to people when I don't know what they're going to do with it," I said, patting the hand that Daniel had put on my arm.

"You're a charming human," the king said, almost disarmingly. "And I don't want to hurt you, but I really do insist that you hand over Lord Sero's steward. I have some...burning questions that I don't believe will be answered without him."

"Look, I get that you're the King of behindkind," I said, "but you're not my king. Athelas is my prisoner, and I'm not giving him up. We've got our own burning questions, and they're more important than anything to do with the succession."

Two very faint lines appeared between his brows—confusion. His head tilted slightly to the side, the king looked more than ever like a golden retriever, trying hard to understand the inexplicable fact that the ball seemed to have been thrown and yet unable to see said ball because it was behind its owner's back all the time.

"There's nothing more important than the succession," he said.

"Yeah, there is," I said. "Zero's more important. So is Jin Yeong. Everyone here in this yard is more important than your little feud with Lord Sero *or* your pathetic attempt to stay on the throne forever and always."

"I beg your pardon? *Pathetic?*"

"Dunno what else you call it when a bloke goes around killing kids to make sure he stays on the throne."

"They were by no means all children."

"That's the stupidest defence I've ever heard," I told him. "That's like saying that you didn't personally kill all the people you had murdered."

"I'm not defending myself to you."

"What are you doing, then? How come you're here?"

"I came to see exactly what had happened to bring an end to the heirling trials early. I suspected that your house would be most likely to return for one reason or the other."

"Scoping out the competition?"

"There isn't much competition here," he said, his eyes flicking around the yard.

We probably didn't look like much; half of us were injured, the other half mucky as all heck, and only four of us around the place were actually heirlings. Of those four, two were technically dead. It wasn't like the king knew that we had the harbinger here, either, so I could understand why he wasn't impressed.

That's all right. Being underestimated has its perks.

"Yeah? So you're just here for the fun of it?"

"I told you. I came to see what—or *who*—had brought about the end of the trials. And I really do insist on speaking with the steward."

"Okay, well you stand there and insist," I said. "We're all going back in to have some tea and bikkies—Morgana'll probably have some brains, but you probably don't want to know about that. You can leave whenever you get tired of standing out here."

To my everlasting glee, everyone turned around when I did and started filtering back into the house. JinYeong, one hand lightly resting on the small of my back like he was afraid the king might have a go at me while I was walking away from him, even grinned, his eyes liquid and amused.

"You should remember that I gave you a gift!" called the king.

"Told you that I didn't owe you anything for it," I reminded him. "And it was mine to start with."

JinYeong's arm tightened at my waist, and I smiled reassuringly up at him. The king had already known that both the book and the name were mine; he had shown as much when he found his way to me in order to give the book to me.

As we kept walking, the king called out again, "I don't like to threaten people—"

"Yeah? 'Cos I'm pretty sure that book was a threat," I said, stopping and half-turning.

"A very polite, non-confrontational one," said the king, shrugging disarmingly. "I'm about to become very much less non-confrontational."

"It's *nearly* worth getting Zero to fight you, just to make sure you can't keep ruling," I said, and this time I turned to face him properly. "But he doesn't want that, so you can go and be confrontational elsewhere, thanks."

"And get out of the street, you bozo!" yelled Kevin. It could have been Kyle, though. "The postie can't get past while you're standing there!"

I heard Daniel's voice say in a gravelly undertone, as if with the last thread of patience, "*Will* you lot stop antagonising the King of Behind!"

I didn't wait to see if the king did as he'd been told; I let Jin Yeong usher me back into the house and felt the faintest huff of air as the door shut behind us. Then I let out a shaky breath and grabbed a handful of his shirt to steady myself.

"Heck. That wasn't fun. Wonder if Zero knows what's been happening?"

"*Hyeong* is busy," said Jin Yeong. He seemed content to lean his shoulders against the wall while I held onto his shirt. "We will tell him later."

"Reckon he's hurt Athelas more?"

"I think that *Hyeong* is trying very hard not to disappoint you right now," he said. "And I think there is not much that can hurt the old man."

"Maybe nothing physical," I said, rubbing a hand over the back of my neck to get rid of the crawling feeling there. "But there's definitely stuff that can hurt him."

Jin Yeong gave me a long, thoughtful look and said unexpectedly, "Maybe you should not spend too much time with the old man, either."

"Maybe," I said. I wasn't sure what disturbed me more: the fact that I could so clearly see how I could hurt Athelas, or what that fact meant. I didn't want to examine either thought too closely, and it was a relief to have Sarah interrupt us.

"What if North and my parents get here while I'm inside?" she asked. She didn't seem anxious so much as determined: she obviously trusted North to safely bring her parents to her. "Can North get in?"

"I've never seen North *not* able to get in anywhere," I said, and added hastily, "unless you count the heirling trials, anyway. But if you're worried, keep an eye on the window: I reckon the lycan-thropes are keeping an eye out for—yep. Join that lot over at the window in Zero's room. If you want to share the window, just shove them a bit. They respond to shoving better than words."

"I noticed that," said Sarah, wrinkling her nose. "I think Zero took the scary fae upstairs, by the way."

"Yeah," I said. I'd already felt that. He'd taken Athelas upstairs to my parents' old bedroom, if I wasn't mistaken. I would have been angry about it if it hadn't already occurred to me that the room, like my relationship with Athelas, was already tainted beyond repair by his occupancy. He couldn't ruin the atmosphere any more than he already had.

So instead of stomping upstairs to tell Zero to move Athelas into another room, I said, "Time for coffee," and went into the kitchen to put both the jug and percolator on, followed by my vampire shadow.

The lycanthropes who had accompanied Zero into the house earlier came back to the kitchen while the jug was boiling. They'd probably heard it—or smelt the shortbreads that I'd dug out of the back of the cupboard in delighted surprise.

"Where's Zero now?" I asked them, frowning. There was a spot upstairs that should be him, but it didn't seem to be very firm, and that worried me.

"He's all right," said Kyle. "Reckon he'll be down in a bit. He's settling the creepy one into his room and making sure he can't get away. He said he wants some coffee."

That sounded promising, but when the tea and coffee were made and everyone was settling themselves around the living room and the dining room, Zero still hadn't appeared.

I met JinYeong's eyes across the kitchen island and picked up

Zero's mug. "I'll go get him," I said. "I don't think he should be up there for too long."

"I can do it," he said, and there was a slight upward lilt to the sentence that turned it into a question. *Do you want me to do it?* was that question.

"It's all right," I said. "I'll only be a minute. Make sure that lot doesn't pinch my bikkies."

I went upstairs with the feeling of lead in my stomach, but it was hard to tell if it was because I was dreading seeing Athelas again, or if I was dreading seeing what Zero might have done to him.

I headed toward the feeling of Zero and Athelas, and was led right toward my parents' room upstairs, as I'd thought. The house still shifted around me a little, but I felt as though I understood and felt each part of it better than I ever had before.

The first thing I saw when I entered the room was Athelas' chair; Athelas in it, bound by magic and Between and something else that I didn't recognise. It was physical but not rope, and it passed through the leather of the chair while binding Athelas to the wood of the chair beneath.

"What a charming surprise," said Athelas, lifting his head as with a mighty effort. "I didn't think I would see you again so soon, Pet!"

"I'm not here to see you," I said shortly. "I'm here for Zero."

"As you see, my lord is not here."

He wasn't, either. I could feel the lingering sense of him being there, but it was fading quickly, as though he'd just left the room. I couldn't help the small step I took toward the door to go and look for him, even though I could already feel that he was nowhere upstairs—nowhere in the house anymore.

"Perhaps you might answer a question for me, Pet?"

I didn't recognise my own voice when it snarled, "What did you do to Zero!"

"May I remind you, Pet, that I am restrained?"

"You don't have to remind me, because I still remember you killing me six times when you were restrained!" I spat. *"What did you do with Zero?"*

I heard yelling from downstairs in the silence that followed my question; the sound of startlement, then fear and bewilderment. Still inclined to respond to the immediate thought that the house had been breached and overtaken by other heirlings, I made another small, involuntary movement toward the door.

"How very interesting," said Athelas, his head cocked. "Perhaps you'll be more inclined to listen to me now that the same trouble is brewing below stairs? You can't think that—"

"What are you talking about?" I demanded, staring at him sickly. "What's happening downstairs? What did you do?"

"My dear Pet, if you would allow me to complete a sentence—"

"I don't actually care what else you want to tell me," I said. "I just want answers to my questions!"

I heard footsteps on the stairs; bounding, swift footsteps that boomed across the top landing and then hurried around the corner toward the doorway of my parents' room. JinYeong, his face as pale as anyone of his complexion could be, darted through the doorway with a wild look and seized me by the elbows, his eyes running over me as though to make sure I was really there.

Daniel, his face ridiculously haggard for someone of his age, caught himself in the doorway behind him and said, "Pet! You need to get downstairs!"

"The heck is going on down there?" I demanded. "Look, Zero just disappeared, and Athelas won't tell me what he did with him. You're going to have to deal with whatever it is yourself."

"Morgana is gone!"

I stared at him, caught between sickness and rage. "Gone *how?*"

"She disappeared—one second she was there, the next she was

gone. I don't even—did someone know her name? I didn't think that worked on humans!"

"Morgana isn't human," I said mechanically, allowing myself to be hugged tightly by Jin Yeong, who was speaking a nonsense of Korean that was too fast for me to comprehend and he was too overwhelmed to translate for me.

"Yes, but that's a *fae* thing! It doesn't work like that for all of us!" snarled Daniel.

"Get Sarah and Ralph," I told him over Jin Yeong's shoulder, cold obstinacy sinking into my bones. "We'll see about this. If Athelas has—"

"My dear Pet—"

"No, you don't understand," Daniel insisted. "They're gone. They're all gone."

"All of who?"

"The heirlings," he said, wiping a shaky hand across his eyes. "It's not just Morgana: Ralph and Sarah have disappeared, too. There isn't an heirling left in the house except you."

In the buzzing silence, I heard Athelas' faint exhale; it bubbled a bit where it shouldn't have bubbled.

"Ah," he said. "The king really does have them, then. It seems as though it's all up to my lord now, after all."

www.ingramcontent.com/pod-product-compliance
Lightning Source LLC
Chambersburg PA
CBHW040522170726
48295CB00012B/294